I0741615

Dress Blues
(Book 5)

By Lea Carter

ISBN 9780988599185

Cover Photo by Jace Carter

Learn more about the author at
leacarterwrites.wixsite.com/wholesomefantasy

Chapter I

Captain Kimberlite squinted into the setting sun as her windship, the *Nadauld*, descended towards the sea. She could feel her own wings twitching slightly with nervous anticipation. "Make ready," she shouted from where she stood on the quarterdeck. She would much rather have been on the main deck with the lads, watching the Water Fairy, Kuntza, prepare. Rotten luck that the pirate Bane—as she had adapted herself to calling Major Layton—had not been efficient enough to fill the fresh water barrels while he was repairing the *Nadauld*'s mainmast and raiding their medical supplies!

"Reduce speed," she shouted. Sails began dropping instantly, until only the topgallants remained. Constance nodded her approval at Miss Dunn, a young but capable officer she had been relieved to find alive and unharmed among the survivors of Bane's massacre. There had been a hundred and seven survivors, out of well over a thousand, most of them skin and bones. Too few to sail a Gyrfalcon-class windship properly, too many for the amount of fresh water they had left. And they had been beating against the wind, fighting for every ship's length gained towards their capitol city Regalis since escaping the pirate stronghold. This gradual circling downwards was a welcome respite from the never-ending zig-zagging of the last few days.

When they had realized they were low on water there had been a heated discussion of the options. That was only natural with three captains all trapped aboard the same windship. They had seriously debated stopping at Port Herio for fresh water, but that would have caused quite a delay on their journey to Regalis with the news—a secret pirate stronghold smashed, a traitor summarily dealt with, and a *fifth* fairy tribe discovered all in less than a week.

Kuntza's casual offer to "make" fresh water for them had stunned them into temporary silence. Young Captain Grant had recovered first, scoffing at the idea. Trevaille had responded to Grant's disbelief by bristling like a challenged cockerel, and Constance had been left with the task of breaking the tie, Prince Cambrian being still restricted to below-decks at the time. Not that it had been difficult to choose between a mostly routine procedure that might save their lives and losing days of travel.

"Cap'n," muttered the helmsman, breaking into her thoughts, "do ya really think this here trick will work?"

"I do not know, Jacque. But I am eager to find out." She flashed the large man-fairy a smile and stepped to the forward rail of the quarterdeck. From her new vantage point, she could see the small knot of windfairies standing in the waists, ready at the hose. Others were forward, clustered loosely around the capstan, waiting in near silence as Kuntza finished stretching a cloth across the top of an empty fresh water barrel.

It was hard to believe that a simple piece of cloth—no matter what it was treated with—could transform the briny stuff the lads were preparing to pump up into drinkable water. Constance worked her tongue around in her mouth but it remained dry. They were all dangerously dehydrated. Glancing at the starboard railing, she saw that they had almost descended far enough to…

"Lower away!" she shouted. As the lads began shoving the hose over the side, she realized with dismay that Cambrian had joined Captains Trevaille and Grant on the main deck. With an effort, she stilled the prickles that ran up the back of her neck every time she saw or thought of him since three nights ago in the infirmary—when their slow-burning romance had skipped the preliminary decades of most maturing relationships and plunged into the precarious terrain of innermost secrets.

She rubbed her forehead in agitation. The memories were still far too sharp to ignore completely. In short, delirium had set in, caused in part by the beating he got from Bane and his pirates and in part by the near hypothermia he got during their time on the midwing. She had been roused from a sound sleep to find Cambrian shouting for his valet, in an irrational panic over having forgotten some minute detail of etiquette while dressing for a state dinner. Over the next few hours his fears had swung wildly from instance to instance, covering everything from intertribal politics to their recent attack on the pirate stronghold. She was still chilled at some of the things he had worried would go wrong during that attack, and deeply concerned at hearing his uncensored thoughts on his own value—or lack thereof. She and Jennings had moved him to her cabin for privacy, and there they had taken turns soothing him, cajoling him, promising him that his fears were ungrounded. That had been followed by nightmares, which Kuntza had eventually dulled with a strong sleeping potion.

Now Cambrian stood by the water barrels, his right arm crossed over his left, no doubt to hide the fact that his left wing and arm were firmly strapped down. Remembering the sorry state of their medical supplies and her own experiences with broken ribs, she reflected that he would be lucky to be up to bowing to his mother when they arrived at Regalis in another four days. Cocking an eyebrow at Jennings, who had stationed himself a twig or so away from Cambrian, Constance was slightly comforted to know that he was on duty. And she felt better for having cried the night before, her mild headache a small price to pay for releasing the myriad emotions she had been keeping bottled up.

"The hose is extended, Captain!" bellowed Miss Dunn from the waists, her voice startlingly loud for someone her size.

Constance nodded sharply. She should have been watching the hose, not Cambrian. "Pumps on and go!" To Miss Dunn, she added, "Call the altitudes!" It was now a balancing act, staying low enough for the hose to reach the sea's surface without sinking below a sailing wind. She smiled grimly. Not to mention the chance of a buffeting gust rising off a swell.

The group at the capstan gripped the wooden handles and leaned into their work. It was slow going, but their efforts drove the pump that began drawing sea water up through the hose, a process designed so that they would never have to carry more than a single sea water barrel, leaving more room for the fresh water that their lives depended upon.

Constance frowned. Something was wrong. No, something was missing. She scanned the deck, trying to find it. The lads on the hose were watching it closely, to keep it from snagging on any surface debris or from losing contact with the water. The lads at the capstan strained along dourly, not a slacker amongst them despite their general exhaustion. Her gaze ran along the system of pumps and hoses, but all was in place. Just then a wind whistle sounded, shrill for a moment before lapsing back into silence.

Constance ran her tongue over dry lips.

Music. The lads usually sang while they pumped the water, or sang for those doing the pumping. Today they worked and waited silently, every available eye on the hose end that they had tied above the fresh water barrel by Kuntza.

Constance blinked. Was she seeing things? But it was no trick of the eye. A few drops of water became a trickle and then a steady stream. Kuntza's cloth slowly softened and sagged with the water. Then the stream stopped. Constance dragged her gaze away from the potential breakthrough and turned it on the capstan. There was too much wonder in the lads' eyes, too much longing in their faces for her to chastise them. She even shook her head at Miss Dunn who was moving forward to discipline them.

A reliable means of freshening water, so small it could be carried in a pouch on one's hip. No more barrels of brackish water, no more searching the skies for sight of a supply ship, no more half rations for windships on long patrols. It was indeed an awesome possibility.

On the main deck, Kuntza took down two battered tin cups from a rack of them and stepped up to the spigot. The sound of water hitting the bottom of the first cup was loud in the relative silence. When Kuntza turned his wrist to bring the second cup under the spigot, all eyes but his followed the water that splashed between the cups onto the deck at his feet.

"Your Highness," Kuntza held out one of the

cups. He had never known thirst before now and was appalled at the idea that this was a common dilemma amongst the other tribes.

Cambrian's bruised mouth quirked up in a smile. "A pleasure." With some difficulty, he straightened from where he had been leaning against a cannon and accepted the cup. "Ah, Master Kuntza," he interrupted when Kuntza began lifting his drink to his lips. "A toast, good sir." He raised his cup and turned to the lads, his smile nearly dying as he met their anxious gazes. True, a guaranteed supply of fresh water was a mere day away at Herio should this test fail. But it was no longer just about the water or the discomfort of going without. They were face to face with the wonder of something new. In a way, face to face with hope.

"Master Kuntza." Cambrian did not completely turn away from the lads. "With the first two cups of fresh water my tribe has ever known through your method, let us toast a fresh start for your tribe and the rest of Fairydom."

Kuntza hesitated. "I am not a pro-mise maker for my tribe," he said apologetically.

"A toast is not a pledge," Cambrian hastened to reassure him. "It is simply a wish."

Kuntza smiled. "I also wish for a peace-ful future." He raised his cup uncertainly, mimicking Cambrian's gesture.

Relieved, Cambrian took a sip. The first thing he noticed as the water passed over his lips was that it lacked the burning sensation he associated with salt and cuts. Then it splashed onto and under his tongue. It was cool, it was sweet—it was fresh! Tipping his head back, he drained the cup and held it up high in a gesture of triumph.

"Strike up a tune, ye lads and lasses of the far winds!" he crowed, surprising himself with his enthusiasm. "Soon we shall have water enough for all!" Amidst the cheering, he looked aft and made eye contact with Constance. His heart, already racing with excitement, did a triple flip. One for love, one for fear, and one for the sheer joy of seeing her. "Jennings," he called to the man-fairy who had evolved into his shadow over the last two days. "A cup for the captain."

"Compliments of the battered man-fairy in the waists, Captain," Jennings cheerily informed Captain Kimberlite, offering her the tin cup. Joking about Cambrian was his way of letting her know that things were going well. No serious mood swings today, anyway.

"Give him my thanks," Constance half-laughed as she bent to accept it and dismiss him to rejoin Cambrian. She hesitated briefly before taking a sip. She would have liked to pass the cup on to the helmsman, but knew it would be unseemly for her to do so. Sloshing the water about in her mouth, she savored the moment, then hastily poured the rest down her throat. "Jacque," she commanded, turning back to the helmsman. "Take this back down, would you?" She held out the cup, placing her free hand on the wheel. "After you have had a drink, make sure you take a turn on the capstan."

"Aye, aye, Captain!" he agreed, reaching for the cup. He had not expected this turn of events, but accepted it gratefully.

Constance had just settled into her position at the wheel, watching the colored strips of cloth fluttering on the wingtips, one ear listening for wind whistles and the other keeping track of the altitude as Miss Dunn called it, when Mister Dixby joined her on the quarterdeck.

"Captain," he began to speak, then paused. "Captain, I am worried." He tugged at his shirt hem, irritated at how it constantly rode to one side, and wished again that Bane had left them with more than poorly cut slops in the ship's store. It was one thing to toss Cambrian's wardrobe while trying to locate his crown; that was almost logical as it might have been hidden anywhere in Cambrian's cabin. It had been sheer spite to toss the rest of their clothes, as those rescued reported he had done.

"Say on," she prompted when he paused again. She had spent too much time below decks, only surfacing to resolve disputes between the other captains, to really know what was happening.

"It is Captain Grant," Dixby said at last. "He is working the lads too hard."

"What else can he do?" she asked directly. "With so few of us on board, it is either do the work of two or let the *Nadauld* crash." She glanced at him as she spoke, noted the way his eyebrows drew together. "Dixby?" She contented herself with his name, experience telling her that he had been about to speak his mind anyway.

"We need not work quite so hard, Captain," he said slowly. "There are other breezes."

"None that take us directly to Regalis." She frowned. Had she really just contradicted her navigator on the subject of their course? "What do you suggest?"

"Take the winter wind," he answered, moving a half-step forward in his earnestness. "It sweeps down this time of year, bringing the cold weather in from the north. One day, perhaps two, of sailing before that and we would be in reach of the higher altitude westward winds."

"Which we could carry inland to the foothills, empty all ballast, and glide into Regalis from the southeast," she finished for him, her mind having dredged up the memory from previous tours. Already lighter than usual with their smaller crew, they would be able to keep what foodstuffs and supplies they had.

"Nonsense." Grant's voice cut through the space between them like a lightning bolt. Glaring at Dixby, Grant leaned on the chart rack. "I told you already, navigator, that we would take the direct course."

"Is that so?" Constance adopted her best bored-officer tone of voice. Without waiting for his response, she looked past him to Captain Trevaille, who had also come onto the quarterdeck. "Did you know about this?"

"I did not," Trevaille denied, glaring briefly at Grant. "I have been mostly occupied with Master Kuntza. Unfortunately." In fact, he had spent the last three days trying to work out the best way to handle the tricky diplomatic situation they were in and it was making him cross. The fact that Kuntza insisted on keeping his tribe's existence a secret for the time being only complicated matters further.

Grant wilted a little before the combined disapproval of two fellow officers. "But surely you agree," he began. "We must get to Regalis quickly."

"Aye," Trevaille folded his arms. "And if we can do that without killing the lads off, that would be even better." He had tried to like Grant. When that had failed, he began avoiding him. Apparently, that had been a greater mistake than he would have dreamed possible.

"Did you know, Captain Grant," Constance intervened hastily, "that the winter wind blows with sufficient force to carry us to the westward winds in less than two days?" She had trusted the sailing of her windship to Grant, including the course they flew, but she was concerned to realize that things had gotten bad enough for Dixby to feel that he needed to circumvent the officer in charge.

"But surely…" Grant scowled when Trevaille cut him off.

"And that the westward winds would carry us to the foothills in another day?" Trevaille scowled back at the younger, less-experienced captain. "Gliding into Regalis from there would take another day at the most."

"It is not faster," Constance threw Grant a point.

"That may be," Cambrian entered the conversation with an allowance. "Nevertheless," he glanced at the main deck, where groups of exhausted sea-fairies savored fresh water and waited their turns at the capstan, "it seems a sound plan."

"Then, with your permission?" Constance barely waited for his nod before turning the wheel. The Nadauld answered smoothly, accepting the more southerly point to her spiral. "As soon as the water barrels are full, bring her back up to altitude," she told Mister Dixby. "Have you had your glass of water?" she asked him next, frowning slightly.

"Aye, Captain," he nodded quickly.

"Excellent. Take the wheel, then," she ordered. "With your permission, Your Highness," she nodded slightly to Cambrian, "the captains and I need to take our turn at the capstan."

"Well really!" Grant's protest ended abruptly when Trevaille good-naturedly pummeled the wind out of him.

"I dare say I can go a turn longer than you, young fella," Trevaille teased and moved cheerfully towards the capstan.

"You will find no competition in me," laughed Constance, moving quickly to join him.

"Tell me, Dixby," Cambrian promptly engaged the junior officer in conversation to prevent Grant from feeling that he had to assert himself, "how long do you think it will take for proper surveys to be completed?"

"Of all the areas incorrectly mapped for the last few hundred years?" Dixby shook his head, dividing his attention between the prince's question and navigating the *Nadauld*, Grant getting completely pushed out of his mind in the process. "It will take decades."

"Yes, I was afraid of that," Cambrian glanced over his shoulder and watched a moment as Grant sulkily made his way forward. "It will be almost as important to apprehend the false surveyors as it will be to correct their work."

"True." Dixby nodded slowly. "But I have been thinking about that. I doubt that Layton would have risked himself by making his plan known to so many." Seeing Cambrian's eyebrow go up inquisitively, he explained, "Surveying teams go out every quarter, here or there, take their measurements, and make a single, painstakingly accurate copy."

"Which is then provided to the Royal Record Keepers. And in turn, they produce copies for the military and civilians alike. Of course!" Cambrian would have pounded his fist on the chart rack if it had not been for his cracked ribs. Breathing was challenging enough. "Why try to manage a fleet of surveyors when one can simply suborn a handful of chart makers?" Noticing the pleased smile on Dixby's face, Cambrian made a mental note to reward his keen thinking. "How about you, Dixby?" he asked, testing a theory. "Did you ever consider surveying?"

"Me?" Dixby looked up at the sky, out over the railing, then back and forth between the wingtip indicators. "No, I think I would rather be a navigator," he said, making a minute course correction. The *Nadauld* rose slightly, then settled back into a level spiral.

"I thought you might feel that way," Cambrian smiled. "Tell me," he paused to glance about, and finding Jennings the only one in earshot, continued, "where are the bags of papers and books that we took from Layton's flagship?"

"They were in an empty water barrel until this morning," Dixby smiled broadly. "But I used the commotion to transfer them to my quarters."

"I see." Cambrian tried to hide his amusement at Dixby's referring to the fresh water experiment as a commotion. "Are they safe there?"

"Any searcher would have to examine my

own books and papers first, to be sure they were not Bane's. And by the time that was finished," he shrugged a little, "I or someone else would surely have had cause to enter the room."

Cambrian took Dixby at his word on that. He had learned from Constance that, because Dixby's passion for learning extended well beyond navigation, his private library was in a constant state of flux.

"Time for mess, Your Highness," Jennings announced from Cambrian's elbow. He had been watching Cambrian closely since following him up on deck. While he was of a mind to let the prince do what he felt he could, seeing the man-fairy's shoulders begin to droop was all the indication Jennings needed.

"Very well." Smiling at Dixby, Cambrian resigned himself to his fate. While he understood that it was necessary to eat soft things for the sake of his teeth, a few of which had been loosened by abrupt contact with the *Kimuxwe*'s deck during his duel with the pirate king Bane, gruel and milk toast were beyond boring. He had tried protesting, but there was no dissuading Jennings. "Do you know how to play Stratagem?" he asked as he turned towards the aft companionway.

"Me?" Jennings scoffed. That was a game for white-handed dandies.

"No?" Cambrian smiled. "High time you learned, my friend. High time."

Chapter II

Constance rubbed her face with one hand and tried to remember what was in the paragraph she had just read. But even after her third time going over it, she had no idea what Bane had decided to write in his logbook. It did not help that she had spent every available moment of the last two days working with Dixby and Cambrian to complete a preliminary review of the material they had rescued when they burned Bane's flagship. She was beginning to hate the chart room, which they had turned into a temporary library as it had one of the few lockable doors on the *Nadauld*.

"More useless bragging?" Cambrian asked from where he sat on the other side of the table. There had been some coolness between them lately, understandable given all that had happened. While he had no intention of losing her, he was proceeding cautiously, giving her the space she seemed to need. He had been discreetly watching her for the last several minutes, waiting for her to turn the page. As she was now showing overt signs of distraction, he decided to try to find out what was wrong.

"What?" Constance blinked at him in surprise. She had thought him absorbed in his own thoughts.

Cambrian tapped the logbook he was reading. "Bane carries on for almost two pages about how the puny royal forces will fall before his bloodthirsty pirates. And here," he flipped back a couple of pages to where Bane had been describing their time at Bakarti, "he documents how tired he is of feigning loyalty to the fop others call a prince." With a wry smile, Cambrian tossed the book onto the table and stretched carefully. They had been at it since supper. "Come on," he rose and offered her his hand.

Still surprised, Constance set aside the logbook she had been trying to read. Taking his hand, she let him lead her out of the chartroom.

"Fresh air," Cambrian announced cheerfully as he headed down the passageway. "That is what we need."

Constance smiled in faint amusement when they came up on deck and he slipped his good arm around her waist, under the pretense of helping her with her safety line. Her silent concern that he was feigning good humor while driving himself to prepare a report for his father dissipated under the soft rays of fading sunlight. When they reached the gunn'ls by the water barrels, she paused, stretched in such a way that her head came lightly into contact with his right shoulder.

"I wish I had two good arms," Cambrian murmured into her hair. A soft evening breeze took a wisp of her hair and tickled his cheek with it.

"You will soon." She gently eased back into

his embrace, mindful of his ribs. "But one arm is enough when the woman-fairy is willing."

"Are you?" Cambrian wondered aloud and kissed her temple. He would never cease to be amazed that she found him, of all men-fairies, worth her interest. He just had to be careful not to let that amazement become insecurity, or worse, self-contempt. It was a matter of concern to him how rapidly his emotions could change, how much effort he was having to expend lately to keep them in line. Thank goodness Jennings was patient!

Constance frowned a little. It would not take much to overthink that question. She was quite willing to let him hold her. If he felt up to kissing her, she would even kiss him back. Why? Because she knew she was willing to marry him. But to carry that line of thinking into speech…?

"Constance?" Cambrian murmured after several seconds of silence. When she still did not respond, he carefully turned her so that she was facing him. Along with everything else on his mind of late was the question of whether or not to discuss with her what was happening to him. Since Kuntza had told him about his delirium, and Jennings had confirmed it, Cambrian had been watching for signs that Constance wanted to—or needed to—discuss it. He was still struggling with the idea of ruining their time together when he asked, "Are you alright?"

Her frown twisted into a smile. Of course

she was alright; and, of course she was not alright. Such complicated answers to such simple questions!

"I," she hesitated. "I was just thinking."

"You mean you were worrying," Cambrian half-asked, keeping his tone light in case he was wrong. Most of what he knew about women-fairies, beyond a certain skill at flattery, came from experiences with those in his own family, and he had learned from them to approach serious topics carefully.

"Yes, I suppose I do," she agreed after a moment's consideration. "About me?" Cambrian felt enormously conceited to even suggest it, but surely if one of them was worried about the other it would help to talk about it. And maybe she would dismiss the idea, which would leave him free to muddle along without worrying about her worrying about him.

She looked up at him sharply, regretting her decision to stop in the half-shadows by the water barrels. It made it more difficult to see his face and read his expression.

"Kuntza told me," Cambrian began to explain but hesitated, suddenly unsure of himself. "That I was delirious in the infirmary."

"Yes," Constance nodded. "You were." It was relatively easy to agree to a plain fact.

"He also said he was worried about you." This was not going the way he had hoped. He began hunting for a way to change the subject, but her response came too quickly.

"About me?" Constance's astonishment was genuine. "Why?" She had done her best to hide her own nightmares, appropriating a cabin for herself and Miss Dunn, the only two female officers on the *Nadauld*, and arranging their schedules so that they rarely saw each other.

"I only know what he told me," Cambrian pointed out quickly. A poor defense at best. And why, he wondered, did he feel a need to defend himself?

"Which was what exactly?" Constance pulled back, bumping into the gunn'ls before she remembered how close she had been to them. Confused, she caught hold of her safety line, gripping it as if she had fallen over the side. If Kuntza was concerned about her, he needed to talk to her, not to Cambrian. Cambrian had more trouble than he could handle already. The daughter of a military family, she had many times seen the emotional damage that came part and parcel with the physical wounds inflicted by violence. She had seen her own parents work through it more than once. Together. So why did she feel so driven to handle her own symptoms single-handed? She bit her lip. Habit?

"He said you were crying." Cambrian watched her closely, her withdrawal from him placing her squarely in the light. "He said he thought you were brave but frightened. And," he held up his hand to prevent her from interrupting him, "he told me in no uncertain terms that we needed to talk."

Constance turned away, looked out over the gunn'ls into the night. "Yes, I cried," she admitted at last. She understood what Kuntza had done. Cambrian would benefit from having someone to help, a positive way to contribute to life around him. Her mother had provided similar exercises for her father, usually in the form of fixing something about the house or with the younger children that no one could do quite as well as he could. But how should she proceed? As honestly as she dared; hopefully she could keep the focus off of herself while she recovered her balance. "I could hardly believe some of the things you said."

"For example?" Cambrian asked, crossing his good arm over his strapped one. Jennings had been vague, then testy when Cambrian had tried to talk about it with him. Kuntza had been simply impossible, answering every question with the admonition to talk to his 'woman-fairy.' Oh, Kuntza had *listened* when Cambrian tried to explain why he could not burden Captain Kimberlite with his unsolvable problem. But he simply would not talk beyond that one bit of advice.

"Do you really believe that you are the most useless member of the royal family?" She turned to face him.

"I," embarrassed, Cambrian paused. "I

sometimes wonder."

"Why?" she challenged, stepping closer. "Because you loathe state dinners and have to bite your tongue to keep from pointing out that bored nobles would be less bored if they would fulfill all of their duties?" How far would she have to push him before he would willingly admit these things? Would that do him any good?

Cambrian cringed away from her words, appalled to hear some of his innermost thoughts being expressed aloud.

"And do you really think that the Wood Fairies would go to war with us if you forgot to wear a medallion their king impulsively gave you?" Constance pressed on, mostly because she could not bear the silence.

"You speak of things you do not understand." Cambrian instantly regretted his tone, his defensive reaction to her honest questions. He saw the fire fade from her eyes and watched her step back to lean on the gunn'ls as though she needed something to hold her up. Sighing, he ran his fingers through his hair. He was sorely in need of a haircut. "And yet everything you said is true. I do loathe state dinners. And I do find myself in the peculiar position of having almost everything I do cross-examined and exaggerated until even I lose sight of how things got started. It is a hazard that every member of royalty faces daily." That he sounded as frustrated as he felt was only further proof of a need for concern on his behalf. He used to be able to hide his emotions better. In fact, until he had met Constance, he had thought himself permanently devoid of emotions.

Constance tried to blink back a wayward tear, one that she should have cried with the others when she had given vent to her feelings, but it somehow slipped past her screen of lashes. Should she even tell him that in his delirium he had called for his first love, Joanna?

"Oh, Constance." Cambrian stepped forward, cupping her cheek in his hand and wiping away her tear with his thumb. "I am sorry. I should not have spoken so sharply."

She looked intently up into his face, thoughts tumbling about in her mind. There was no need to tell him; she had accomplished her goal for the moment. Facing fear began with acknowledging it. Besides, her bruised heart would heal more quickly by actively caring for him than by dwelling on something he had not *chosen* to say. Anyway, he was apologizing for snapping at her just now….and doing it rather nicely.

"Cambrian." She let out the breath she had been unconsciously holding and stepped closer, wrapping her arms carefully about him. "I remember my mother telling me that communication and miscommunication were so much alike that I should always expect to have both in any relationship." While she would have enjoyed a little more carefree time with Cambrian before any major challenges had surfaced, she would not abandon him because under his calm, self-assured surface he had carefully guarded fears. She had fears of her own, some kept private for so long that she would rather be grounded than give voice to them. She could certainly empathize with his being emotionally unsettled by their uncontrolled surfacing.

Cambrian laughed softly as he put his arm about her shoulders and gently tugged her braid. He was going to have to talk her into wearing her hair down again while they were at Regalis.

"Your mother sounds like a wise woman-fairy."

"She is." Constance smiled into his shirtfront. "Now, you must allow me to admit that you were not solely at fault."

Cambrian raised eyebrows that he temporarily forgot she could not see. "How so?"

"I should have given you time to think." She closed her eyes, unhappy with her behavior. *How boorish she must seem to him! He finally says something,* she sighed inwardly, *and I attack him. It had seemed a good idea at the time.* It had turned out rather like using a cannonball to deliver a message to a friendly windship. Not for the first time she wished that she could counsel with her mother.

"Oh, that." Cambrian chuckled. His outburst fresh in his mind, he weighed his next words carefully. "We are only two days out from

Regalis, capitol city of the Sky Fairy Tribe, home to the Royal Family," he allowed his tone to change to the monotone of a tour guide, "and scene of some of the fiercest verbal battles fought in our tribe." Smoothing her hair, he kissed it. "If I cannot keep my wits about me, I shall be of even less use to my family than I feared. Of course," he gently tipped her head back so he could watch her face, "by now I should know I do not think clearly where you are concerned."

After a moment's hesitation, she went up on her toes, feeling strangely shy as she pressed a kiss to his cheek. Her gasp of surprise was purely spontaneous when his arm caught her about the waist, preventing her from settling her heels back onto the deck.

"Cambrian," she began to protest, worried about his injuries. "I..." She forgot what she had been about to say, something about his cracked ribs or perhaps his bruised jaw, when he leaned closer.

A clanging bell signaled the changing of the watch, but she stayed where she was, warm in his embrace. Despite herself, her thoughts turned to the future. Her experience with state affairs ranged from formal dinners at the academy to defending the kingdom, always with the protection her military status afforded her. So many times in the past she had figuratively donned her captain's bicorn and been excused her social shortcomings. Windship captains had early mornings, and could be pardoned for leaving a boring party early. Windship captains spent all of their time on the wing and could hardly be expected to know every custom in every port. But what would be what would be expected of her as Prince Cambrian's flame? For she understood that their relationship would become public knowledge and a matter of common speculation once they arrived at Regalis.

"Cambrian," she said at last. "I would like to help." *If I can*, she added silently.

"Help?" he asked. "With what?" As far as he was concerned, everything was perfect.

Laughing softly, she pulled away. "Cambrian," she raised both eyebrows at him. "I would like to help *you*." It would be easier with his permission. She hoped.

"Me?" He frowned thoughtfully, then grimaced. "Do we have to talk about that right now?" he asked. He had just been indulging in the most delightful vision of the future. Constance had been about to come through the door, wearing a dinner gown…

"Yes." She answered seriously, though she did not turn her face away when he bent to kiss her again. "The sooner the better," she added softly when he straightened away. While she did not know how much help she could offer, she knew it was more than physical pain that had caused such a dramatic change in him, making the charming, unflappable prince she fell in love with have to work so hard at maintaining a minimum of self-control. Jennings had told her a little about Cambrian's behavior, enough that she knew he needed their help whether he wanted it or not.

"Very well." Releasing her, he stepped back. If anyone had a right to discuss his flaws with him, it was Constance. "I think you should know," he said bravely, "that my temper may be my biggest weakness."

"It may *have* been." She wilted a little under the effect of his wounded gaze, but he had a right to the truth. "Jennings and I have both noticed you struggling, but not just with your temper." She spoke quickly, anxious to have the admission done with. "In fact, we have both been watching out for you."

Cambrian blinked, not sure how to respond to that. "Watching *out* for me," he emphasized her words. He felt himself beginning to flounder and fought to focus on what she had said rather than on the dozen or more thoughts and emotions it sparked inside him. "Like the other day, with Kuntza?" he asked. He had been trying to explain something to Kuntza, something that had seemed relatively simple until he realized he had been 'explaining' it unsuccessfully for over twenty minutes. Suddenly Jennings had appeared at his elbow, telling him that Dixby wanted to see him. That had been happening a lot lately, come to think of it.

"Are you upset, darling?" Constance blushed a little when she heard the endearment slip out. Some women-fairies gauged the progress of their courtship by the kind of gifts they were brought; for now she would have to make do with the hints that they both dropped and hope one of them was not progressing faster than the other. Or regressing. That thought left her so cold that she shivered despite his warmth.

"Is Toby in on this?" he asked abruptly. Upset? Yes, that and more. But with whom? With himself for needing help? With them for offering? With the whole of Fairydom for daring to go on after Joanna died? In a word, yes.

"Toby?" She shook her head. "Unless Jennings told him. Why do you ask?" It had not even occurred to her to ask for Toby's assistance.

Cambrian started to shrug, then checked himself. It would never do to go around his father's court shrugging, however much he enjoyed his brother Oliver's exasperated response.

"Little things. Things he has done or said." He frowned. "I think it started after I shouted at him the other day."

"You shouted at him?" Constance frowned, too. Very little happened on her windship that she did not hear of, one way or another. Usually. "When was this?"

"Two days ago." Cambrian did not have to stop to think. The moment was indelibly etched in his memory. "Jennings was late and I had been trying to dress myself when Toby knocked on the door. First I shouted at him to come in; then I shouted at him to get over and help me."

Constance remembered bumping into Toby later that same day. He had been leaning on a cannon, chewing a bit of hardtack with a thoughtful expression on his face. She also remembered being puzzled at his reluctance to talk to her about what was bothering him. Now she thought she understood. Cambrian was something of a hero to the boy-fairy, and it was always sobering to realize one's hero was not perfect.

"The point is," she sorted through her thoughts to find what she had started out to say. "The point *is*," she repeated, "that there are those who would help you."

"I am not…" He paused, searching for a way to express what he knew was the truth. "I am not accustomed to needing help." Certainly not to *admitting* it.

"I wish I could say the same." Constance smiled. Seeing his eyes narrow and his mouth harden, she realized that she would have to convince him. "A windship captain who believes they are flying without help is only fooling themselves. I shudder at the thought of flying the *Nadauld* without Mister Dixby, or…" She bit her lip to steady herself, the loss of her officers too recent to be easily spoken of. "Fortunately," she added sardonically, "I have Captains Grant and Trevaille to help."

Cambrian smiled faintly at that. Trevaille seemed capable of flying a windship blindfolded and with both hands tied behind his back. But because Kuntza required so much of his time and attention, and because Constance was spending her energy with him and the investigation, the flying of the *Nadauld* had been left mostly to Grant.

"What?" Constance asked. "You sighed just now," she clarified when he looked quizzically at her.

"I was just thinking." Feeling suddenly drained of energy, he turned and leaned back against the nearest water barrel. When Constance stepped closer, he reached out to gently guide her to stand by his right side so that he could put his arm about her shoulders.

"Hold that thought," she told him. Unclipping her safety line, she untangled it from his and clipped it back onto her safety harness. "There." Finished, she leaned against him, his chest rising and falling under her hand. From where they stood, looking forward, it seemed as if the bow of the *Nadauld* was dipped in the gold of the setting sun, the sails afire with its slanting rays.

"I was just thinking about Grant," Cambrian mused aloud. Privately, Cambrian thought he must have been promoted prematurely, perhaps as a result of the vacuum of officers created by the pirate offensive. He was not quite sure what to do about it, though. "It might be the best thing for him to do another decade or so as a junior officer," he hazarded at last.

Constance did not respond immediately. After she had set aside her surprise, she had to decide whether or not she should follow his lead. Was he just trying to change the subject? Or was he slipping back into his former role as investigator for the crown?

"I certainly can see how it might help," she agreed slowly. "Are you planning to suggest that to your father?"

Cambrian had just been asking himself that same question. "I do not know. That, my dear," he scowled at himself, "is my true weakness." The words left a bitter taste in his mouth, but somehow his heart felt a little lighter at having someone to express his innermost thoughts to. Not that it would be easy to explain why he blamed himself, his self-confidence, for their nearly getting captured. For the loss of over a hundred windfairies and the *Kimuxwe*. For—so many things. He had played right into Layton's hand.

Constance opened her mouth—and shut it. There was something in Cambrian's tone that made her think listening was more important than rushing to reassure him.

"Miss Dunn," a querulous voice called from

the quarterdeck, interrupting the peaceful evening air. "Miss Dunn, how many times must I tell you that I want those cannons ready to be loosed at a moment's notice? No, no excuses." He was biting the words out now. "Assemble the lads. I will address them myself."

Constance grimaced and stepped away from Cambrian. Of all the rotten timing on the wind! From somewhere in her store of muscle memory, she summoned up a cold smile. And turned it in Grant's direction.

"That will be all for now, Miss Dunn," Constance informed the junior officer, who jumped at the unexpected voice. "Captain Grant will stand the rest of your watch." Grant, she knew, had retired shortly after breakfast and arisen just before supper, making him the perfect choice for the second dog watch.

"Captain, I can," Miss Dunn started to protest.

"I know you *can*," Constance interrupted, raising her eyebrows and her voice slightly in a bid for the younger woman-fairy's full attention. "I also know you are exhausted. Now go below and get some sleep."

"Aye, aye." Miss Dunn snapped a salute and spun on her heel, taking care to use the forward hatch so she would not have to pass near Grant, the insufferable little despot.

Constance fixed her gaze on Grant while she waited for Miss Dunn to move out of earshot. "I think you will find, Captain," she addressed him by his rank for both their sakes, "that the lads will do better with a sound night's sleep than a lecture." While their new course had made flying the *Nadauld* much easier, many of the lads were recovering from sleep deprivation caused by their earlier course as well as wounds and malnutrition. Those that were sleeping now would, of course, hear of the altercation before morning mess, thanks to the open ears scattered about the deck from the night crew.

"That is your opinion," Grant snorted. "Captain." He smiled wanly.

Constance did not have to think very hard to understand Grant's hastily tacking her rank onto the end of his belligerent sentence. Obviously he had noticed Cambrian. Her smile dropped a few degrees in temperature. Officers like Grant were lower than courtiers in her mind. At least courtiers were honest about their intentions to climb socially by seeking favor with those of higher station.

"I will stand the first watch," she announced firmly. Mister Dixby had originally been slated for that, partly so he could take a lunar sighting, but if Grant knew *she* was to relieve him he would probably cause less trouble between now and then. Besides, Mister Dixby could still take his lunar. And then spend the first watch reviewing the strange map she and Cambrian had found in the oilskin pouch.

Chapter III

On the morning of the fourth day of their voyage, the entire crew stood out to help bring the *Nadauld* into Regalis. Even Jennings was required on deck, which left Constance, as one of three captains, tending to what had been Jennings' duties for the bulk of their voyage. Below decks, Constance smiled and took up the sling from Cambrian's bunk. "Almost done." Taking care to position it so that it would ride comfortably on the sensitive wing area, she wrapped it around his chest and looped the back strap up over his shoulder. Ordinarily this was Jennings' task, but he was busy above decks. The steady winds had brought them gliding over the foothills right on schedule.

"I detest that thing," Cambrian growled even as he obediently held out his elbow for her to slip the sling onto. "I thought fleet windships were better equipped when it came to treating traumatic injuries." He waited for her to respond to his unjust criticism, to snap back at him, but she only glanced up, her gorgeous blue eyes piercing his bubble of selfishness and letting the warmth of her love in. It was not her fault that Bane had looted the *Nadauld* and her stores. It was Bane's fault, something he had to remember to keep from blaming himself. "I am sorry," he sighed, running his right hand through his dark

~ 34 ~

blue hair. "For the dozenth time," he began.

"Shah," she dropped one end of the strap to press a finger to his lips. "You talk too much," she teased, smiling softly. They had agreed that more thinking and less talking would save him from most of the embarrassing predicaments he anticipated at court. Deliberately, she picked the strap back up and fastened the ends together, glad that the strap ran above the line where he had been kicked in the ribs by the pirates. She was a little worried that his mood would only worsen when he tasted the vile potion the doctors used for bone healing. Perhaps it tasted better now than it had a hundred years ago? She shook her head. "Do you really think I am counting your smiles and frowns?" she asked, fluttering up a little so that she could smooth his hair and straighten his collar.

"No," he admitted, "but surely you have a right to resent being barked at." He watched her settle to the ground, wishing there was time for him to steal a kiss. It might make him feel better. Or at least less anxious.

"A right?" She chuckled. "Yes, I suppose I have." To keep her hands busy she fastened the lower two buttons of his open-necked uniform shirt, leaving the last one undone so he could breathe. They were all wearing slops by now, liberated windfairies and princes alike, and grateful for them. "Perhaps I will resent it, once you are a bit more healed. But for now," she took a half step back, "I am disposed to be patient with you." She tried to project the cool, detached air of a nurse-maid. Her composure slipped a little when Cambrian frown-smiled at her.

A wanderer and a poet. A windship captain and a prince of the realm. Two very different fairies, deeply involved in their own lives. Yet somehow, with everything else that had happened since they left Fort Bakarti, she had managed to fall in love with him. She had known that from the first time she let him kiss her, had loved him despite the sacrifices that had immediately followed. Of course, his previous announcement that he had very serious intentions towards her had weighed on her mind, tipping the scales in his favor. Now, as Cambrian cupped her cheek in his right hand, a fear welled up inside her—fear of losing him to his family and responsibilities. Aboard the *Nadauld* they had at least been able to find each other. At Regalis, there would be affairs of state, military debriefings, boards of inquiry, hours of paperwork. They would be like puppets, the strings that made up the tapestries of their lives pulling them every direction but closer…with more of the same every day for the foreseeable future.

She turned away to hide the tears pricking at her eyes. "Is it in the usual place?" she asked briskly, already moving towards his sparsely equipped clothes cupboard as she spoke.

Cambrian watched her go, feeling twice ashamed of himself for making her cry. Why was he taking his frustration out on her? She had done nothing to deserve it—except turn his heart inside out. He inhaled slowly, forcing himself to take a step back from the current incident and look at the root of the problem. As much as he loved loving her, it seemed he could not pick and choose which emotions he experienced. All of them—anger, fear, frustration—had been revived with happiness and love, powerful even after their years of lying dormant. The worst was when they flooded into his brain so that he was not experiencing one emotion, but several at the same time. He frequently felt angry and pleased at the exact same moment, which left him fumbling for an appropriate way to express himself. All too often he failed, inflicting wounds upon those to whom he owed so much. And it seemed to be getting worse, not better.

Think more, talk less, he reminded himself.

"Constance," he opened his mouth to try to explain, to apologize just once more. But when she turned to face him, his crown in her hands, he was tongue-tied. Realizing that she was waiting for him to continue, he said the second thing that came to mind. "I still cannot believe I told you about that hiding place." Rewarded by her smile, he shook his head as she returned to him, more to delay having her place the crown than to express actual disbelief. He had opened his soul to her many times during the last four days. Somehow, they had never gotten around to putting their feelings for each other into words. And if they had, he would have been at a distinct disadvantage. There were no words that could convey half so much as her gentle patience and intelligent listening. What could he offer to match that?

"Hold still," she admonished, fluttering so that she was at eye-level with him. "In less than an hour we will be docking at Regalis and the last thing we need is for your mother to have to hunt through rows of windfairies in slops to find you."

Cambrian grinned and rubbed the stiff collar of his uniform shirt with his right hand. "You make an excellent point," he acceded. According to Mister Dixby, who had been aboard the *Nadauld* when Major Layton, the pirate king Bane, was searching for Cambrian's crown, Bane himself had thrown Cambrian's wardrobe over the side, item by item. "I must say I do not regret the loss of my plum-colored satin suit."

Constance raised both eyebrows and mouthed the word 'plum' to herself as she went to hunt for his sash, more to complete the uniform than because she thought he wanted it.

"I suppose you realize Jennings would find your court wardrobe a constant source of entertainment?" She threw the observation over her shoulder as she shook out the sash she eventually found hidden under the pillow. She was of the opinion that Cambrian should ask Jennings to be his valet sooner rather than later, but Cambrian insisted that Jennings at least deserved a look inside the Crystal Castle of Regalis before being asked to make that kind of a choice.

"Yes." Cambrian chuckled, amused at the thought. Jennings was certainly a more complex man-fairy than his last valet, Robert. Best of all, underneath Jennings' rough exterior was a ramrod straight spine and a true heart that bridged any gap between his education and the position. If Robert had been like that, how many lives would have been spared?

Constance wound the sash expertly around Cambrian's waist and tied it with a flourish. It reminded her so much of helping her father dress for formal events that she closed her eyes. She missed her father more than ever since she met Cambrian. When she was a little girl-fairy, barely old enough to be a cabin lass, she had imagined the man-fairy she would one day introduce to her father. The two men-fairies were to have become good friends, and when her father was too old to be on active duty, they would all spend the long winter evenings playing Stratagem and discussing the latest news. Or the oldest. Winter months seemed like years, sometimes, every windship and town shut down against the weather. Travel via tunnels was possible in the larger communities, but most chose to avoid them as a an unpleasant reminder of the deadly conditions outside.

"Constance?"

Captain Constance Kimberlite opened her eyes to find Cambrian looking down at her, his head cocked to one side and a half-smile on his face as if he were not quite sure smiling was the correct response to her silence. Disciplining the urge to kiss away his half-frown, she took two steps back.

"I should go on deck," she said quietly, squaring her shoulders. "We will be in sight of Regalis soon and I must see that your flag is run up." She waited for his nod before turning to leave. Truly their relationship could be complicated at times! Making her way briskly through the passageway and up to the quarterdeck, she exchanged salutes with Captains Trevaille and Grant.

"The winds are a bit rough this morning, Kimberlite," Captain Grant informed her brusquely. "I recommend circling Regalis and coming in from the north."

"Nonsense." Trevaille scowled, as he often did when Grant was around. "This breeze is barely stiff enough to support a docking maneuver. Altitude is what we lack."

She stifled her frustration with their constant bickering and fished her telescope out of a waist pocket. "Is Kuntza safely below?" she asked.

"Aye," Trevaille answered. Frowning, he continued, "I think he is happier below decks, to tell the truth. Something about being able to see to the horizon seems to make him uncomfortable."

Captain Kimberlite lowered her glass. "Or perhaps, homesick? Like us when we are on patrol. We can see our mountains, but we cannot go to them."

Trevaille nodded slowly. "Aye, there is that. After my time among his tribe, though, I have noticed that they do not much care for open spaces, even with solid ground beneath them." He added the last with a sardonic smile, remembering how cramped their underwater cities had seemed at first.

"I see." She made a mental note to pass that along to Cambrian, just in case he was not already aware of it. Shutting her glass decisively she called, "Miss Dunn." When Miss Dunn looked back from where she was supervising the sail crews, Constance nodded. Almost immediately a windfairy ran to the flag locker for Cambrian's flag. Returning her attention to her fellow captains, Constance advised Trevaille, "We are approaching the docks rapidly now and this will be another new experience for Kuntza. It might be better if you were with him."

As soon as a reluctant Captain Trevaille had gone below, she turned her attention to Captain Grant. "Take your station, please." It had been something of a struggle to regain command of her windship during their meeting last night, but she had been determined and not even Grant's thinly compressed lips was going to change her mind. With barely a third of the crew complement ordinarily assigned to a Gyrfalcon-class windship, this was going to be an interesting docking maneuver even with her expert touch.

As it happened, she did not agree with either of them about the docking. Gliding in from the north would be too easy, even with a skeleton crew. Coming in straight from the foothills, on the other hand, would require sharp attention to detail by the officers and strict compliance by the crew. The breeze was quite brisk enough as it was. And she thought they could handle the challenge, that they needed it. Some of these windfairies had been grounded for months. Today's successful docking maneuver would be a pleasant memory for them while they eagerly waited for their families to be informed that they were alive. Mister Dixby had the list of names ready to turn over to the dock officer at his first chance.

Just then a flag officer on the docks presented a challenge. The *Nadauld* was not assigned to the area around Regalis and for all her military trappings, she could be fired upon if the correct answer was not promptly returned.

"Steady as she goes," she ordered the helmsman as Captain Grant used the signal flags to respond, asking for assistance with the docking as well as identifying their windship. The entire crew had been rousted to manage the sails, the flaps, and the mooring cables. They all waited tensely until the flag officer returned an 'all clear' and a green flag went up over an empty cradle. "Off the port bow," Constance instructed the helmsman even though he had probably seen it first.

"Aye, Captain." The helmsman gripped the wheel a little more tightly. The *Nadauld* would be slowing soon and it was his job to direct her safely into reach of the mooring cables.

"Miss Dunn," Captain Kimberlite called, her eyes fixed on the dock. "Begin taking in sail." It was earlier than she normally would have given the order, but it would take them longer than usual to get the sails secured. "Captain Grant," she ordered, "stand by for the cradle."

Captain Grant stowed the flags and went forward. Wing crewmembers were already in position by the winches that controlled the flaps on the *Nadauld*'s six short wings. Grant clasped his hands behind his back and tried to look nonchalant as he waited for Captain Kimberlite's command.

"Steady," she called from the quarterdeck as the *Nadauld*'s nose dipped slowly. Mentally calculating and recalculating the *Nadauld*'s rate of approach as the sails were furled, she began to wonder if they were going to make it. It was always simpler to theorize than to apply! "Forward flaps down!" she ordered as the windfairies began furling the topgallants.

"Down and locked!" Captain Grant answered her order. The Nadauld's nose rose sharply, levelled and resumed a lazy earthward tilt. He smoothed his hair nervously.

"Mainflaps down!" she ordered after a brief pause. She was relying on the staggered lowering of the flaps to control the descent of the gradually slowing *Nadauld*, allowing her to arrive at the cradle at the right speed, altitude, and time. "Mizzenflaps down!"

The *Nadauld*'s nose rose sharply one last time and she eased forward. In answer to their signaled request, the dock lines were accompanied down by six members of the docking crew and hauled hastily under her hull. They were met on the other side by six more of the dock crew, who executed the emergency cradling procedure of strapping a second set of lines to the first, just below the level of the main deck. The noise the *Nadauld* made as she settled into the straps sounded almost as if she were sighing in relief at her safe arrival.

"Ahoy, Captain," called a voice from above. "Permission to come aboard?"

"Permission granted!" Captain Kimberlite responded a moment before Captain Grant could. She watched the dock above, puzzled at the delay. To be sure, they were facing more than an inquiry into their emergency docking maneuver, but what was keeping the docking crew captain? She gasped and reached for her sword as an armed squad of mounted marines suddenly swarmed the *Nadauld* from below. She felt a little dizzy as she remembered that she was not wearing one. Bane had taken every weapon that was not affixed to the windship—including her father's sword.

"At ease," Captain Kimberlite called to her lads as they began reaching for belaying pins, wrenches, and buckets. These were no pirates to be fought off, but their own military. Forcing herself to relax, she repeated the command. "At ease, there!"

"Who is in command of this vessel?" snapped the squad's officer. He and his lads ignored Captain Kimberlite's efforts at peace, keeping their weapons at the ready.

"That depends," answered an amused, male voice from the aft companionway door. "Militarily or diplomatically?" Realizing that the squad's officer was looking to see who had spoken, Cambrian stepped to one side so that the mainmast was no longer blocking the officer's view. Then he smiled, broadly. "I suppose no matter how one looks at it, I am ultimately in command." It was almost easy to slip into his old role.

Constance bristled reflexively at the thought of someone else in command of her windship— but only for a moment. Had she not shared command of the *Nadauld* for the last several days?

Besides, it was entertaining to watch the squad officer scrambling for his formal manners.

"Your Highness!" the man-fairy half-barked, half-croaked. "What are you doing here?"

Cambrian just raised his eyebrows. *Talk less, listen more.* Even if the officer only continued asking questions, he should be able to deduce quite a bit about what had been going on during his most recent absence from Regalis.

"He is returning home," Captain Grant bit out impatiently. "Did you not see his flag on the mast?"

Cambrian glanced at Captain Grant in annoyance, but still said nothing.

"Indeed they did," called a voice from above.

Cambrian watched, dumbfounded, as his father descended from the dock. He barely even took notice of the tall, lithe man-fairy that descended with the king.

King Jasper hovered a moment, taking in the state of things, before dropping lightly to the deck.

"I ordered them here to determine if it was a ruse," he explained quietly. He had many times seen his sons in uniform during their obligatory decade in the Royal Marines, but never had he seen Cambrian in such an ill-fitting outfit as this. On the other hand, it had been years since he had seen him looking so happy.

"Salute!" Captain Grant shouted, snapping to.

Jasper blinked, the only outward expression of his surprise at the command. What did he care for salutes when his younger son was safely home again?

"Thank you," he smiled, returning Captain Grant's salute. "And, Captain," he acknowledged the woman-fairy on the quarterdeck. "Kimberlite, is it not?"

"Aye, sir," she smiled and lowered her salute.

Jasper's smile widened. Of course he remembered the handful of captains that he had awarded medals to after the successful—but costly—pirate offensive. What luck to find his son in the care of the best of them!

"At ease." He chuckled, to the relief of the windfairies scattered about the deck. "Well," he approached Cambrian and clapped him on the right shoulder. Whatever he had been about to say died on his lips when Cambrian's face went white. "Well," he repeated, lowering his hand to his side, "I can hardly wait to hear your reports on all that has happened since you left Bakarti." Suddenly noticing Captain Grant drawing an eager breath, Jasper continued hastily, "Of course, I understand that the windship comes first."

"I will see to the *Nadauld*," Constance volunteered, flying up and over the quarterdeck's forward railing to land beside Cambrian in a rare, dock-side maneuver. As she had expected, Captain Grant frowned. She really was spending too much time with Cambrian, she thought. She was picking up all sorts of bad habits from him. Still, Trevaille would have to go along to take care of Kuntza and somebody needed to get the windship squared away.

"I can see to the *Nadauld*," Captain Grant objected. It was the sort of thing a proper captain would do, after all.

"Yes." Cambrian pursed his lips slightly as though suppressing a doubt. "I am sure you could."

Constance put her hand lightly on Cambrian's good arm, as if to prevent him from protesting. "Captain Grant is a qualified officer," she said reassuringly. She was relieved to see the color returning to Cambrian's face after his father's unintentional jarring of both collarbone and ribs. "Although," she hesitated, "a record of his report must be taken."

"As must yours," King Jasper inserted smoothly. It was a clever tactic, one that he used routinely to get things done at court without having to subject his friends to orders. He tapped one finger on his jaw briefly before snapping his fingers in triumph. "I have it. Lieutenant," he turned to the nearly-forgotten squad of marines, "send for a scribe. Captain Grant can give his statement while he settles the *Nadauld*."

"Capitol idea," Cambrian agreed briskly. "But Lieutenant, I suggest you send for two scribes. It will take two to keep up with Captain Grant." An understatement if ever there was one; the man-fairy had a highly annoying habit of trying to be everywhere, overseeing everything, at the same time. He did not bother to explain that to the lieutenant, of course, who disappeared with a salute, the rest of his squad trailing after him.

The thought of a scribe following him about while he gave orders to the crew made Captain Grant's chest—and head—swell a bit. "With your permission?" he squared his shoulders and saluted King Jasper, who readily released him with an answering salute.

Constance somehow maintained a straight face. "Captain Trevaille and I will have to join you at the castle, then." She mentioned Trevaille mostly to give Cambrian a lead-in as to why they needed a discrete transport.

"Ah yes." Cambrian faced his father directly. "Have you room for four, um, five more in your carriage?" he asked, adjusting the number as he remembered Jennings. Funny how easily he had slipped back into his role of prince. It was almost as if he were the same man-fairy he had been for the last fifty-some years.

"There is always room for more," Jasper responded breezily. Truthfully, he had not come by carriage at all, though one could be acquired in short order. He refrained from asking who the other passengers were, satisfied to know that Grant was not among them.

"Excellent," Cambrian smiled. "Perhaps it could meet us at the captain's aft window?" he suggested. It was his intention to transfer their plunder from Bane's windship and Kuntza to the castle at the same time. It was also his intention not to let those bags of books and papers out of his sight until they were safely locked inside his father's treasure room. Constance had the care of the oilskin pouch and wall map from the same raid, and while he was ever reluctant to be away from her, he had to admit that she was perfectly capable of looking after herself.

King Jasper nodded and turned to his bodyguard to relay an order.

"Spare me a moment to see to the lads?" Constance asked Cambrian, leaning closer so that she could lower her voice.

"Of course," he nodded. "It will take Ian a few minutes to conjure up a carriage anyway." He was only guessing, of course, but his father had probably taken the first available dragonfly when he heard his son's flag had been sighted on an incoming windship. It was the only way he could have arrived so quickly.

She smiled, aware that Ian Longfellow was his father's bodyguard. "You royals," she teased and squeezed Cambrian's good arm gently.

The dock crew captain had finally boarded and there were things she needed to discuss with him, like temporarily quarantining the crew for the sake of Kuntza's secret; and making arrangements for the medical supplies to be restocked for the care of the more seriously wounded lads. She would have liked to remain aboard with them, if only to make up for leaving Grant in charge for so long during their voyage, but Trevaille would have his hands full with Kuntza—which left her to go along and help Cambrian explain 'all that had happened' since the courier windship *Dispatch* had crashed at Bakarti.

Chapter IV

"Father," Cambrian hesitated in the passageway, his hand hovering over the handle to the door of the captain's cabin, "how are you feeling?" He had debated for hours with himself about how to tell his father of the Water Fairy Tribe, without coming to a firm conclusion. Even if his father already knew of the fifth fairy tribe, and an argument could be made that he did, finding a Water Fairy aboard the *Nadauld* was still bound to be a shock.

"Well enough," Jasper answered, one eyebrow slightly elevated at the question. His son stood before him, the skin around one eye a ghastly yellow-green, left arm and wing in a brace, and was asking after *his* health? Why?

"It is good to hear that." Cambrian might have hesitated further but for Constance's slight shrug. "We have something of a surprise for you." Opening the door, he motioned for his father to precede him.

King Jasper waved Ian back when the man-fairy made as if to move forward. He was unsure of many things at the moment, but he trusted his son implicitly. Fluttering forward, he entered the cabin and looked around. A desk, a chair, windows—what he saw by the windows startled him sufficiently that he dropped to the deck with a thump.

"King Jasper," Captain Trevaille, feeling more than a little foolish in his slops and stained bicorn, bowed at the waist. "May I have the honor of presenting Kuntza, a truth-seeker for the Water Fairy Tribe?" The question was as rhetorical as ever one was, but he hoped to relieve the situation of some of its awkwardness by at least sounding as though he were deferring to the king's authority.

Kuntza did not bow. Standing by the window, his hands clasped behind his back, he looked at this king of theirs with open curiousity. Even admitting that the circumstances of his meeting Prince Cambrian were unusual, he had not expected such a lack of formality at this presentation. Not that he was displeased. Had this meeting taken place at his own capital city of Cachora, there would have been a roomful of solemn-faced scholars watching their every move, evaluating everything from the smallest stitch on his hem to the unruly wisps of hair on his head. Surely this was a better way to greet a stranger. Bringing his hands forward, he offered them both to the Sky Fairy King.

King Jasper remained frozen in place for several heartbeats. It was just as his great-great-great-grandfather's notebook had described the first meeting with the Water Fairy ambassador, from the proffered double-handshake to the pink hair and soft light in Kuntza's eyes. *Almost as if they are lit from within*—the passage sprang to his mind as he had read it just the night before. Were his fears about to be realized? Surely not. Why break several thousands of years of silence by sending an ambassador just to declare war?

"Welcome, Kuntza," King Jasper stepped forward, placing one hand inside both of Kuntza's and setting his free left hand on the outside of their joined hands. He took care not to put his left hand on top of the handshake, lest he be mistaken as one trying to intimidate or assert his authority, of which he had none over this member of another fairy tribe. "May rainbows brighten your stay." Water Fairies, unless they had changed overmuch since they had cut off diplomatic ties with all the rest of Fairydom, preferred their enclosed cities, complete with the brilliant displays of color that the sea life surrounding them provided.

Kuntza did not attempt to deny the relief he felt at the ancient greeting. True, it meant the king had known of his tribe all along, but would he trouble himself with such politeness if he truly sought war with the Water Fairies? There was much to discuss—about the pirate invasion of his world and the Sky Fairy colonies with their mines poisoning the waters—and to observe before he had a solid basis upon which to begin forming a recommendation to his leaders.

"May the sun warm your lands," Kuntza responded politely. Personally he found the sunlight above water a harsh thing, heating his skin to uncomfortable temperatures and making it difficult to see things from their softer angles, but he understood that those unfortunate enough to live on dry land treasured the very things that made him uneasy.

"We owe Kuntza our lives, Father," Cambrian said quietly, feeling steadier than he had in days, a fact that he attributed to his father's presence.

"A debt that cannot be repaid," Jasper responded, his eyebrow quirking up again as he wondered just what *had* happened since his sons parted at Fort Bakarti.

A tap at the window alerted them to the fact that the carriage had arrived. Trevaille moved quickly to insert himself between Kuntza and the window.

"Kuntza is not yet ready to reveal the existence of his tribe," Cambrian answered his father's unspoken question immediately.

King Jasper nodded sharply. "I agree." In fact, he had been prepared to insist upon that, for the time being. He shuddered inwardly at the thought of the penalty described in their treaty should the knowledge of their tribe be revived after fading from memory. The Water Fairy Tribe was one enemy that Fairydom could not afford to make. His mind had settled on one thing, at least. Kuntza would have the truth; as much as he could absorb, about all of Fairydom. And Jasper would dispatch communiques to the other tribes as soon as Kuntza agreed, even if it meant risking winter travel. They had to understand.

Constance bent to pick up one of the pillow cases that they had liberated from Bane's flagship. It was stuffed almost to the brim with papers and books swept from the shelves of Bane's cabin. Most of the wall map, all but what had been left behind when Cambrian tore it free, was neatly folded and hidden within her tunic. She had taken pains to secure it along with the fat oilskin pouch against the small of her back, where the loose-fitting uniform shirt hung straight down off her shoulders, revealing nothing.

"Trevaille," Cambrian prompted.

"Best cover your hair," Trevaille admonished Kuntza and leaned forward to open the cabin window.

Ian went first, inspected the inside of the carriage, then held the door for King Jasper. Kuntza, Trevaille, Jennings, and Cambrian followed in short order. Constance handed out first one sack, then the other. It was a tight fight after that, but somehow she was able to wedge herself between Cambrian and the side of the coach. That left Trevaille, Kuntza, and the king on the forward wall, travelling backwards, while Ian sat up with the driver.

King Jasper reached back over his right shoulder, smiling apologetically at Kuntza, who had to move a little to accommodate him, and rapped on the wall. At his signal, the carriage moved smoothly away from the *Nadauld.*

"Forgive me," King Jasper apologized to Kuntza, speaking loudly to be heard over the hum of the horseflies, "I should have given you a window seat. We will be flying through some of the most interesting parts of Regalis on our way to the castle."

Kuntza shook his head somberly. "I cannot risk being seen." Then to be polite, he added pleasantly, "But what I can see from here is ver-ee nice."

Constance smiled at Kuntza's speech, noting that some of the stiffness in his pronunciation had eased since they had first met him. She had at first been surprised that he spoke their language at all and told him so, at which point he had explained that there were still some few among his tribe who regretted the severing of diplomatic ties. While much of the fluidity of the spoken language common in Fairydom had been lost to time, several hundred Water Fairies could read it with great skill. She had waited for him to tell her why they had withdrawn from among the rest of Fairydom, or perhaps why they were reaching out now, but he had simply smiled and begun lecturing Cambrian on the importance of wearing his sling.

Cambrian tapped Constance lightly on her near hand. With a wink, he began raising his right arm until he had slipped it about her shoulders, which allowed her to relax back from the uncomfortable-looking position she had taken, leaning far forward—he suspected in an attempt to keep from compressing his battered frame. He was careful to avoid making eye contact with his father, who was sitting on the bench opposite him, choosing instead to direct his gaze out the narrow coach windows. He could see Regalis slipping by, below and about the carriage.

It was all so different and yet so familiar. He supposed he had not really *seen* it since Princess Joanna's death. A group of child-fairies were playing rob the nest on the bottom level of a market they passed. The glimpse he got of their mothers, at the various shops on the second and third levels, made him wonder about their lives. This one was sampling perfume, that one counting out payment for a basket of groceries, and several others had gathered themselves about a booth draped with expensive-looking jewelry. Was there a party that night, or the next? Or were the occupants of Regalis so well-to-do that they could afford ornaments whenever they chose?

The feeling of Constance taking a slow, deep breath brought him back to the cramped inside of the carriage. Parties. Ribbons. He looked down at his clothes, at where Constance's hand rested carelessly against his knee. Slops were fine while on the wind, enormously suitable in some respects. The rough cloth held up against the various abuses of windfairy life, the dark color hid most of the stains, and the loose cut kept it from binding its wearer at inopportune moments, such as while taming a wildly flapping sail. At court, however, the standards were somewhat different. He made a mental note to ask his mother to find a way to provide Constance with some suitable clothes. The thought made him smile. He was really looking forward to seeing her in a ball gown.

"Look," he tried to point with his left hand, then hurriedly pointed with his right at a building they were flying over. "That is the town library. I used to spend hours there." He congratulated himself on stopping before he said all that was in his mind, telling how he had hidden there for days after Joanna's funeral. As extensive as the palace grounds were, he had been too easily found there.

"Are we near the castle, then?" Constance asked, looking up at him instead of out the window. The prospect of meeting his mother dressed in her current garb was not a pleasant one and she was eager to have done with it. As she leaned back against Cambrian's good shoulder, she saw King Jasper out of the corner of her eye. One of his eyebrows started to rise, causing her to hastily sit forward again.

Cambrian chuckled as the carriage passed through a gap in the outer wall of the Crystal

Castle, the steel netting blocking out neat squares of sky over their heads. "We are there."

Moments later the carriage was drawn up beside the royal family's private entrance to the second level of the castle. The moment the skids touched down on the marble outcropping, Ian leapt for the door, inspecting the area scrupulously while he held the door for the king.

Trevaille ushered Kuntza inside but King Jasper remained to hand down his younger son and the windship captain he had quickly come to perceive as a woman-fairy of about his son's age. Winking at Cambrian, he went before them through the heavy wooden door that led inside the castle.

Constance turned back at once for the sacks, lifting them out onto the outcropping. To her surprise, Ian closed the carriage door and sent it on its way promptly.

"Allow me," he said simply, bending to pick up both sacks in one hand. "I will keep them safe," he promised, gesturing with his left hand for them to precede him into the castle.

"Thank you, Ian," Cambrian smiled and offered Constance his elbow. Grinning at Jennings, he tried to decide if the man-fairy's face had gone any whiter since they got in the carriage. What effect would meeting his mother have on the tough windfairy?

"Yes," Constance smiled, relieved to have their care off her mind, "thank you very much."

Taking Cambrian's elbow, she squared her shoulders. She could hear several voices coming from inside, most of them female. Which one of them, she wondered, belonged to the queen? Stepping through the door, she discovered that there were five women-fairies inside! She felt quite at a loss when Cambrian dropped her arm to hold up his own in self-defense. Not as lost as poor Jennings looked, though. She sent him an encouraging smile.

"Easy," Cambrian warned his three younger sisters. "I have more than one cracked bone and would greatly appreciate it if you could content yourselves with a simple 'welcome home.'"

"A likely story," scoffed one of them, folding her arms across her chest to keep from racing forward and hugging him until he turned as blue as his hair.

"Who *is* this man-fairy, Father?" another asked in turn, raising her left eyebrow in a gesture that she had obviously inherited from Jasper.

"What an assumption, sir," baited the slightest of the three as she demurely smoothed the front of her exquisite rose petal skirt, "that we would wish to hug *you*."

Cambrian raised both his eyebrows, turned towards his mother, and pretended to stumble. All three of the girl-fairies reacted, from gasping in alarm to starting forward to assist him. Cambrian regretted his choice the moment his mother's hand flew to her lips.

"That was wrong of me, Mother," he said, without trying to excuse himself or hide his words from the others. "I ask your pardon." There was a great deal more he wanted to say, but his throat had tightened up so that further speech was impossible. That was probably just as well.

Queen Marta stepped forward, folding her son in a gentle hug. The rest of the room watched and waited in respectful silence.

Constance felt, as she supposed Trevaille and Jennings must also, a keen longing for her own mother's embrace. Such was the life of a windfairy that seeing family was all too rare a pleasure. She also felt as if a weight had been lifted from her shoulders as she watched the queen, who was only fractionally shorter than her son, ruffle and smooth his hair fondly. She had felt that Cambrian's wounds went deeper than sword cuts, without knowing how—or even if— they could be healed. Who better than his own mother to nurture him in his emotionally fragile state?

"Mother," Cambrian did not completely disengage from his mother's embrace even when he turned and sought Constance with his eyes. "Permit me to introduce my travelling companions. Captain Kimberlite," he paused while she bowed, "Captain Trevaille," another pause and corresponding bow. "Jennings," he grinned as the windfairy touched his forehead respectfully. "And this is Kuntza, a truth-seeker for his tribe." Cambrian held his mother tightly with his good arm while Kuntza lowered the hood of his cape. To his surprise, she took her introduction to a pink-haired, hazel-eyed man-fairy quite calmly.

"I am honored to meet you, sir." She curtsied deeply.

Constance watched in amazement as the entire royal family, including Cambrian, who, of a necessity had bowed with his mother's movement, curtsied and bowed before this stranger. Even Prince Oliver and his wife, Gemma, acknowledged Kuntza's arrival in a manner to match the queen's. Constance felt herself going pink when she found the triplets watching her curiously.

"Welcome to our home," the queen continued, rising slowly. "All of you."

"I suppose the best welcome would be a hot meal served on a stationary table," offered Oliver jovially, no stranger to travelling by windship.

Constance and Trevaille exchanged amused smiles, both of them wondering why it was that those fairies who ventured onto a windship only when absolutely necessary seemed to assume that windfairies agreed with their definition of comfort. Jennings' face remained mostly blank.

"Thank you," Trevaille responded, inclining his head slightly.

"You are very kind." Constance forced herself to use the same gesture of gratitude that

Trevaille had rather than allowing herself to be caught deciding between curtsying, bowing, or nodding.

"Seeker Kuntza," King Jasper stepped forward, "permit me to show you to your rooms."

Kuntza hesitated, not so much out of distrust as discomfort. He had spent most of his time in the company of books prior to Lay-ton's arrival and was not eager to leave the company of the friends to whom he had grown accustomed.

"Jennings and I will accompany you, if we may," Cambrian suggested, forcing past his worry about leaving Constance with his sisters. He would have liked to save Constance from a deluge of questions, or worse, the combined silence of his younger sisters. Still, his mother was there and for now they would be using their company manners, which might well make it the safest time for Constance to be left with them.

"And you, Andrew," Oliver fluttered forward and smiled at his old friend, "I suppose you would like to see where we have you slated to bunk." As if he had not noticed Kuntza's hesitation he went on easily to add, "I would let my father show you, as your chambers are quite near Kuntza's, but I had hoped to do a little catching up before supper."

"It has been a long time," Trevaille agreed, accepting Oliver's suggestion gladly.

The six men-fairies left in a loose group,

together but travelling in twosomes, Kuntza listening to Jasper while Trevaille and Oliver traded gentle jabs about how the years had changed them. Cambrian shot a final, reassuring glance at Constance before preceding Jennings out the door.

Constance felt about as out of place as a tin cup at a royal banquet as the doors closed behind them. She jumped a little when a hand came to rest lightly on her arm.

"You must not worry, my dear." Gemma, Oliver's wife, smiled encouragingly at the tense woman-fairy captain. "We have not forgotten you."

Constance looked at the woman-fairy who might someday become her sister-in-law and smiled weakly. Then she looked at the triplets, who seemed intent on surrounding her with cheerful smiles when she would have preferred a little space. Alas, what could she do? Reject their attempts at friendship?

"Indeed, no," Queen Marta inserted, smiling kindly, smoothing her crushed gown with practiced hands. "I am sure you will be very comfortable in the women-fairies wing." She referred, of course, to a small area of the castle set aside for their single female guests, where by time-honored tradition no man-fairy would intrude upon their privacy.

"It did not occur to me that she might be relegated to the women-fairies wing," Gemma mused aloud, carefully inserting the proper inflections into her voice so that it sounded more of a question than a suggestion. "If you would permit me, Your Majesty," Gemma erred on the side of formality, as she always did with her mother-in-law in public, curtsying slightly before continuing, "the rooms assigned to my cousin have not yet been assigned to another. I am sure the captain would find them comfortable." She had a sense of what the captain might be feeling, as much from her own experience of meeting this fearsome female foursome as from the way the captain's arm muscles had remained tense under her hand. By offering rooms in the wing of the castle designated for her and Oliver's private use, she hoped to shield the captain from the…inquisitive nature of the triplets. For a while, anyway.

"A generous offer," Marta responded, trying to fathom the motivation behind it. To be sure, she loved her daughter-in-law, but was distressed to realize upon occasion that Gemma was not always at ease with her husband's family. "What say you, Captain Kimberlite?" She turned her attention to the woman-fairy in question. "That wing of the castle is a bit removed from the daily entertainments; perhaps it would be too quiet for your taste?"

"By your leave, Your Grace," Constance responded carefully, "I fear I shall have little time for entertainments during my stay here." Also, a quiet room sounded marvelous. "If the rooms are available, I would be only too happy to stay there." Up until now she had had no idea as to the method of arranging quarters in the Crystal Castle. It certainly was not something included on the public tour! And no matter where she was quartered, it was not likely to be down the hall from Cambrian, as it had been on the *Nadauld*.

"'Tis settled, then," Gemma stated brightly. She waited half a heartbeat for her mother-in-law to excuse them with a slight movement of her hand, then began moving towards the door. "We must hurry," she told the captain kindly. "There is water to heat and clean clothes to find if we are to have you ready in time for dinner." She hated to sound so patronizing, but announcing a rather dull set of plans was the surest way to make the triplets lose interest.

"Oh!" Constance forgot herself when she remembered the sacks. Turning back to retrieve them, she came face to face—well, face to chest—with Ian. Looking up at him, she somehow felt better about having let her responsibility slip her mind.

"Shall I place these in the strong room?" Ian offered, correctly reading their importance in the captain's face.

"Yes, please," Constance agreed. She would have liked to hand over the map and pouch right then, but that would have proven awkward.

Ian bowed respectfully, first to the queen,

then to the royal family, and finally to the captain. There was about her something that he recognized, something that seemed almost to draw him to her. True, it was the king's own nod that had prevented him from dropping the sacks to follow him with both hands free. He nevertheless felt better knowing the fate of the young woman-fairy. She would be safe with Princess Gemma.

Gemma, who had found a silent friend in Ian when she first arrived, took note of Ian's respect for the captain. "Come," she bid her new friend gently.

Constance flicked a glance, and half a smile, in Ian's direction even as she bowed to the queen, the map crackling a little as she did so. When the queen and her three daughters responded by dropping curtsies, Constance cringed. A bow was good enough in terms of military courtesy, but she was not here merely as a windship captain in the King's Fleet. She was…what, exactly?

Chapter V

Cambrian laughed with the others at his father's account of a humorous incident at court, but his mind was not in the luxurious rooms where Kuntza and Trevaille would be staying. How could he have forgotten the sacks? He struggled with the anger seething in his chest, trying to set it aside before panic set in. Ian had them, he reminded himself. Ian would take care of them. Constance would see that they were alright.

"Cambrian," Oliver spoke from where he leaned against the fireplace mantle, a false smile hopefully hiding his concern, "do you still have that suit?"

"Not likely," Jennings snorted when Cambrian did not immediately respond. "Bane threw his whole wardrobe off the *Nadauld*." The overstuffed chairs and thick carpet were so unlike his natural habitat of a sparse windship hold that it made him nervous. So nervous that he could not help being himself.

Cambrian smiled at Jennings' intervention. The spontaneous gesture relaxed him, permitted him to think a little more clearly.

"That is correct, I am afraid," he sighed, feigning sorrow. "Even the plum-colored suit Mother was so fond of." At first he had worn it just to please her. Then he had realized how effective it was in disarming the fairies he was investigating. It seemed that they just could not take a man-fairy dressed in a velvet, plum-colored suit seriously.

"Ah." Jasper raised his eyebrows in an effort to keep himself from sighing in relief. "It is fortunate that you left a few suits in your chambers. I suppose they will do until you can schedule an appointment with Mark." Mark was the royal tailor, and had promised the king faithfully never to make another plum-colored suit for Cambrian.

"Of course," Oliver grinned knowingly, "Mother will insist on accompanying you."

"Your mother," Jasper intervened before they could get too far into family matters in front of Kuntza and the others, "will certainly insist upon your having a medical examination."

Cambrian sobered slightly. While he was looking forward to tossing the sling, he was not looking forward to the potions and therapy that the doctor would prescribe. The effectiveness of potions seemed directly proportional to their ghastly taste.

"I am alright," he said quietly. It was all he dared say for the distress of memories. Every time he thought about challenging Bane, it was with an overwhelming sense of astonishment at his own audacity. A fear at all he had risked.

"Your son is bet-ter than alright," Kuntza interrupted gently, misinterpreting the distress in the younger man-fairy's eyes. "A few weeks of care and he will be fit to resume limi-ted use of his wing and shoul-der."

"Weeks?" Jasper repeated, shocked. "Is your injury that serious?" "

No, Father," Cambrian held up his good hand. "Kuntza *is* a physician, as well as a truth-seeker." He looked at Kuntza, a wisp of an idea solidifying in his mind. "Kuntza, does your tribe not have potions for mending broken bones and repairing injured muscles?"

Kuntza blinked. "We do not."

Cambrian smiled. "This knowledge has been part of medicine in Fairydom for a few generations, but must have been discovered after your tribe separated itself."

"Indeed," Kuntza nodded. It was knowledge worthy of desire. He filed it away in his mind as something to include in his report.

"Too bad Bane plundered our medical stores to replenish his own," Trevaille growled.

Jasper and Oliver exchanged glances, intrigued. This was the first they had heard of what had occurred. Kuntza was an astounding development, but clearly there was more to be told.

"Bane?" Oliver asked his friend. "The pirate?"

"Aye." Trevaille shot a look at Cambrian. There was no reason he knew of not to speak, yet he was not sure. A nod from Cambrian prompted him to continue. "During the pirate offensive, the magic silver mirror on my windship, the *Talon*, was damaged to the point that it became unusable. We got lost in the Mists pretty quickly after that, despite our best attempts at following the sound of cannon fire." He turned to the fireplace, holding out his hands to the heat. It was warm for fall, but still too cool for his liking. "When we reached the edge of the Mists, the lads cheered. A windship was coming up, flying the Sky Fairy flag. An officer came aboard and told us the battle had been won. All that remained was to smash the pirate fortress on a nearby island."

Cambrian leaned back in the overstuffed chair, thinking it was just the sort of thing Layton-Bane would have approved of. Completely unexpected, nearly foolproof. Nothing to tie it back to him.

"Like a fool, I followed him. There had been no time for orders to be written out, he said, no time for us to gather and discuss things. Haste was the word of the day." Trevaille's tone was bitter at best. "When we reached the island, we were ready. Hull patched, cannons primed, our battle flag flying. Suddenly the lookout shouted—he had sighted two more windships. Then it was too late. Our escort ran up a pirate flag and it was three windships to one." His shoulders sagged at the memory of being defeated without firing a shot. "It was almost anticlimactic to discover that Major Layton was the pirate Bane."

Oliver was too stunned to respond. A glance at his father's white face showed a similar reaction there.

"Bane kept him and a few of his lads alive." Cambrian took up the story to ease the pressure he sensed Trevaille was feeling. "Those who would not turn to piracy, or at least, appear to turn," he reminded himself of Trent, "were murdered." He paused a moment, until he had regained control of his voice. "Then I arrived at Fort Bakarti to investigate 'Major Layton's' command capacity." He shook his head. "I was too tempting a prize for him to resist, so he baited a trap. Giving up the *Talon* was a small sacrifice if it would net him a prince of the realm. I overrode Oliver's common sense and went whistling where Bane led me, straight to the same island where he captured the *Talon*."

"If I might?" Jennings interrupted, concerned by the changes he could hear in Cambrian's tone of voice. While he could understand Cambrian feeling responsible, he hoped to avoid the type of emotional outburst to which the prince had recently become susceptible. "We did not make it all the way to the island on the *Nadauld*."

"No, you are right," Cambrian nodded and passed the story on with a wave.

"Bane made his move before we could realize how close we were," Jennings said, leaning forward fractionally, voice lowering dramatically. "Set on us with three sideboats of pirates and blood in his eye. Boarded the *Nadauld* as if she was his own," he added bitterly, "pompous as you please and looking for the prince." He jerked his head towards Cambrian. "But the cap'n had already sounded the alarm, rousting the lads and starting a fearsome battle."

Cambrian smiled a little at how Jennings' retelling had captured the attention of everyone in the room. Even Trevaille and Kuntza were still, almost holding their breath as they listened.

"She used one of the aft cannons to repel those boarders, then…" Jennings paused and licked his lips, suddenly unsure of himself.

"Then used the second one on the mainmast," Cambrian finished. "I had put together an emergency sailboard, so after she gave the call to abandon ship, we hopped off. Bane was so busy keeping the *Nadauld* aloft and searching for my crown that we were able to escape." Watching his father and brother nod, he hoped the military board of inquiry would be as understanding of Constance's actions as his family. Of course, the story of the *Kimuxwe* remained to be told.

"A few of us found each other on an island," Jennings picked the story back up. "Figured a way we might get the *Nadauld* back and took our chances."

"What a chance it was," Trevaille

acknowledged gravely. Turning from the fire to face King Jasper, he explained, "Bane outmaneuvered us. Again. He had a heavy guard on the windships, so that when we reached them half of us were recaptured before we knew what was going on. If it had not been for Prince Cambrian, we would have all died that night."

Cambrian's face, which had been growing paler, abruptly turned an unbecoming shade of red.

"Aye," Jennings agreed before Cambrian could speak. "He distracted Bane whilst the rest of us took the *Nadauld* away from her guards."

"Distracted Bane?" Jasper asked, not so much because he wanted to know the answer as because he wanted to learn it in relative privacy instead of during a public inquiry.

"Cambrian chall-enged Bane." Kuntza spoke directly. "They fought with swords. Bane's pirates fought with boots."

Oliver's brow puckered briefly, until he remembered seeing Cambrian wince while hugging their mother. Boots—brought into sharp contact with ribs—could cause such a lingering physical reaction.

"Dirty maggots," escaped him before he controlled his rage. He was at once ashamed and glad that Gemma was not present.

"Yes," Kuntza nodded seriously. "Filthy, in fact." He was surprised at their response to his honest observation. They all laughed, including the king, who had a moment before been staring at Cambrian with wonder and pain in his eyes.

"He is right," Cambrian gasped, holding his ribs and still unable to stop himself from laughing. "Of course, we were a few days past clean ourselves by the time we got the *Nadauld* back." Something he would never forget was Constance sliding towards him on the deck of the *Kimuxwe*, her blouse stained with gunpowder and blood from the fighting, her hands reeking of kerosene.

Understanding at last, Kuntza smiled. Concerned by Cambrian's situation, he took up a clean goblet from the table at his elbow and filled it with water from the crystal pitcher that was beside it. Adding a pinch of powdered medicine from a pouch on his belt, he swirled the water carefully in the goblet.

"Drink this," he told Cambrian after the thin film of powder had dissolved into the water. "It will ease the pain."

"Will it make me sleepy?" Cambrian asked, eyeing it warily. "Because I intend to eat dinner at the king's table tonight and I would hate to fall asleep in my soup." Also, he had been looking forward to finding out if returning to Regalis would ease the nightmares.

Kuntza smiled kindly, understanding much of the hopes and needs of the young prince. "No, it will not," he shook his head. He watched Cambrian drain the goblet and nodded in satisfaction. "Good." Kuntza planned to eat in the very rooms they were currently occupying. There would be time enough tomorrow to expand his investigation.

"I suppose we had better go," Oliver remarked. "There are a few things to be done before dinner." For example, he wanted to suggest that Cambrian be put in charge of investigating Arnold Mosley. It was the perfect job for him, something that would make use of his talents yet light on physical requirements. Mosley was almost too powerful for his own good and seemed primarily focused on obtaining more power, which made his interest in the metal smith Edgar Twain all the more puzzling. But Oliver was confident Cambrian could sort it out. Also, it would relieve Oliver and their father of the concern, leaving them free to pursue other obligations.

"Yes," Cambrian agreed, allowing Jennings to help him after his first attempt at extricating himself from the plush chair failed miserably. Laughter was definitely off his list of things to do for the next few days.

"Well," Oliver clapped Trevaille on the shoulder, "I realize these are not the kind of accommodations you are accustomed to." He cast a look of mock sorrow about the spacious room, with sleeping chambers on either side of it and a window almost large enough to fly a sideboat through. "But do you think you can manage for a few days, at least until Master Kuntza has had some time to evaluate the situation in Fairydom?" The apology in his tone was real. Oliver's determination to set his friend free as soon as possible was motivated as much by expedience as friendship. If ever there had been a time when qualified officers were needed on the wing, this was it. And he knew that however short the stay on land, it would seem too long to Trevaille.

Trevaille responded seriously, "I am a windfairy, sir, accustomed to taking the bad with the good." Then he grinned. "Now that is settled, it is time for you to be off." He elbowed Oliver gently. "I know that look you are wearing and I know my way about a room. Go on, then, and take care of your important business." It made sense, he had to admit, bunking him with Kuntza. He could deal with the butlers or maids, order the food, and just generally become the face of the rooms, relieving Oliver and the king of some of the worry of keeping Kuntza's secret.

"Thank you, Andrew," Oliver smiled gratefully at his old friend. "I will eat breakfast with you and Kuntza tomorrow," he promised, "and we can talk then." With that, he hurried to follow his father and Cambrian across the hall.

"What, and scare Kuntza with our stories of academy life?" Trevaille joked even as he waved his friend off. Closing the hall door behind him, he ran his hand over his chin. He had been looking forward to being at the business end of a razor for the last few days and this was his chance.

Oliver made it to Cambrian's rooms just in time to open the doors for them. Signaling his father, who might have otherwise gone off to reassure his wife, to come in as well, Oliver considered Jennings carefully.

"That is better," Cambrian sighed as he settled himself into one of the handful of chairs arranged around his sitting room. Unlike the chairs in the royal guest rooms, these chairs were only cushioned to the point of being comfortable, not dangerous. The periwinkle upholstery and a handful of warm oil paintings gave a pleasant lift to a room otherwise dominated by the dark walnut of the chairs, tables, and woodwork.

"Jennings," Oliver spoke as if to a social equal, "in the other room you will find…"

"Jennings," Cambrian interrupted, "is perfectly trustworthy. Whatever you were planning to say can be said in front of him."

Oliver stopped, surprised. Consulting his father with a glance, he nodded.

"Very well. Jennings, we can almost certainly use your help in this." He took care to look the man-fairy in the eyes, hoping to impress upon him the seriousness of what was about to be discussed. "There is a matter that Father and I have been trying to solve for the last few years, a matter of intriguing delicacy."

Cambrian, recognizing the sound of a new assignment, discarded half a dozen possibilities as being too straight-forward for the adjective 'intriguing.' Mentally he arrayed the few remaining options before himself and tried to puzzle out what his brother was about to say. His fear of failure was somewhat alleviated by his relief at the idea that he might still prove useful.

"Excellent, Oliver," Jasper was quick to agree. "I was also thinking that Cambrian could untangle this for us."

Encouraged, Oliver determined to lay it out quickly enough to give them all time to prepare for dinner. "It may surprise you to learn that the secret of Kuntza's tribe has been passed down from king to king in our tribe since the treaty was signed nearly ten thousand years ago." His lips twisted up in a half smile as he added, "It certainly surprised me."

Cambrian said nothing, simply gestured for Jennings and the others to seat themselves. This was a time to listen, to absorb, perhaps even to comprehend beyond what was said. And he was still hoping to deduce what they were going to ask him to do.

"That is why Father was so reluctant to grant the miners and the colonists approval to expand to the east," Oliver explained, choosing to remain standing. He thought best on his feet. "Enough time has passed that even the stories have faded, leaving our tribe with only the knowledge that there remains unsettled territory, untapped riches," he gestured broadly.

"It has grown more and more difficult to resist their petitions," Jasper said quietly.

"Which is why you permitted Feo'lyn and Port Herio to be built," Cambrian deduced aloud. "Being bound by the terms of the treaty not to reveal the Water Fairy Tribe once it had been forgotten, you hoped that the challenges inherent to such a remote colony would discourage others."

Amused at his own surprise, for Cambrian had always been a quick study, Jasper nodded. The treaty did indeed set clear terms, from physical boundaries to the very stipulation Cambrian had inferred. And the penalty for any breach of the treaty. He wished his ancestors had exercised a little more foresight, anticipating a day when the Sky Fairy Tribe might need room for growth beyond what they had.

"It was also the best way," Oliver added from where he now stood by the fireplace, "for us to put a military presence close to the mining operations in that area."

Cambrian smiled. He knew who they were going to ask him to investigate.

"Arnold Mosley," he said simply. "A man-fairy with significant power and wealth at his disposal. As I recall, he inherited the Burdina mines when his father died." He watched Oliver and their father exchange sober looks. "What exactly is he suspected of doing?”

“We have fairly solid evidence,” Jasper answered before Oliver could, “that he has broken several regulations regarding safety and that runoff from his mines is poisoning the water in that area.”

“But there is more,” Cambrian asserted. That was enough, certainly, to draw out the Water Fairies. It was the way his brother stared out the window, hands clasped tightly behind his back, that made Cambrian assume the telling was not done.

“At the beginning of this year, Mosley came to us to renegotiate his military contracts.” Oliver turned to face him, his face dark with anger. “He claimed he had run into difficulties with his mines and would only be able to provide a fraction of what he had in years past.”

“His mines are the primary sources of iron and saltpeter in all of our territories,” Cambrian said for Jennings’ benefit. Then, as he had been away on minor investigations throughout most of the year, somewhat detached from the problems of their economy, he speculated aloud, “A reduction in his supply could drive up the price of steel significantly.”

“Which is exactly what happened,” Oliver agreed, raking one hand through his hair. “We have spent more this year for less than we needed.”

“What is most troublesome,” Jasper

intervened before his elder son could get caught up explaining what the financial council had taken weeks to resolve, "is that we have reports of supply wagons leaving his mines more heavily laden than when they arrived."

Cambrian sat up a little, the prospect of a good mystery—and Kuntza's pain potion—restoring some of his strength.

"You think he is producing as much ore as ever, then selling it elsewhere?" That was the only explanation that fit.

"He knew he could not simply withdraw from his military contracts," Oliver clasped his hands behind his back again, "but if we believed his output was reduced, he could go about his business unimpeded."

"We want to know to whom he has been selling it. I have sent discreet enquiries to the other kingdoms, none of which admit to or have indications of stockpiling ore." Jasper shook his head. He had run out of ideas some time ago, though he and Oliver had continued taking turns puzzling over it for the last few months.

"No," Cambrian agreed quickly. He was surprised that they had not brought this to him sooner. "It is not another kingdom. The Plant Fairies and Silver Fairies prefer to buy our finished products, not raw ore." He shook his head. "And while the Wood Fairies require a significant amount of ore for their windship production and military outfitting, I trust them not to agree to something so underhanded."

"If he went to the governments directly. And assuming he would have felt it necessary to explain his methods to them," Oliver raised his eyebrows to express his doubts on that score.

Cambrian leaned back in his chair. "I assume he found an even bigger buyer."

"Who?" Jasper asked, eager to have the riddle solved.

"The pirates."

They all stared at Jennings, Cambrian as dumbfounded as the others. That was exactly the conclusion he had come to.

"Lying, cheating, needing supplies to make weapons and trouble with," Jennings shrugged, uncomfortable under the steady gaze of three pairs of eyes. "Sounds like pirates t'me."

"I could not have said it better," Cambrian managed at last. "Has Mosley recently entered the uncut gem trade, by any chance?" The Wood Fairies were fantastic jewelers, capable of turning a sliver of sapphire into a drop of sky to be worn for decoration. And they had lost a large shipment of uncut gems to a pirate attack barely two months ago.

Chapter VI

"Enter," Constance called when someone rapped at the door to her borrowed chambers. "Your Highness," she dropped a clumsy curtsy to Gemma, grateful that the robe she had found with the towels was comfortably sized.

"Now, none of that," Gemma protested, laughing. "You will have your fill of that within a day's time, or I miss my guess."

Constance smiled a little at the sound of the other woman-fairy's friendly laugh. "I am not accustomed to it," she admitted.

"Then let us have no more of curtsying between us, at least not in the privacy of our own chambers," Gemma smiled. Gesturing slightly, she bid her maid enter the room behind her.

"Oh!" Constance gasped when she saw what the maid carried into the room and hung in her armoire. Wrist-length sleeves billowed slightly and the rose petal silk skirt whispered against itself as it settled into place.

"I hope you will not take this amiss," Gemma began, feeling her old shyness coming upon her. It was so difficult sometimes, striking the right balance between helpful and friendly. "It is a dress that I commissioned a few months ago." She touched the delicate fabric wistfully. "I thought you might like to wear it tonight."

"I?" Constance squeaked, overcome by the

very idea. "But surely you should wear it!" That certainly sounded better than just objecting to wearing the garment, which was far too fancy for her taste. The vertically pleated dress had a wrap-around look to the bodice that would accent her excellent posture in a very unmilitary fashion. And just below where the two sides of the bodice met above the waist on the right side, a belt of miniature golden roses hung loosely.

Gemma blushed and dismissed her maid with another gesture. "Shall I tell you a secret?" she asked when the door had closed.

Constance hesitated. Cramming one more secret into her mind might sprain something!

"How do you know I will keep it?" she evaded.

Gemma's smiled only broadened. "I know." That being said, she fluttered close to Constance and held out her hands. "But there is one other thing I must know before I tell you."

"Yes?" Constance asked, feeling more than a little anxious as she placed her cold hands in Gemma's warm ones.

"Your first name," Gemma giggled.

Constance let out a burst of surprised laughter, which quickly became genuine laughter when Gemma joined her in it. It felt good to laugh for no reason, such a contrast to the wear and worry of her life since the fateful day when the pirate offensive had been announced.

"I…Constance," she gasped at last. "I am

Constance."

Gemma's own laughing subsided as she said, "Constance.   Constance Kimberlite."   She squeezed her friend's hands. "A lovely name."

Constance lapsed into silence, still not sure she wanted to know any more secrets.

"I cannot wear that dress tonight," Gemma blushed, "because I am no longer that size."

Stunned, Constance stared at her. Women-fairies, in her experience, only spoke of gaining weight with smiles and blushes when there was a baby involved.

"Oh Gemma." Constance shook her head, momentarily speechless. "That is wonderful!"

"I know," Gemma giggled again, a little delirious with the joy of a shared secret. "This will be our second child."

Constance remembered suddenly that Cambrian had mentioned having a niece. The image of a tiny Gemma popped into her mind, bringing on more smiles.

"You say this is a secret?" she queried, wanting to be sure she understood.

"Oh yes," Gemma nodded. "Oliver knows, of course, and my doctor. And you."

Concerned, Constance broke away, turning her attention back to her damp hair, which she had been toweling when Gemma knocked. It had already soaked through the shoulders of her dressing robe, despite the towel she still wore. A stray thought crossed her mind about getting it cut shorter—much shorter.

"Why tell me?" she asked, automatically rubbing a soggy strand of hair between two, almost equally soggy, ends of the towel.

Gemma, her shyness having beaten a hasty retreat, considered the question seriously. "Because you needed a friend." She had little experience with women-fairies of military backgrounds, but she had heard Oliver and Cambrian both speak of their appreciation for the directness of the women-fairies they had met during their time in the marines.

"Yes," Constance agreed slowly. "An ally would be even better." The concession having escaped her tired mind, she waited for Gemma's reaction.

"Perhaps you are right." Gemma took up a dry towel and guided her new friend over to the chair by the vanity. "But I should warn you. While here," she placed the wet towel in the hamper, "if you go expecting a pitched battle, a battle is what you shall have." With hands grown expert during hours of tending first her sisters' hair and then her daughter's, Gemma began toweling Constance's hair. "I recommend preparing for a sparring match, for here the swords are blunted and the arrows tipped with paint."

Constance smiled at Gemma's reflection. "Even a blunt sword can hurt."

"True," Gemma returned the smile as she

settled the towel on Constance's shoulders. "However," she took up a wide-tooth comb, "at court, the truth is your best defense and a pleasant demeanor your best offense." A glance at the clock reminded her that they had very little time before the supper hour, so she began combing Constance's hair. Her own hair having already been arranged while Constance took her soak, her maid, Natalie, would return to help Constance finish dressing.

"I suppose I should have waited until after supper to wash my hair," Constance blinked a few times to help keep her eyes from closing for the night. "I meant to," she added with a sigh of contentment as the comb swept through her hair.

"Nonsense." Gemma began twisting here and plaiting there, using a variety of hair implements from the vanity to keep her creation from coming undone while she worked on its several parts. "It is easier to arrange damp hair, you know."

Constance reflected that she probably had known that at some point, if only because her mother had told her. Since she had no use for elaborate hairstyles, though, it had eventually been filed under 'trivia.'

"There." Gemma's verbal expression of triumph was mostly to open Constance's eyes again, for they had drifted closed. "It looks lovely."

"Oh my." Constance stared at herself—or at

least, at the reflection of the woman-fairy seated at the vanity table. It blinked when she did, and turned its head this way, then the other while she tried to see as much of her hair as possible. "I hardly know myself," she managed at last. It probably was an attractive hairstyle, she trusted Gemma that much. After she had gotten used to it, she might even like it. That would take a while, however.

"Ah," Gemma tossed the comb into the hodgepodge of discarded ties and pins on the vanity when someone rapped on the door. "Come in. This is Natalie," she introduced her maid to Constance. "She will help you finish dressing." Gemma looked wistfully at the airy concoction, its full skirt gloriously puffed out and dainty looking. "Every time I commission a new dress I remind myself that I want something simple, something that I can get into on my own," she ran one hand down the sleeve, enjoying the feeling of the cool silk on her fingertips. "And every time, I find myself with something that requires an extra set of hands or double-jointed arms to fasten up in the back."

Constance eyed the coral pink dress with even less enthusiasm after hearing that description. More important to her than getting into it was the fact that she hoped at some point to get *out* of it and into bed. While she had been sleeping fairly well since they had changed course, it was so wonderful to finally be at Regalis, the prince delivered and most of Bane's paperwork safely locked away (she underlined her mental note to ask Cambrian about transferring the map and pouch from her care), that she felt almost exhausted with the relief.

"She does not know the schedule, Natalie," Gemma dropped her hand from the dress. "Be sure to have her ready in time."

"Yes, Your Highness." Natalie smiled agreeably. When her lady had left, she turned her attention to their guest. "Has the captain ever worn one of Madame Karan's creations?"

"I think," Constance frowned, "that I have heard of them." She rose and looked at the dress again, even more put off at the idea of struggling into it now that she knew it was the work of a renowned designer. She was woman-fairy enough to know that it took a certain flair to successfully wear that kind of dress. What if she got into it and it looked awful on her? It was a beautiful dress, so that left only one conclusion.

"Are you ready to dress?" Natalie asked. She did not want to rush the captain, but they were running out of time. Besides, something about the odd expression on the captain's face worried her.

"Very well," Constance sighed. Untying the sash on her dressing gown, she slipped out of it and stood waiting in her undershirt and bloomers. "At least we are of a similar coloring," she muttered under her breath, meaning herself and Gemma, as she watched Natalie carefully take the dress down. "What will the men-fairies be wearing?" she asked, suddenly curious about Cambrian.

"Suits," Natalie answered cheerfully, her fingers deftly undoing the clasps on the back of the dress's bodice. "With bowties and cummerbunds."

"Oh." Constance had no difficulty picturing Cambrian in that costume. As handsome as he was in slops, he was very striking in a suit. Sadly, the charcoal grey suit Cambrian wore when they had dinner on the *Nadauld* a few weeks ago was thrown overboard with the rest of his wardrobe while Bane was searching for the prince's crown.

"Here we are," Natalie held the dress out.

Constance took a deep breath and lifted herself off the ground. Holding position like a supply ship during a transfer, she waited anxiously for Natalie to position the dress beneath her. She did not let the breath out until her bare feet sank into the plush carpet.

"Come now," Natalie smiled as she helped the captain slip her arms into the sleeves and raise the bodice into position. "That was not so bad." She took great care redoing the clasps, counting them so as to be sure she had not missed any. "Shall I lay out the powders and colors for you, m'lady?" she offered when she was done.

"No, I think not," Constance sighed, rubbing her tired eyes. She knew the basics of face painting, as most women-fairies did, but she doubted that what little she could do would sufficiently improve her appearance to be worthwhile.

Natalie hesitated. A bare face would draw more attention than she felt this particular woman-fairy would be comfortable with.

"Perhaps you would allow me?" she suggested after a moment had passed.

Constance turned to the maid, wondering what to make of the offer.

"Even the queen wears a *little* face powder," Natalie said, hoping the captain would understand and not take offense.

"When at court, do as the queen does, eh?" Constance sighed. "Well, if you are sure there is time…" She found herself back in front of the vanity before she could finish the sentence. A thin, soft towel was tucked under her chin and the powders produced before she could change her mind.

"This will only take a moment," Natalie assured her. "You have a lovely tan already, so," she popped open a bottle of plain moisturizer and hastily dabbed it into place. "Perhaps just a little lip color and some eye embellishments?" Meeting the captain's gaze in the mirror, Natalie demonstrated how to flex her lips so that the color would have maximum coverage. "Perfect," she beamed and brushed a thin layer of tinted gloss onto the captain's lips. "Now, your eyes," she hesitated, her hand poised over the tray of powders while she considered the colors of the gown, the precise hue of the captain's eyes and, most importantly, the captain's character. "Here," she took up a section of pearlescent colors. "Perfect," she exulted again when she set it down a moment later. A pale beige with a hint of yellow had taken the color out of the circles under the captain's eyes, and the pearlescent blue on her eyelids brought out the captain's wonderful dark blue eyes. Carefully removing the towel, she gently smoothed the dress's high collar. "Is there anything else I can do for you, m'lady?" she asked out of habit.

Rising, Constance turned to face the full-length mirror to the right of the armoire. Her hairdo was still a bit breathtaking, but it was the dress that worried her the most. The stiff collar was reminiscent of her dress uniform, except that this was almost uncomfortably high. The bodice was modest and sensible at the same time, the top third of it being formed of some opaque, lightweight material that would allow body heat to escape, then cleverly transitioning into the rose petal silk that composed the bulk of the bodice, the wrist-length sleeves, and ankle-length full skirt. Flexing her wings a little, she was relieved to find that the wing slots were practically perfect. She and Gemma really were of a size. As she stepped into the slippers Natalie produced, which fit well enough, she felt shorter somehow. It was a moment before it occurred to her that the slippers were lacking the half inch heel that was the military standard.

Whatever was she going to do with her hands? Letting them rest against the skirt would crush the layers of tulle that kept it from draping lifelessly about her hips.

"Here," Natalie slipped a soft cord over her left wrist, the fan a necessity in her mind. "Even though fall approaches it is still sometimes uncomfortably warm at large gatherings." Taking the captain by the hand, she led her away from the mirror and towards the window. "Tonight the dinner will be outside, followed by musical entertainment." Opening the window, she pointed. "They are assembling already."

"Right." Constance took a deep breath. Bread and water served in the privacy of her own quarters would have been immensely preferable to the delectable scents and bits of conversation that were floating up to her window. "Thank you," she adopted almost the same tone of voice that she used with Toby, the *Nadauld's* cabin boy. To her relief, Natalie dropped a curtsy and vanished, closing the hall door behind her. With some effort, Constance managed to close the windows behind her, but still hesitated on the balcony. She jumped when someone spoke to her.

"Captain," called a voice from her left. "Will you join us?"

Constance watched Oliver and Gemma fly towards her, having just come around an ornate bulge in the outer wall that she now recognized as a privacy partition. The idea of arriving at the dinner *with* someone was much more appealing than going alone, though she still thought bread and water was the best option.

"Yes," she called back, lifting off. "Thank you." She was pleasantly surprised when Oliver offered her his free right arm, and shot Gemma a quick look before accepting it with her approval. As they slowly approached the dinner, she began looking for Cambrian. She almost hoped that he was not present, that he had been sensible and suggested to Kuntza that they and Jennings all dine together. Kuntza, in turn, would have the good sense to insist that Cambrian retire early. It would be much better than having Cambrian exhaust himself on his first night back in Regalis. She had almost decided that was what had happened when Oliver guided them in a quarter turn to the right. And there Cambrian was, laughing at something one of the triplets had said.

Cambrian, meanwhile, had been watching anxiously for Constance. It would just be the two of them on public display tonight, Trevaille and Jennings having begged off to keep Kuntza company, the lucky louts. He arched his itching back, adding to the ache in his shoulders. His empty stomach, which was rapidly losing patience with the delays protocol insisted upon, growled, causing him to quickly clench his abdominal muscles. The rumble passed and he sighed. So far he had been successful in keeping his temper because he was restricting his interactions to the triplets, for he had decades of experience at remaining calm around them.

"Ah," Queen Marta appraised the approaching group. "Your captain cleans up rather well."

Cambrian turned sharply in the direction his mother was looking. He looked at, then past, Oliver and his group. Suddenly he returned to the woman-fairy on his brother's right arm. She was lovely. The hairdo was almost as severe as the braid she usually wore, but somehow a curl had escaped and was lovingly nestled just below and behind her ear, visible to him only because she was looking towards his father. Not *at* his father, he realized as he followed the line of her gaze, but at the man-fairy beside his father. She seemed very interested in him, in fact.

Welcome," King Jasper smiled at them, especially at the captain. His most recent guest, he felt a particular concern that she be able to relax and enjoy herself. "Permit me to introduce the rest of our dinner table for this evening." He put his hand lightly on Edgar's shoulder. "This is Master Twain, a metal smith of Feo'lyn."

"Captain Kimberlite?" Edgar gladly extended his hand to Port Captain Braxton's friend. "Remember me?" he added hastily, the slight gathering of her eyebrows ample evidence that she was trying but without much success. "We met at the Wandering Tattler."

"Oh, of course!" She smiled and shook her head at the same time that she watched Edgar raise her hand to his lips. "How could I have forgotten?"

Edgar grinned and released her hand, though he could have held it longer so glad was he to finally find callouses on somebody else's palm!

"I was one face among many," he shrugged off her forgetfulness. "The Tattler is a fine eatery, the most popular at…"

"Yes, no doubt," Oliver interrupted gently. They were fairly safe at the king's table, but even so the guest list was liberally sprinkled with merchants, lobbyists, and others who were overly interested in understanding how a simple metal smith came to be in such close company of the king. "I do hope that tonight's menu is more to your liking, Master Twain." With that, he transferred his smiling gaze to his father's face. They were both at their wits' end as far as tending Master Twain was concerned, and had begun seriously debating the merits of allowing the triplets to take up the task.

"One thing is certain," Master Twain offered his arm to the captain, "I shall have the loveliest dinner companion." He lowered his voice for the last few words, which resulted in her having to lean closer to hear them.

Finding herself practically in his arms, Constance hastily put her hand on the one he was holding out to her. This was not going as planned. Before she could decide whether or not she dared send an apologetic glance in Cambrian's direction, a lone trumpet call was heard over the general bustle of the gathered fairies.

"Prepare yourself," Master Twain warned Constance, his voice still low to avoid being overheard. He did not wish to speak ill of his hosts, but every so often he did permit himself to remember that he would rather be at home by now. "I mentioned last week that I was accustomed to having heartier meals." That had been one of many unsuccessful hints that he was ready to leave. "And the queen was kind enough to consult me about the menu for tonight."

Constance noticed a slight emphasis on the word 'kind,' as if Master Twain was thinking one thing and saying another. "And what am I to prepare for?" she asked, deciding to play up her curiousity instead of choosing sides.

"Thick stew in bread bowls is what I asked for," he sighed even as he stepped forward to take his place behind Oliver and Gemma. Having Captain Kimberlite for a dinner companion would make the evening tolerable, at least. While he had finally gotten to where he could tell the triplets apart despite their actively working to fool him, he looked forward to an interesting conversation for a change.

When he did not expound upon what he actually expected to find, Constance gladly let the subject drop. It was a short trip to the king's table and they arrived just as the last guest located their place card. Constance almost laughed aloud when she saw one of the triplets trying to pull a chair out for Cambrian.

"Here you go," Master Twain smiled at her from behind the stiff-backed chair he had pulled out for her. They were heavier than they looked and he did not want her struggling to tug it closer to the table after she had seated herself. It had been bad enough when he found himself in that position!

Surprised, Constance shot a quick glance at the queen and king, then waited by the chair until the king had seated his wife. Her anxiety dissolved when she made eye contact with Gemma, who smiled and nodded almost imperceptibly as she slid into the chair Oliver was holding for her. Taking the cue, Constance slid into her own chair, hovering until it had been pushed in sufficiently. "I suppose," Master Twain said as he hitched his chair forward, "I should have known better than to request my favorite dish." In answer to Constance's furrowed eyebrows he leaned a little closer and remarked, "Nobody makes stew like my mother."

Determined not to let the dinner go solely to Master Twain's complaints, Constance airily replied, "While I am sure your mother makes excellent stew, you have never had stew until you have tasted *my* mother's stew." She cringed inwardly at how childish she sounded.

"I look forward to it." Master Twain grinned, taking up his napkin.

Startled, Constance stared at him. And then she laughed. She could not help herself! The idea that he might misconstrue her words as an invitation had never entered her mind.

Queen Marta looked up at the sound of Constance's laughter, then over at Cambrian. "Is something wrong?" she asked, concerned by the dark look on his face.

"I hope not," he answered obscurely. "I certainly hope not." With that, he rescued his napkin from Lila, who was reaching over to help him, and spread it deftly across his lap. One day at a time, he told himself. One day at a time.

Marta considered his reaction for a long moment, wondering if his concern with the attractive captain meant what she thought it did.

Chapter VII

Constance came awake with a start, fumbling for her sword. Between the yards of bed sheets and the disorientation, she soon found the edge of her bed the hard way.

"Ouch," she muttered, rubbing a sore spot and blinking rapidly. Where was she? Daylight, reflected by a full length mirror in one corner and the vanity mirror beside it, nearly blinded her when she peeked over the top of her bed. "Oh." She sank back onto the floor. "I remember." The racket that was pouring in through the windows with the daylight was a nearby bell tower. It was announcing the hour, not calling for all hands.

"Ten bells?" she yawned. "What time is ten bells?" she asked nobody in particular. As the mist cleared from her mind, she began chuckling at herself. "Ten o'clock." With a sharp flap of her wings she was on her feet. "Ten o'clock?" she half-shouted. The day was half gone. Throwing back the blanket and top sheet, she rapidly smoothed the bed sheet. Moving with military precision, she had things ship shape in a matter of minutes.

Meanwhile, her mind was working rapidly. She had made a point of thanking Gemma for her graciousness—for the loan of the gown as well as the room—in Cambrian's hearing before the end of the dinner, but no one had come for her in the night. Did that mean Cambrian had not told Jennings where to find her? That he had slept well? Or just that her assistance had not been required? She wished she knew an easy way to find out.

Taking a short cut between the bed and its canopy, she reached the other side of the room quickly. When she opened the armoire, she stopped short. Dresses. Gemma had explained her idea of exchanging dresses with her cousin, the last guest in this room. Having a dress made over was apparently much less expensive than commissioning a brand new one, and was a fairly common practice at court where wardrobes had to appear new every season. Even so— Constance reached unhappily for the most likely looking one, wishing that she had thought last night to send Natalie, a page boy, or even one of the more adoring courtiers to the nearest military outfitters for a uniform. *Any* uniform, including formal wear, would have been preferable to the self-consciousness she felt just looking at her options.

"Here goes," she sighed. Closing the armoire, she hung the dress from the hook on the armoire door. Zipping over to the full length mirror, she hastily poured water into the basin and washed up before slipping out of her nightgown and tossing it over the mirror. The main difference between daywear and evening gowns being sensibleness, she was pleased to find that the dress she had chosen did not require double-jointed arms when it came to fastening up the back.

No one had said anything the night before about breakfast, but her stomach was lecturing her severely by the time she had finished braiding her hair. "Alright," she said, pouring a glass of water from the pitcher on her nightstand. "I heard you!" Draining the glass in a single swallow, she paused to consider. Should she exit by the heavy outer doors into the maze of hallways, with the hope of meeting someone who could point her in the right direction? Or should she exit by the windows and chance following her nose to breakfast?

Tap tap tap. She froze, the glass hovering just over the nightstand. Someone was at the frosted window less than a twig from where she stood debating.

"Captain," called a male voice softly. "Captain, are you awake yet?"

Setting the glass down silently, Constance flexed her wings and curled her fingers around the water pitcher.

"Who is it?" she called back.

"Twain," came the reply. "Sorry if I woke you," he continued, his tone bearing out his words, "but breakfast is the one meal they do properly around here."

Relaxing, Constance released the pitcher and

opened the window. "Lead on, Master Twain," she instructed, pulling the window shut behind her.

He grinned and pointed towards the east. "The kitchens are over yonder, where the winds blow the wood smoke clear of the grounds."

"Excellent," Constance grinned back. "How did you know where to find me?" She threw the question in without preamble, as much because it had just occurred to her as to take him off-guard.

"Simple," he shrugged. "My room is down the hall." He scowled. "Easier for them to keep an eye on me that way."

"Keep an eye on you?" she repeated, confused. When Braxton had introduced her to Edgar Twain, master metal smith, over lunch at the Wandering Tattler, she had never expected to see him again. Finding him at Regalis was actually quite puzzling, even without his allusions.

"I suppose I can tell you." He looked about, but there was no one else near their altitude. "Braxton sent me here with a secret dispatch." He saw her start to frown and began nodding. "Truly he did. I was to deliver it to the king, then report back. Unfortunately, I failed miserably." Shoving his hands in his pockets, he flew along silently for a few seconds. "I was doing fine until I tried to go home."

"Then you have been here since I met you?" she asked, surprised. Thinking back on their brief encounter at Port Herio, she frowned slightly.

The brief, confidential conversation the two men-fairies had engaged in was probably when Braxton had enlisted Edgar's help.

"Well, the last twelve days, anyway. Even by dragonfly it is about a five day journey here from Herio." He began gradually descending, for the kitchen door had come into view.

Constance heard and understood the wistfulness in his voice. However long or short her stay ashore, she missed the feel of a deck beneath her feet. That was home to her. On the other hand, if there was even the slightest chance that he suspected anything about the Water Fairies, what else could King Jasper do but keep him on, even as an unwilling guest? That information simply could not be made generally known. It was too dangerous. She bit her lip.

"So you must know where everything is around here?" she prodded further. While she understood Edgar's wish to return home, there was nothing she could do for him but try to make his stay seem more like his idea. With the right approach, she might be able to keep him happily occupied for a few days at least. Jennings and Kuntza could take care of Cambrian for that long, and he had his family for support as well.

"More or less," he agreed, landing easily. "Why do you ask?"

"Because I do not know where anything is," she confessed, rolling her eyes slightly as she touched down beside him. She had more experience being chummy than she did flirting, which was just as well under the circumstances. If Edgar was unattached, she did not want to give him the wrong idea. "And I am going to have back to back meetings before much longer."

"Really?" He cocked an eyebrow at her as he opened the door. "Military stuff?"

"For the most part," she nodded. "Debriefings, and at least one board of inquiry. It is sure to be rather dull." Not that dull would be bad for a while.

"Sounds to me like you could use a guide," he suggested. He kept his tone casual, not wanting to let her see how much the idea appealed to him. Women-fairies were few and far between at Feo'lyn, and while he doubted a windfairy captain would give up her commission for a quiet life in the backwoods, he could at least enjoy her company for the present "Maybe I could even find some not-boring things to show you."

"What a wonderful idea," she smiled. Simultaneously she clenched her stomach muscles against the threat of another growl. Whatever was for breakfast smelled delicious!

"Matilda," Edgar called ahead of them as they entered the kitchen. "Look who I found!"

"Spring winds!" exclaimed a tall, angular woman-fairy, fluttering over to them. "If it ain't Captain Kimberlite!"

Constance smiled a little uneasily. What had she gotten herself into?

"My brother was in the last pirate battle," Matilda proudly informed everyone in earshot. "And many of the stories he tells are about the way you handled the *Falcon*. Almost won it all single-handed, he says," she grinned as she wiped her hands on the brilliantly white apron tied about her slim waist.

"I?" Constance clamped her mouth shut before the flat denial could escape. Insulting a cook was never a good idea and insulting the cook's brother was just as bad. Try as she might, she could not think of a single member of her crew that resembled the woman-fairy, which left her at a loss for words.

"Of course," Matilda gestured for them to seat themselves at a wooden table that stretched almost the full length of the kitchen, "Barry is a terrible tale teller."

At that, Constance grinned. She might never have heard of Barry, but Matilda's wink set her at ease.

"I have spun a few myself," she acknowledged, thinking back to her days as a cabin lass. Perhaps I could trade one for a plate of breakfast?"

"A fine idea!" cried Matilda, swooping up and over to where two junior cooks were tending to food being brought back from somewhere. "Will you be having it on tin plates?" she joked even as she reached for the mid-range pewter dishes that she kept for visiting couriers.

"I will be having mine with a tall, cold mug of milk, if you have it to spare," Edgar chuckled. "And some of the fantastic gravy and biscuits you make."

Matilda rolled her eyes. "Keep your compliments for the serving lass at home," she admonished him. Winking again at Constance she remarked, "You can always tell a bachelor by his silver tongue." Filling the plates generously with fried eggs, bacon strips, and sautéed vegetables, she added hot biscuits and a brought a pot of honey along for good measure. "I hope you eat better than them," she jerked her head in the direction of the door that presumably led into the formal dining area. "A village could live for a week on their leavings." At her signal, a scullery maid returning to the kitchen flew over with a tray of open jam jars, pitchers of juices, and a large wedge of cheese dominating the center.

Constance smiled back indifferently and took a sip from the mug of milk a lass had brought her. At her elbow Edgar, the bachelor, did the same. If she read the situation correctly, the trays of food being brought back into the kitchen were coming from the main dining hall. She had not missed breakfast by much, it seemed. Stifling a sigh, she focused on the situation at hand. She knew just which story to tell. It was not the funniest thing that had ever happened to her, but she hoped it would secure Edgar's image of her as an ordinary woman-fairy who just wanted to be friends.

"Well, then," she took a deep breath, enjoying the fragrant smells wafting off the plate of eggs and herbs before her. "About that story." Taking up her fork, she plunged it into a heap of golden deliciousness. "I started out as a cabin lass on my father's windship. And one of my duties was to help in the galley." Between bites she regaled them with a story of her ineptness and confusion, topping it off with a slightly exaggerated account of the resulting chaos. "If the cook had stayed topside a moment longer, the stew would have not only been burnt, it would have decorated the rest of the galley!" She laughed with them, amused to see Matilda wiping away tears. "As it was I had to spend the rest of the day mopping up flour from the bag that had exploded."

"Ah, you poor wee thing," Matilda gasped. "Did you ever learn to balance the pot properly?"

"After some practice," Constance chuckled. "It has to be done just so...and then latched to the wall with the hook that I did not see until too late." A fresh round of laughter greeted that revelation. On a windship, where up was sometimes the only direction to be sure of, things had to be secured if they were not to roll about.

"What is it, lad?" Matilda asked, spotting the page that had appeared on the edge of the gathered group.

"The king is asking after the captain," the lad

responded, nodding at where Edgar and Constance sat. He almost mentioned how long he and half a dozen other pages had been searching for her once it was discovered that she was not in her room. "He would have you meet him in the smaller library."

Edgar sighed and wiped his mouth with his napkin. "I should have known. We are off, then," he stood up. "Thanks for breakfast, Matilda. Never had better!"

"You say that every time, Master Twain," Matilda retorted dryly. "Keep an eye on him," she warned Constance in a stage whisper.

"He is to keep an eye on me," she returned jovially. "Else I shall become permanently lost." Setting her napkin beside her plate, she rose. The rustling of her dress reminded her of what she had been able to forget in this comfortable kitchen, that she was most definitely in strange currents. "Thank you for a lovely breakfast," she smiled.

"Thanks to you for a fine tale," Matilda escorted them to the outer door. "A meal for a tale so long as you stay, in fact."

"Thanks!" Constance lifted off, prompting the reluctant Edgar to do the same.

"I suppose we should take the shortest route," Edgar said glumly. He had been to the library many times, and there were several other places he would rather go just now.

"So long as we take it slowly," Constance put

her hand on her stomach. "That was a big breakfast for me."

"A grand idea," Edgar grinned. "But we had better take the short route. The king does not like to be kept be kept waiting."

"I can understand that," Constance nodded seriously. She expected the meeting to outline her schedule for the next few days, heavy on the debriefings. She was certainly surprised to find the three military commanders in the library with the king. It was not the first time she had saluted in a dress, but she did not like it any better this time than she had before.

"At ease," Admiral Taylor said. "Take a seat." He nodded at the library table nearest her.

King Jasper stepped forward, hands clasped behind his back. "We understand that you had a most interesting voyage, Captain Kimberlite."

"Aye, sir," she nodded. She started to glance questioningly towards Edgar, and stopped herself just in time.

"That will be all, Master Twain," the king said.

"Ah, but I am the lady's guide," Edgar bowed from the waist. "I..."

The king interrupted firmly. "You may return for her in an hour."

Deflated, Edgar took himself off, closing the hallway door behind him.

Left to herself, Constance wished she had remained standing. Even though the table hid most of her dress, it was awkward to be the only one sitting. "Suppose you begin at the beginning and tell us how you came to return with two extra captains, one windship, and less than half a crew?" The admiral prompted.

Constance looked at the four fairies curiously. Was she to debrief them now? Surely not. Where was the scribe? Where were the other officers and windfairies of her crew? Where was Cambrian? She took a deep breath.

"I was at Fort Bakarti, waiting for the *Nadauld* to be refitted. Prince Cambrian was there as well, investigating Major Layton." She paused while the others exchanged glances. If she read the surprise correctly, they knew of the investigation and had not expected her to. "A courier vessel crashed on its approach and the captain delivered a communique from Port Herio." Abbreviating wherever possible, she outlined the events of the voyage. Their brief stop at Herio—she glanced at the king and proceeded at his nod—which had apparently prompted Port Captain Braxton to send Edgar to Regalis with a pouch filled with reports. The uneventful three-day flight towards the mysterious island, followed by the completely unexpected attack by the crew of the *Kimuxwe*, led by Layton. Escaping, sabotaging the *Nadauld*, planning the counter attack—meeting Kuntza in the lava tube maze beneath the island. The stunning discovery that Layton was none other than the pirate Bane. At the king's nod, she included Kuntza in her explanation of their escape from the pirate fortress to the windships.

"We had no choice," she finished quietly. "Bane was waiting for us aboard the *Kimuxwe*. Prince Cambrian distracted Bane and the pirates while Mister Dixby and I slipped our captured crew members off the *Kimuxwe* and onto the *Nadauld*."

"Distracted?"

She looked up at the king. It was the first time he had spoken since dismissing Edgar.

"Yes, sire," she nodded slowly. "He challenged Bane to single combat." She watched the blood drain from his remarkably straight face and correctly deduced that he had heard something of it the night before. "The pirates gathered round to watch, to…intervene," she chose the politest word she could think of for kicking someone when they were down, "where they could. With their attention so fully occupied, I was able to rig an explosive charge, which was set off just before Cambrian and I quit the *Kimuxwe*."

"Was Bane killed?" This question came from the marine general. Layton had been a marine, a disgrace.

"Yes. I killed him." She swallowed hard and wished for a drink of water. How long had she been talking? It felt like more than an hour.

"*You* killed him?" This remark of surprise came from the army general. She would have expected Cambrian to have been the one to accomplish that as a natural extension of the duel.

"Yes," Constance said again. "He followed Cambrian and me to the *Nadauld*'s wing." Too late she realized she had slipped into the familiar way of speaking of her prince. "I was in the better position, so I threw my dagger at his heart. The last I saw of him was as he fell into the darkness below." She shivered at the grim memory.

King Jasper turned away, focusing his gaze on an ancient collection of plays. It was not wrong, he knew, for his thoughts to turn to his younger son, a man-fairy injured in the defense of others. But he had called the commanders in from their other duties on short notice and could not spend their time on his private concerns.

"A most unusual tale," the army general said quietly. "It speaks of a continued pirate presence…"

"There are always pirates," grunted the admiral.

"And speaks of a tribe I have not heard of since my great-grandmother told me stories before sending me to bed," the army general continued. "Have we proof that such a tribe exists, beyond this testimony?"

"We have." King Jasper rejoined the group. He was not yet prepared to introduce that evidence, as per Kuntza's particular request, but did not consider informing a handful of his senior officers to be the same as revealing the existence of the Water Fairies to all of Fairydom. "That information is not to leave this room." He made eye contact will all three of them. He was already sure of Constance's discretion and understanding. "You will not tell your aides. You will not tell your spouses. You will not even discuss this with each other if I am not present. You will also not begin looking up vague and obscure references to mythical tribes." He raised both eyebrows, a commonly accepted indication of his complete seriousness. "Is that understood?"

"Aye." The three answered as one.

"Dismissed."

Constance sat still as if pinned to her chair by the king's direct gaze. What now?

"Captain Kimberlite," King Jasper began, then hesitated. The door to the hallway closed, but not without him catching a glimpse of a rather anxious-looking Edgar. "I will not keep you much longer." Pulling out the chair opposite her, he seated himself. "May I call you Constance?" he asked. It was his experience that some fairies were made more uncomfortable by his use of their first names and that was not the direction he wanted this conversation to go. But it would make *him* uncomfortable to call the recipient of his son's affections by her title.

"You may," she assented breathlessly. Not even a trip to the commandant's office while at the academy had set her heart to beating this way.

"Constance, I would have you understand that I am more than just the king of the Sky Fairies." He watched her face carefully, but it told him nothing. "I am the husband of Marta Nash, and the father of five wonderful children. Children," he repeated, "that are mostly grown now. Still, I could not help but notice that you referred to my second son by his given name just now."

Constance smiled unexpectedly. When the king did not continue, she presumed to speak. "Now I see where he gets his directness from." Was this her chance to learn if Cambrian had nightmares last night?

King Jasper blinked. Her smile and words transformed her from a polite officer in his fleet to a young, attractive woman-fairy. "He has spoken to you…like this?" he asked carefully.

Constance blushed. She could not help it. "Not exactly," she replied just as carefully.

King Jasper read the signs skillfully. Constance was very different from Gemma in some respects, it was true. However, Gemma had been just as demure and vague when he had spoken to her. And look where that had led!

"There will be formal debriefings tomorrow," he said slowly. "You will not mention Kuntza or the Water Fairies in your explanation of your escape."

She nodded. His tone and manner had not changed, so she expected more of a private nature was coming.

"You will have to remain at Regalis for the time being, to help with Kuntza. The *Nadauld* needs work, of course. And your lads will remain as well. Their families are being brought in."

"So many fairies," she said, mostly to herself. "Where will they be staying?"

"There is an old school building just beyond the walls of the castle, complete with dormitories. It is being cleaned and set in order for their arrival. Tutors have been summoned to continue the education of the children." He recited the steps they were taking to make the lads comfortable, his mind still on the startling development of his son's courtship.

"There is many a good lad and lass aboard the *Nadauld*," Constance interjected. "Some would make fine officers."

King Jasper considered the statement, intrigued. "Of course," he nodded. "Academy instructors will interview them. That will help take the edge off their anxiety."

"And put them in a controlled situation," Constance agreed. She found herself liking this man-fairy who was her king. "I would prefer to stay at the dormitory with them," she hazarded.

He turned the idea over in his mind, inspecting it from its various angles. It made a great deal of sense. If all three of the captains stayed there, it would vastly reduce the chances that something would go wrong. On the other hand, Tremaine was Kuntza's primary contact. Grant, unfortunately, was in eminent danger of a reduction in rank, which would go hard with him were he left amongst lads he had previously captained. And Cambrian was falling in love with Constance. What a quandary.

"For now I would prefer," he used her wording, "you to remain in the guest room." He saw honest disappointment on her face. "With the privilege of visiting the dormitory whenever you have time."

"Thank you." It was only half a victory, but who was she to complain? "There is something," she spoke quickly, for she saw that he was about to speak again and wanted to get this off her mind, "else that you should know."

Jasper looked at her, wondering uneasily what she was about to say.

"In addition to the two cases of papers and books that we gave to Ian last night, we took a map and an oilskin pouch from Bane's flagship." The words came out in a rush, leaving her limp with relief when they were all spoken.

"And where are they now?" King Jasper asked, leaning forward.

"In my guest room. Between the head of the bed and the wall." She had been a little surprised to discover that the carving on the footboard was recreated so perfectly on the headboard, which was destined to spend its life snugged up against a wall where no one would ever see it, but the map and pouch had fit there nicely.

"Ian."

Constance almost jumped out of her chair when the bodyguard materialized from behind a bookshelf.

"You heard?" the king asked. When Ian nodded, Jasper instructed, "Retrieve them and put them in the strong room."

Constance watched Ian disappear as abruptly as he had appeared, the bookshelf moving ever so slightly when he had gone, so that it was again flush with the wall.

"If I may suggest it," Jasper hesitated.

Women-fairies could be very sensitive about their clothing. "There is a military outfitter at the academy. Since you are here in an official capacity, and at my command," he included that as a stroke of sheer brilliance, "you will need a full military wardrobe, dress uniforms and so forth." Taking up quill and paper, he wrote a brief note. "Give this to the supply sergeant. They will provide what you need, courtesy of the realm." Folding it, he held it out to her.

"Thank you." Constance took the paper and stared at it. All of her clothes had been aboard the *Nadauld* when Bane took her. She had been dreading the expense of replacing them. More than that, though, she sensed in the king's hesitation a desire to help her, to rescue her, even, from the frills and fancies common to court styles. "Thank you," she repeated, looking him in the eye.

Smiling, King Jasper waved away her thanks, content that he had not offended the woman-fairy he would be pleased to welcome into his family. She was not only an outstanding officer, decorated for bravery and gifted with ingenuity. She seemed lovely inside and out.

"You will be very busy over the next few days," he remarked as he stood. "I recommend placing your order today so that you will have some things for tomorrow."

"Aye," she began to salute, then stopped when he held out his hand. "May I ask, sire," she paused. Should she reveal Cambrian's secret? Was it a secret still? "Do you know if he slept well?"

He frowned slightly at her breathless question. Had Cambrian slept well? What did she mean?

"I assumed so," he answered slowly as he took her hand in his. "But I shall inquire." King Jasper looked her in the eye. "My son is quite taken with you," he pointed out gravely. As her cheeks pinked and her gaze dropped in obvious confusion, he smiled. While it was too early to assume that there was a marriage in the offing, he was glad to see that she reciprocated. "That pleases me." He met her gaze directly, for his words had brought her eyes up sharply.

Stunned, Constance watched as her king brought her hand to his lips. Heard him say, "Welcome to court." And allowed him to guide her to the door, which he closed between them.

"That took over an hour," Edgar said reproachfully. He had not bothered to get up from his chair beside the door this time.

"What?" Constance asked, looking down at him blankly. Her thoughts were still anchored to the king's words. *That pleases me.* Had she just been welcomed to the family?

"I said," Edgar would have repeated himself except that it was not really important. "Never mind," he shrugged as he rose. "What have you got there?" he asked, nodding at the paper she held.

"A requisition," she said, holding it up. "For the academy outfitters." Suddenly remembering her decision to keep him occupied, she added, "Can you take me there?"

"Oh," Edgar took her by the elbow, drawing her towards a window. "I am not allowed to leave the castle grounds," he said a little too loudly while he looked carefully about. "But," he added in a lower tone, "I sometimes do anyway. Come along." Dropping her elbow, he captured her hand. "A friend showed me a back way out." Diving out the window, he pulled her along with him.

Constance glanced over her shoulder as they left and was startled to see the king watching them from the library window. Her imagination might have been a little overwrought with all that had happened—or else the king really did nod before turning away. Remembering something Cambrian had told her about how observation was his primary tool in an investigation, she wondered if he had learned that from his father.

"This way," Edgar grinned back at her. Seeing a half-frown on her face, he hastened to assure her, "I promise this will not take long. I will be back at the castle before anyone realizes I am missing."

Deciding that the king would stop them if he wanted to, Constance played along. "You had better be right," she retorted, hoping that was in character.

"They have not caught me yet," Edgar gloated.

Constance rolled her eyes after he had looked forward again.   As much as she liked his easygoing directness, he apparently knew nothing of the subtle undercurrents that always existed in large groups of fairies. His 'friend,' for example. What sort of friend helped by providing a way to disobey a simple command? A misguided friend? Or a self-serving one? She resolved to get Edgar to point out this fairy to her. She might be reading too much into the situation, of course. With stakes as high as keeping Kuntza and his tribe a secret, though, that was a mistake she was willing to risk.

"We have to speed up a little," Edgar explained, letting go of her hand, "because the hole is quite small. Have to tuck up to get through." Shooting ahead for a distance, he suddenly tucked his wings and disappeared into the hedges that lined the southwest wall.

Shaking her head, Constance briefly debated finding the main gate and letting Edgar find her later. Instead she marked the spot in her mind before following Edgar through.

"Pssst." Edgar's whispered hail drew her attention to where he stood at the bottom of the wall. "Down here."

Constance tucked again, falling until it was almost too late before spreading her wings and abruptly self-arresting for a light touchdown.

"Nice," Edgar complimented her on the move. "We have to go softly here, or the parapet guards will hear us." He caught her by the shoulder as she turned towards the academy, which was visible from where they stood. "And then there are the marine patrols to watch for," he added, drawing her into the shadows as a patrol came around the curve of the castle.

Constance was taken aback at the type and number of weapons that each marine carried. Why were they so heavily armed? They were at peace except for the occasional pirate skirmish or bird attack, neither of which was likely to happen at Regalis. And why Ian? It was the duty of every fairy in the castle to protect their king and their tribe. So why did the king need a bodyguard?

"Safe now," Edgar murmured. "C'mon."

They had reached the next building before she realized he had taken her by the hand. Tugging it free, she pointed.

"There it is." Rubbing cold hands against her upper arms, she flew into the sunlight. That was better. Fall was teasing them with cool winds and warm sunlight on the same day, a bit unusual for this late in the year.

"There is an eatery over there," Edgar gestured to the east. "We can have lunch there, if you like." He hoped she would say yes. He was meeting a friend there, someone he wanted to introduce her to.

"Lunch," she laughed. "How long do you think this will take?"

The clang of the entry bell on the door to the outfitters cut off any response he might have made. Constance took a deep breath, enjoying the scent of fabrics, detergents, and new leather boots that hung in the air. There was no one behind the long counter on the other side of the room. The curtain that separated the front room from the fitting rooms in the back stirred, though whether that was due to the air moving or actual hands on the curtains she did not know.

"Over there," she nodded forwards and grinned at the bewildered Edgar. "The shelves on the left are the army, on the right are the marines, and the fleet is dead ahead."

Edgar whistled. "What could possibly be on all of those shelves?" he asked, staring left to the far wall, right to the far wall, and from the ceiling down to where the counter blocked his vision.

"Boots, harnesses, jumpsuits, dress uniforms…" She held out her hands, palms up. "You name it. The fleet has the most variations on equipment and uniforms, so we take up the most space."

Edgar considered remarking on how little space *she* took up, and how nicely she used it, but decided against it. She did not seem like the type of woman-fairy he had been meeting at court, that begged for compliments the way a child-fairy whined for sweets.

"Yes?" asked a voice as the curtains parted. "What is it?"

"I have a requisition," Constance announced, holding up the paper the king had given her.

"Bring it here, please." The curtains swished slightly behind the older man-fairy who entered the room to back up the command. He was still fit and square-shouldered, but his hair that had faded over the years to a powder-blue. "Well," he said, taking the paper and looking at it through spectacles he had slipped on, "a most interesting requisition." Lifting the spectacles off his nose, he dropped them into his breast pocket. The action jostled the soft measuring tape he wore on his shoulders, causing it to swing slightly from side to side until he stilled it with his free hand. "See here," he frowned, "is this a prank?"

Astonished, Constance stared at him. Perhaps she should have read the note before handing it over!

"Why do you ask that?" she returned after collecting her thoughts.

"It is signed by the king," he waved the paper, "and authorizes a Furstenberg wardrobe."

Constance swallowed. A Furstenberg wardrobe was made of the finest materials, by the finest available tailors, and was well out of her pay range. Admirals and a few officers from wealthy families indulged in them, but most windfairies took their clothes off the shelf. She opened her mouth to respond, but Edgar beat her to it.

"Then a Furstenberg wardrobe she shall have. The king wrote that with his own hand," Edgar sniffed. He smoothed the front of his own finely tailored suit, reclaimed from Oliver's wardrobe and made over by his valet. Bowing to Constance he added, "I see you shall require some time here, though I hope not too long." Taking her hand, he kissed it with all the suaveness of a veteran courtier. "I shall return in time to collect you for our luncheon." Winking with the eye the clerk could not see, he turned with a flourish and flitted out of the shop, letting the door slam behind him. Going shopping with the triplets had not been a complete waste of time after all, he chuckled to himself as he made speed towards the businesses that dotted the far side of town.

Constance jumped when the door stuck home. Apparently Edgar had no experience with military outfitters! Unless she was very much mistaken, Edgar's performance would simply have made the supplier more upset.

"This way," said the older man-fairy, holding the curtains open with one hand.

She blinked in surprise, then preceded him into the back room.

"Martine," called the man-fairy, stepping around to the back of a short counter. "You have a job."

A woman-fairy, smartly but simply dressed in the workwear of a military tailor, stepped out from behind one of the sets of curtains that lined the far wall.

"Good day," she greeted Constance. "Please enter." She held back one of the curtains that blocked off the fitting room she was using that day.

Constance obeyed, still in something of a daze. When the king had promised her a new wardrobe, she had never thought he meant to do it on such a grand scale. Meekly she allowed Martine to remove the gown so that she could take her measurements. The curtains closed off most of the light, but a set of frosted windows near the ceiling let in sufficient to see by.

"Do you suppose I might have something to wear out of here?" she asked, that being the one hopeful thing about all this.

"Of course," Martine agreed, making notes as she efficiently measured shoulder to elbow and elbow to wrist. "If you do not mind a short wait, that is."

Constance listened to the bells striking in the academy tower. "My friend will be back in about an hour," she estimated aloud.

"Plenty of time," Martine nodded, folding up her soft ruler. "Stand over here, please, at attention." She made more notes of Constance's height by head, shoulder, wing, waist, and knee using the ruler carved into the far wall. "Very good. Now, we will start with the uniform you will be wearing out of here." Pocketing her notepad, she handed Constance a smock. "What branch?"

"Fleet," Constance answered, slipping the smock on and buttoning it. It was such a pleasure to be in a simple garment again!

"Ah," Martine frowned. "I am afraid we do not have much in the way of fleet dress uniforms at the moment. The recent ceremonies cleaned us out of those."

Constance paused, remembering the ceremonies Martine was referring to. And now Captain Trevaille would have to present himself to the academy and claim the medals he had been awarded in absentia.

"I will not need a dress uniform today," she said quietly.

Matilda eyed her skeptically, then nodded. "Rank?" she asked briskly, throwing open the curtains and fluttering over to a row of cupboards.

"Captain," Constance answered, folding down the collar on the smock as she followed.

"Fleet Captain," Martine muttered to herself as she flung open a cupboard. "Here is something," she drew out the trousers of a plain dock-side uniform. "A little too tall, I think." She held them up to the vertical ruler on the inside of the cupboard door. "I will have to turn the cuffs up." She stretched the waistline across the horizontal ruler. "And take in the waist." She hung it from a knob on the outside of the door and dove into another cupboard in search of a tunic. "Very good," she announced when she resurfaced. "This will not take much adjustment at all."

"It looks good enough to wear as it is," Constance observed happily. Her statement was met by two rather serious frowns.

"A Furstenberg wardrobe is perfectly tailored," the old man-fairy stated firmly.

"Oh, of course," Constance agreed, her heart sinking. "But surely I could wear that today while a dress uniform is being made for tomorrow. And then this could be altered tomorrow."

"I suppose it could be done," Martine said, still frowning. "We do have less than an hour until her friend returns."

The man-fairy sighed unhappily. "Very well. I will work with her while you alter the trousers."

And so Constance found herself with a lapful of cloth swatches.

"In the fall," he told her, "our best dress uniforms are made of polished cotton twill."

Constance listened patiently as he launched into a detailed description of the available fabrics. This one held its lines well, but that one was more durable… She found herself wishing that she had waited and brought Cambrian along. He would have breezed through the decisions that she was having to struggle through with a great deal of coaching from the head tailor.

"Finally," the man-fairy held up a book of swatches, "the inside of the cape has no regulation color. I am afraid these are all the options we have at the moment. We are expecting one more shipment of materiel before winter sets in, but with so much of the fleet in dry dock at the moment..." He sighed eloquently and shook his head.

Constance took the book from him with a barely suppressed sigh. She automatically flipped past the brilliant yellow with blue threads and the plum with gold threads.

"Oh," she exhaled softly when she reached the back of the book. "This one." She held it out to him.

He took it and made a note of the color code. "Any others?" He was pleased that something had at last caught her interest. Up until that point he might as well have been picking fabrics and colors for himself.

"That will do," he advised her, noting down the color codes in order of her preference. "I believe Martine is just about ready for you," he informed her as he began sorting the swatches back into order. When she nodded and left, he paused to consider her color codes. By regulation, military uniforms were a combination of varying shades of blue, depending on one's branch and rank. Also by regulation, personal touches of color were permitted in the accessories, gloves, sashes, et cetera. It was always a pleasure for him to add color to the drab uniforms.

"Here we are," Martine closed the curtains again, nodding at where the adjusted trousers and tunic hung on the wall. "If you will hand me your slippers?" Taking them, she disappeared through the curtains, leaving Constance to change in peace.

Constance hung the smock on the clothes tree and slipped the tunic over her undershirt. She let the button flap hang loose while she stepped into her trousers. "Finally," she sighed as she fastened the inner waist buckle and secured the three midnight blue, braided loops from the right side of the waistband around the over-sized buttons on the left side. She smiled at herself in the mirror as she buttoned each of the seven buttons that cut her tunic into two right triangles, marveling at the fact that the tunic buttons and the trouser buttons were exactly the same shade of sky blue. All she was missing was a bicorn and rank insignia. Besides boots.

Opening the curtains, she stepped into the back room, shoulders squared.

"Your dress," the man-fairy held out a neatly wrapped box. "And your insignia," he added, holding up a much smaller box in his other hand.

"Thank you," she smiled and returned his salute. Setting the dress box on a chair, she used another mirror to guide her hands as she fastened the two sets of silver, crossed feathers on her lapels.

"These should fit," Martine said, approaching with a pair of knee-high black boots in one hand and a bicorn in the other.

"Thank you." Constance took the bicorn with a barely repressed sigh. Wearing the more balanced-looking tricorn was, at the moment, the biggest attraction of the rank of admiral. She set the bicorn on top of the dress box and held onto the back of the chair while Martine helped her on with the highly-polished boots.

Constance flexed her feet in the boots after Martine had stepped back. Then she took a few experimental steps.

"A perfect fit," she said, some of her surprise evident in her tone. "And they are so soft!" She almost did not notice the pleased expressions on the faces of Martine and the older clerk as she step-twirled her way around the room.

"Ah," the man-fairy said when the entry bell clanged. "That must be your friend." Picking up her bicorn, he brought it to her. "Where shall we have the dress box and slippers delivered?"

Chapter IX

"Navigating Regalis is a bit tricky," Edgar admitted as they zipped along a few minutes later. "Children and older fairies use the walks below," he gestured. "But the airways can get clogged during the busier times of day. So they put up these posts," he tapped one as they passed it, "as airways to keep folks from getting mixed up."

"So, just follow the arrows," Constance abridged his explanation. She had been to Regalis once before, and moreover, she knew that every town with over a thousand inhabitants was set up in the same way. Markers separated the height of the pole into two airways and one walkway, with the arrows at the top of the way pointing which direction each section was to go. "Very efficient."

"Once you get used to it," Edgar chuckled.

"And how did you learn of it?" she asked as he eased them in with the flow of the top lane, heading east, away from the academy and the outfitters.

"The triplets," he sighed. "I used to go shopping with them when I first arrived, with," he added quickly, "the understanding that I would not talk about where I was from or why I was here." He shook his head. "I barely know why I came here, let alone why I am still here."

She slipped her arm through his and tugged

him out of the way of a heavily-laden errand boy-fairy. "Tell me about the triplets," she suggested, hoping to get his mind off his misfortunes.

"You make it sound so easy." He was back to chuckling. "Lesley, Laura, and Lila. That is in birth order," he explained gravely. "I have been warned that the walls of the castle have eyes and ears—and I am convinced they belong to the triplets. I stumbled over one or the other of them every day my first week."

"They sound like a lot of trouble," she mused, hoping she was wrong.

"Not so much." Edgar shrugged. "Just always underfoot. I thought they were following me until I met Arnold."

"Arnold?" she asked, her mind still busy with the subject of the formidable triplets. She had five younger siblings of her own, counting her own twin, but it was possible to approach them singly. Somehow she had the feeling that the triplets functioned like an elite marine unit, none of them quite complete without the others.

"Aye, the friend I wanted you to meet." Edgar smiled. "I was going crazy inside those walls," he nodded in the general direction of the castle. "Then Arnold came on his annual business trip and Oliver introduced me to him." He practically had to force the introduction, which still struck him as strange. It had been worth it, though, to meet someone with ties to Feo'lyn. And for being the owner of two of the largest mines in all of the colonies, Arnold was a pretty decent fellow. "He was the one who showed me that private exit," Edgar grinned.

"Oh, yes." Constance came back to the conversation. "I am looking forward to meeting him."

"Good." Edgar drew her onto the roof of a nearby building. "Here we are."

Constance smiled as she took in the roof dining area, a quaint approach to attracting passersby, complete with an open fire pit and roasting meat. There were few insects that troubled them at this altitude and the birds had learned long ago that it was not worth the trouble to come here for a meal. Not that they did not have a crop of new birds try it every so often...

"Edgar," called a deep, rich voice. "Over here, lad!"

"Arnold," Edgar waved. Resting one hand lightly on the small of Constance's back, he began deftly propelling her through the tightly packed eating area. It was safer to walk, for the eatery's staff filled the air, zipping back and forth with heavy trays as they served their guests.

Constance looked at the speaker, looked again. Somewhere between two and five hundred, he stood just over five twigs tall, his shoulders broad enough to make him look unusually triangular as his body narrowed down to his feet. Short-cropped hair made guessing his age more difficult, and seemed odd on someone wearing such a fancy suit. When she politely offered him her hand, his lacey cuffs tickled her fingers until he lifted her hand to his lips. There were no callouses on his hand and she was glad to get her hand back, though she did not wipe it on her trousers as she would have liked to.

"Sophie!" The man-fairy hailed a passing waitress as he took his seat. "Along wid ye lass," he continued in the casual parlance of the colonies and border towns when she did not even stop, "would ye have us starve?"

She had disappeared in the general direction of the fire pit but her voice called back reassuringly, "Comin' I am."

Constance allowed Edgar to seat her while she watched the scene play out. When Sophie arrived Arnold gravely informed her that he was perishing from hunger. A grain of gold, pressed firmly into her palm, secured her devoted service. After ordering for them all, Arnold quickly turned his attention to his guests.

"So, Edgar," Arnold leaned back in his chair and squinted at them, "what brings you out on this fine fall day?"

"If you will believe it," Edgar leaned forward, planting both elbows on the table, "I am playing guide for the lady." He nodded in Constance's direction.

"Ha!" Arnold laughed in surprise. "You? A guide in Regalis? Ah, you have been here too long, me lad." And yet, he added mentally, not long enough to know where to take such a woman-fairy for lunch. To be sure, the open-air cafes had their charm, but he knew a restaurant with hand-embroidered tablecloths, chandeliers of the finest crystal, and utensils that were made of silver, instead of just being called 'silverware.'

"Aye," Edgar's face darkened a little. He perked up when Sophie set a steaming platter of food before him, followed by a tankard of nectar. Drawing his dagger, Edgar began sawing his meat into chunks of a more manageable size.

"The finest pork and taters in the city," Arnold boasted as he picked up his fork. That was true at least. "Dig in," he added with a wink aimed primarily at Constance.

Constance felt her skin crawl at the idea of accepting something as small as a casual compliment from this man-fairy, let alone an entire meal. But she forced down her revulsion and took up her fork. The food was hot, freshly cooked, the perfect antidote for the slowly dropping temperature. The bite of potato she sampled was nicely seasoned from being roasted with the meat.

"Thank goodness you are here," Constance smiled at Edgar, taking the dagger from his hand before he could set it down. "I might still have been wandering the grounds of the castle otherwise." Or she might have been with Cambrian. She chose to focus on Edgar for the time being. He was smiling again. She deftly carved her meat into bite-sized portions and then offered the knife, hilt first, to Edgar. "But what brings you to Regalis," she paused, gathering her eyebrows slightly and hoping Arnold would provide his last name.

"Arnold," he offered, resizing his meat with his own dainty dagger. "I come here every year at this time," he grinned. "I have contracts to supply ore to the military metal smiths," he added, watching to see if that impressed her. He was intrigued to see her simply accept the information. "My grandfather brokered the first deal, and the responsibility has been passed from him to my father, and from my father to me." At the end of his speech, he seized his tankard, quenching his thirst with a long draught.

"What a wonderful tradition," Constance murmured, not sure what else to say.

"He also inherited the Burdina mines," Edgar explained with a grin.

Constance absorbed the information while she chewed a large bite of the bread she had taken from the plate in the middle of the table. It was rich, brown bread, worth savoring. The Burdina mines were some of the biggest in the colonies. In the north east colonies. They were, in fact, part of the reason that Port Herio had been built where it was. The miners had torn up a town or two before the port, with its sizeable marine population, had been installed. They still caused trouble occasionally, but nothing like they had in the past. And this man-fairy owned all three of those mines. Interesting. What did he want with Edgar? She instantly felt guilty for asking that question.

"Enough about me." Arnold smiled faintly, for he was his own favorite subject usually. "Edgar tells me you brought our young prince safely home."

"Aye," she nodded and took another bite of bread.

"The only windship that has arrived recently is the *Nadauld*," Arnold pretended to think aloud. He had deduced quite a few things already. "Rough voyage, eh?"

Edgar looked at Constance in surprise. "You said nothing about that," he protested, thinking back over their conversation at dinner the night before.

"I would hardly call it rough." She dabbed at her mouth with her napkin. That would be too much of an understatement. "We had some heavy work for a few days until we came to the winter wind; smooth sailing after that." She smiled reassuringly in Edgar's direction. This was a new exercise for her, juggling two fairies at once while keeping her own secrets.

"Ah, perhaps I heard incorrectly," Arnold shrugged, though he was sure he had not. "Something about an emergency docking and a quarantined crew?" He kept his tone light, furrowing his brows into a quizzical expression.

It was a calculated risk, to show some of what he knew in the hopes of shocking a response from one of them. Constance, however, reflected only mild astonishment. Edgar's face was even less telling, remaining simply surprised.

"How do these rumors get started?" she evaded with a half-laugh. For all of an instant, she had considered telling him about the plans she had discussed with the king, just to show how wrong his information was, but quickly decided against it. In the first place, he already knew too much. In the second place, she remembered just in time that observation was the key to a good investigation. That involved listening, not telling.

Arnold smiled thinly. Neatly parried, he thought. He leaned back in his chair, chewing a bite of pork and wondering about Constance. His information also indicated that she was more than friends with Prince Cambrian. If that was true, which he firmly believed it was, she could be important to him. But how to get information from her? Bribery? Subversion? He dismissed the ideas. She had appeared last night in a dress made of the finest rose petal silk, yet was out the next day in uniform and looking significantly more at ease. Her choice of apparel implied a deep loyalty as well as a lack of interest in expensive fripperies.

Edgar rose and excused himself, making his way over to the small band that occupied one corner of the eating area.

Constance watched him in an effort to ignore the way Arnold was watching her. She smiled when she saw the band leader nod his head. The music was unfamiliar at first, until she recognized it as the ballad of *Bold Brody Pike*, who had headed the first expedition into the north wilderness a thousand years ago. As she had expected, Edgar dropped a coin into the band's plate, but did not immediately return to the table. Seeing the wistful expression on his face twisted her heart terribly, so that she resolved to speak to Cambrian about letting the man-fairy return to his home as soon as possible.

Arnold watched her watch Edgar, puzzled as to how to read the situation. He was intrigued to see that Constance cared so much for one man-fairy at the same time that she was reported to be in love with another. Sympathy was foreign to his character, except as a tool for manipulating others. He was out of practice, though, having restricted himself for the last hundred years or so to dealing strictly with others of whose emotional makeups resembled his own. It made business much simpler.

These were strange times, though, with the king publicly considering drawing back from the colonies. If he redrew the borders as Arnold's source was indicating, Arnold's mines would be on the wrong side of the line. And no amount of 'remuneration' would make up for the loss of power and prestige he would suffer, not to mention the loss of the one thing that he felt made life bearable—winning at business. Getting a better deal, getting the first option, beating the other fairy to it. There was a thrill in that unlike anything he found elsewhere.

"I am relieved that you are here," Arnold said, leaning forward. He tried not to laugh when Constance's eyebrows went up in surprise. "I am worried about Edgar," he lied. "The poor man-fairy has been half a month away from his home, his smithy. That can be too long," he explained, glad to find something he could speak sincerely about, for he doubted she would be easily fooled, "in such a small colony. When things are needed, they are needed at once, and even the most loyal customer will have to move on to what is available."

Constance felt herself beginning to frown and let it happen. He had made a valid point. It did nothing to ease her mind on the subject of his interest in Edgar, unfortunately.

"Perhaps you can help," Arnold dared to put his hand on hers, "to keep his mind off his troubles." If he could just win her trust, she might be willing to help him win his point with the king. It was not such a stretch, after all. Feo'lyn would also be on the wrong side of the line.

She wrapped her legs around the chair legs to keep from standing up and pouring her tankard over his head.

"I will be too busy with military business to be anybody's playmate," she responded brusquely. Removing her hand from under his, she took a soothing sip of nectar. It was just the common peach nectar, available every year in quantity and cheap enough for even the poorest restaurant to provide at a reasonable price. Still, it was a familiar taste, unlike the rose nectar they had served at the castle the night before. She smiled in relief as Edgar returned.

"Say," Edgar upended his tankard in a giant swallow, "we had better be getting back. Someone may have missed me."

"What, already?" Arnold rose swiftly to help pull out Constance's chair. "And I was just about to suggest a flit down the promenade."

Edgar rolled his eyes and wiped his dagger on his napkin. "You know I cannot be seen there," he admonished Arnold while returning the blade to his belt sheath. "Nor would Constance have any interest in watching a bunch of overdressed, pompous peacocks flying nowhere in particular just so they can show off their new clothes."

Constance laughed aloud, the sound drawing looks of surprise from some of the eatery's rougher clients. "If I had to guess," she slipped her arm through Edgar's, turning him slightly away from Arnold, "I would say the triplets had something to do with your knowledge of that area." On the surface it was a wild guess indeed, save that she could not think how else he might have been coerced into such a situation as the one he had described.

"Right you are," he chuckled. With a wave to Arnold, they were off. He briefly sketched the story of his one and only visit to the promenade for her as he guided her back the way they had originally come.

She listened, laughed, and found herself mentally adding little Cambrian-isms, as she had dubbed his manner of storytelling. When Edgar had finished describing the line of fashionable shops where the gentry went to compare their wardrobes, sometimes while they did some actual shopping, she giggled at what she imagined Cambrian would have added. An extra witticism here, a dash of descriptive color there, a first-hand anecdote of ridiculousness, all tied up neatly at the end with a soft poke at his own finery so that no one could doubt his intent in the earlier narrative.

"Shh," Edgar admonished her as they came to a corner. "Tis open ground between here and there," he pointed at the outer wall of the castle grounds.

Constance set her amusement aside for later. This was a serious matter, after all. Her decision to find out how Edgar left the castle so that she could meet the man-fairy who had shown him the way, well, in hindsight it had probably not been as wise as it had seemed. If they got caught, she would have to explain, very convincingly, why she had thought it was worth the risk.

"Now," Edgar murmured, catching her by the hand. Swiftly, silently, he flew across the open area, tucking them into a sliver of shadow just before a squad of marines appeared. When the coast was clear again, he slipped carefully into the hedge and let her precede him through the hole in the wall. Going this way there was a place to grip with one's hands so the legs could be pushed through the small opening. "There," he said once they were safely back on the inside of the wall. "What next?"

"I suppose I should find C...Prince Cambrian," she hastily inserted his title. "I just remembered that there was something I needed to tell him." The location of the breach in the wall, the safe transference of the oilskin pouch and map, where she had been while she was not at breakfast...

"Hmm," Edgar frowned thoughtfully. "I cannot help you with that," he admitted after a moment. "If we knew where he was, I could take you straight to him, but I do not know his pattern like I do the others."

"Oh?" Constance asked, lifting off slowly.

Edgar followed her. "I know where most of them can be found. The triplets will be outside somewhere, perhaps playing rob the nest or planning the winter festival. The queen is most likely in her salon, reviewing paperwork or playing with her granddaughter. The king and Oliver are discussing the events of their day before dinner, trying to figure out who actually wants what from whom and why. They might be in the library, though they sometimes fly through the gallery at this time of day. It is fairly open, so they can see who is trying to eavesdrop on them."

Constance listened in amazement as Edgar opened the royal family before her like a book he knew by heart. Clearly he was not as naïve as she had thought. As Arnold seemed to think.

"And Gemma?" she asked, curiously.

"If the queen has the little princess, Gemma will be tending her herb garden," he mused, looking to the north. "If not, she will probably be in the herb garden anyway." He chuckled. "She says it helps her unwind before supper."

Supper. Constance felt a twinge in the pit of her stomach that had nothing to do with cheap peach nectar. At least tonight she would not have to borrow another gown.

"Wait a moment." Edgar's brow furrowed further, then cleared as he snapped his fingers. "The doctor's," he announced. "I overheard one of the palace staff saying the prince had an appointment after lunch." Thinking back to the last song the bell tower had played he added, "He might have finished by now. This way."

Eagerly Constance followed him through the winding halls and open windows of the Crystal Castle. They dodged clumps of chatting fairies, narrowly missed a tour group, and startled at least two guards as they zipped along their way.

Chapter X

Edgar stopped at last before an imposing oak door. "Will you be alright from here?" he asked.

"I suppose so," she laughed, landing. "Will you not come inside?" she asked, puzzled.

"I do not like doctors," he shook his head vigorously. "And this one keeps muttering something about wanting to run tests on me." He shuddered.

Constance laughed again. "Go on," she waved him away. "Save yourself!" she added dramatically. As she watched him fly away she reflected that even if Cambrian was not inside, she could probably ask a page to help her find him.

"What is going on here?" roared a voice from behind her, startling her so badly that she jumped.

"Why," she turned and found herself face to face with a woman-fairy in a neat white suit. "Who are you?"

"I am the nurse," she barked. "Who are you? And why are you making so much noise?"

Constance wondered briefly which of them was making the *most* noise, then answered politely, "I am Captain Kimberlite, of His Majesty's Fleet. And I was laughing because I was amused." She was beginning to see Edgar's point, however. If this was the nurse, what was the doctor like?

"I thought I recognized that laugh," said the queen's voice softly from somewhere inside the room. "Admit her, please."

The nurse glared as if to impress upon her that laughing was not appropriate at a doctor's office, then stepped aside.

"Your Majesty." Captain Kimberlite saluted without hesitation.

"Captain," Queen Marta nodded politely. "Will you join me? I am just waiting for the doctor to finish examining my son."

Captain Constance Kimberlite flew into the room, her reluctance growing with each flap. Whether she tried too hard or not hard enough, there was enormous potential for disaster here. Tucking her new bicorn under her arm, she landed near the queen but did not sit down.

Marta smiled, mildly amused that she had not anticipated this as her first one-on-one encounter with her son's sweetheart. She had run through a dozen or more scenarios as she lay in bed the night before, unable to sleep.

"After we are through here, Cambrian and I are going to the tailor's for a fitting," she said after several seconds of silence. "Would you care to join us?"

It seemed an odd invitation to Constance, who had never really thought of being fitted as a spectator sport. While she was trying to think of a way to politely decline—what she really wanted was to talk to Cambrian alone—the door to the examination room opened.

"Your Majesty," a middle-aged man-fairy appeared in the doorway. "If you would come with me?"

Marta rose at once and almost without thinking took Constance by the hand. "He will want to see you, my dear," she gently informed the surprised captain.

The doctor would have protested if it had been anyone but the queen. "This will not take long," he said instead.

Flying past him, they entered a short hallway with three doors. One was marked 'Office.' The other two were simply numbered, with the nurse waiting outside of the first door.

Constance was disappointed not to find Cambrian in the room they were shooed into.

"Please, sit down," the doctor instructed them. Taking a pencil, he scribbled something on a notepad and handed it to the nurse. When she had gone, he put his hands in his pockets. "Your Majesty, your son has several injuries, ranging from cracked ribs to loose teeth. His shoulder, as you know, has been severely bruised and his collar bone broken." He paused, hoping one of them would enlighten him as to how a prince had come to him in such a state, but neither of them spoke. They did not even move. "I have written a prescription for two potions and a pill. If," he stressed the word, thinking back to the last time he had treated the king, "he will take them as prescribed, his ribs and collar bone will heal within the week. Therapy can begin for his shoulder and wings almost immediately after that. I have already administered the first dose." Withdrawing the prince's sling from his pocket, he held it over the trash bin. Dropped it in.

"Oh, thank goodness," Marta exhaled her relief aloud.

"But," the doctor held up his hand, "he must avoid strenuous use of his left arm. Reinjuring it at this stage could set his treatment back significantly."

"Of course," Marta smiled confidently. "I can assure you that he will lift nothing heavier than a reference book until you say otherwise."

Constance maintained a straight face despite her doubts on that score. The Cambrian she knew had always been stubborn, prone to doing what he set his mind to doing. She was further puzzled by the doctor's admonishment regarding the potions and pills. When Cambrian had (stubbornly) worked until his hands had blistered and bled on the *Nadauld*, Toby, the cabin boy, never reported any difficulty getting him to take his medicine.

"If you would like to see him now, he was just finishing dressing when I left him." With a half-smile, he opened the door to the hall for them.

Constance stepped back to let the queen exit

first, then followed her into the hallway. The nurse being nowhere in sight, Constance automatically reached for the doorknob. It turned just before her hand reached it, but somehow she continued with the motion so that when the door opened inwards, she was holding fast to the knob.

"Well," Cambrian laughed as Constance was plunged into his arms. "What a pleasant surprise!" He was still laughing when he made eye contact with his mother. Transferring Constance to his right arm, he steadied her without releasing her. "Mother, would you grant us a few moments?"

Constance felt her face warming as the queen nodded and Cambrian shut the door.

"What are you doing?" she whispered, caught between mortification and indignation. *What would his mother think?* Her bicorn slipped and she fumbled for it, her composure slipping further.

"I will ask the questions," he informed her firmly. Turning her suddenly, he placed her against the door and held her there. "You did not come down to breakfast this morning. Where were you?"

"I overslept," she answered honestly.

"And lunch?" he asked, stepping closer.

"Edgar," she began, then stopped, biting her lower lip. She decided to think about it some more before she told anyone exactly what had happened that day.

"I wish you would not do that," he murmured, gently taking her chin in one hand. Tipping her head back, he brushed his lips against hers. "That is about all we have time for right now," he sighed, stepping back. "Will you tell me more, later?" he asked, his eyes warm and his tone appropriately persuasive.

"I…" For a moment she could not speak, so torn was she by the variety of emotions vying for dominance. Discarding the embarrassment, she sighed and reached for his shirt. "You missed a button," she told him, fixing it. "Later," she admonished him when he bent towards her.

"Yes, ma'am," he agreed, smiling happily. Moving her gently, he opened the door to the hallway. "Thank you, Mother." Standing between them, he offered each an arm. "I fear I am still walking for now, but if you do not mind?" His smile grew as they complied without hesitation. "I trust the doctor has informed you of his conclusions?"

"Yes," his mother answered for them both. She could not help noticing the exchange taking place between her son and Constance. Separately they were polite, reserved fairies. Together, they seem to fairly burst with an unaccountable energy. "He said you must take your potions and pill," she continued, "if you want to get well as quickly as possible." She felt silly talking to him as if he were in his fifties again, but the doctor's concern was well founded. When it came to taking care of themselves, the men-fairies of her family needed serious supervising.

"And I do," Cambrian agreed quickly. "One dose and I am already without that wretched sling." Hearing the heat in his tone, he checked himself. "Alas, the good doctor's warnings are well placed." He left their sides long enough to open the door that led outside, then resumed his place between them. "I suppose Father has told you about my new assignment?" It was as much an opportunity to inform Constance as his mother, but he still waited politely for her to respond.

"Oh dear, you cannot leave now," Marta protested. "Your medicine, your therapy…"

"No, Mother, no," he hastened to reassure her. "I am not leaving Regalis." He was glad to feel Constance gently squeeze his arm, conveying her shared relief. "I am to help the tax investigators with their review of Arnold Mosley's mines." He tried to make it sound as boring as attending a fashion review.

Constance tripped on a loose brick and almost fell flat on her face in surprise. *Arnold Mosley?* Could that be the man-fairy she had just eaten lunch with? And were his mines really under investigation? Somehow tax dodging had not seemed his style. He had struck her as being much, much worse.

"Are you alright?" Cambrian asked, turning to

her anxiously. She was, unfortunately, on his left side, and he was concerned that she had not dared put her weight on his arm for balance.

"Fine," she agreed swiftly, righting herself with a flick of her wings. Reseating the bicorn on her head, she excused herself by saying, "New boots."

"And a new uniform." Cambrian inadvertently allowed some of his disappointment into his tone. She had been so lovely in her ball gown last night. Not quite what he had hoped for, but it had been a *borrowed* gown after all. Remembering that his mother was standing patiently beside them, he abruptly resumed walking. He nodded to the guard at the gate and changed directions, heading for the nearest row of shops.

"The king advised me that I would be in need of a new wardrobe," Constance explained. "The formal inquiries begin tomorrow." It was beginning to sink in that he had already accepted an assignment. She had been told, not asked. Well, what had she expected? That he would consult her on every detail of his life? "We shall see each other at those, at least," Cambrian remarked quietly. "Still, you must have a few gowns, for…" He stopped speaking, at a loss as to how to continue. As a captain in the Royal Fleet, she could wear a uniform to every event that he could think of.

"For the entertainments," Marta inserted

smoothly when Cambrian's voice trailed off. "Especially the winter festival," she added seriously. It was something of a risk to anticipate the captain's spending the entire winter at Regalis, though things were definitely pointing that direction. And while the triplets had taken over most of the festival planning, Marta's delicate touch was still required in some areas, such as seating arrangements, explaining delicate things like attire constraints, et cetera. "If the military inquiries are to begin tomorrow, we must get your gowns started today. How perfect that you chose to come with us to the tailor's," she beamed.

Constance cringed away from the shop they were closing in on. She was not sure she could stand more measurements, more cloth samples to decide between, or more questions she had never bothered to learn to understand. And it would be far worse at a civilian establishment.

"If you do not mind, Cambrian," Marta released his arm and held out her hand to Constance. "I really feel that I should accompany Constance."

"Of course," Cambrian agreed, his free right hand going almost of its own volition to rest on Constance's hand. He did not have to look at her to see the distress that had no doubt prompted his mother's change of plans. "Perhaps we should all go," he suggested hopefully. "Mark has my measurements, he has been tailoring my clothes since I was a lad."

"No," Constance interrupted. It would only make her more nervous if Cambrian came along. "Where would be the fun in that?" she asked in response to his wide eyes, desperately racking her brain for some other reasoning to back up the protest. "If you saw everything I chose, there would be no surprise for you when I finally wear it to…an event. Besides," she squeezed his arm gently, "if you leave your wardrobe up to Mark, you might get another plum-colored suit." She dropped her voice for the last few words, more to tease him than anything.

While Cambrian was willing to admit that he probably should be annoyed at her implication that Mark had designed that suit without consulting him, he was too busy being pleased with himself for seeing the humor in her remark. So far, it had been a long but good day, with the exception of his outburst at breakfast.

"Very well," he chuckled and kissed her cheek. Then, he turned and kissed his mother's cheek. "I shall see you both at supper." He looked sternly at Constance, adding a discrete wink for good measure.

Constance tried to look dignified as she waved goodbye to him. Her years of captaincy stood her in good stead in that undertaking, for a captain was many things, but almost always she had striven to be dignified.

"Now my dear," Marta took Constance by

the arm and began leading her towards the dress shop, which was only a few doors away, "what fun we shall have!" She meant it, too. She loved watching the designers in action. She was especially interested in seeing what they would construct for this young woman-fairy with her erect carriage, clear eyes, and tanned skin.

"Mother!" called a cheerful girl-fairy's voice. "Mother, wait for us!"

Constance's heart sank still further when she saw that they were being joined by the triplets and Gemma. A council of war, an academy banquet, even a board of inquiry—anything sounded better than this!

Gemma disengaged herself from Lila's arm and took Constance by her free arm before Lesley or Laura had the chance. "Are you alright, my dear?" she asked Constance in a low tone, smiling for effect. "We missed you at breakfast." That was a polite understatement. The triplets *and* Cambrian had all sulked through the meal. In fact, Cambrian had nearly snarled at his mother when she suggested that they meet with the doctor later that day.

"Fine," Constance answered stiffly. Dignity was the best course of action in public. A dignified woman-fairy would never say or do anything she was going to regret.

"What are you two up to?" asked Laura, raising both eyebrows as she took her mother's free arm.

"We are going to the dress shop," Constance announced. They were going to be told anyway, and a statement of fact was a safe, dignified thing to say.

"Yes," Marta agreed. "The captain…now tell me," she turned her attention to her guest, "what is your first name? I cannot go on calling you by rank," she laughed.

"Constance," Gemma answered for her. "I think it is quite lovely."

"Oh my, yes," smiled Marta. "That is beautiful." She would have liked to grant her son's sweetheart permission to address her as Marta, but doubted that a fleet captain would agree to such an informality so soon. "Constance," she resumed her previous thought, "needs a few gowns to see her through her stay at Regalis."

"Perfect," Lila said enthusiastically. "We were just looking for something to do until it was time to dress for dinner."

"Are your studies completed for the day?" Marta asked automatically.

"Yes, Mother," the triplets chorused.

"And we have reached the end of our patience with the plans for the winter festival," Lesley informed her, shaking her head. "Though we have agreed to and arranged for the services of the young Count DuBois' estates for the food supplies."

"What, the entire menu?" Marta asked in

genuine amazement. While she applauded their efforts to use the winter festival as a way of supporting the families and communities that had lost so much in the recent pirate offensive—including the young count's dear father, who had gone down with his windship—she found it quite incredible that an estate given primarily to harvesting birds for meat had agreed to provide vegetables, nectars, breads, desserts…

"We were doubtful, too, when he first approached us," Laura answered her mother's unspoken thought, "but that is the best part."

"He has contracted with several of the neighboring estates to represent them all as a group, so the monies spent on this year's menu will be well dispersed amongst our tribesmen," Lila finished.

"Well done, my darlings," Marta applauded her daughters, truly pleased at their intelligent managing of affairs.

Somehow, in the course of their conversation, the group had begun moving towards the dress shop again, so that Constance was inside the building before she quite realized it.

"Your Majesties," a middle-aged woman-fairy in a pale green dress curtsied to them.

Constance gave up and curtsied with the rest of the group in response as this was clearly a situation that a salute did not fit.

"How are you today, Madame Karan?" Marta asked pleasantly.

"Superb," Karan smiled, clasping her hands in front of her. "This weather is unseasonably beautiful, is it not?"

"Gorgeous," Marta agreed despite the nagging feeling that it was a little *too* much so. Turning back to the dress designer, she smiled. "We require your expert assistance today, on behalf of Captain Kimberlite."

Madame Karan turned appraising blue eyes on the one fairy she did not know. She had heard just that morning how an unknown woman-fairy had dined at the king's table the night before—wearing what was obviously one of her creations. While she would never have chosen coral pink for such a reserved fairy as the captain appeared to be, her real regret was not having seen her in the gown. It would have complimented her darker coloring and brought out the sun-lightened strands of her hair.

"Welcome to my shop, Captain," she smiled. Clapping her hands, she summoned her youngest apprentice. "Fetch extra chairs for our guests," she instructed. Her middle apprentice was already waiting, a fresh pad of paper and newly sharpened pencil in hand. "Shall we begin?"

Constance reluctantly took a seat between the queen and Gemma, opposite Madame Karan. Her interest was caught almost immediately by the precise strokes of the designer's pencil.

"If you will permit me," Madame Karan began, "to make a suggestion?" Without waiting for an answer, she sketched a gown unique in its simplicity. She had grown tired of the gowns most of her patrons ordered, where each must be more stunning than the last, until 'stunning' had lost much of its meaning for her. "The high waistline," she explained, turning the pad so that her guests could see it, "accents your stately carriage. Sequins add a subtle accent against the smoke-gray wrist-length sleeves and bodice, then flair into small star-like bursts of color trailing down the long midnight blue skirt." Pleased at the captivated expressions on her guests' faces, including the reluctant captain, she continued, "A fine chiffon material will float along with you, adding grace to your every motion."

Chapter XI

Constance was still in a daze later that evening when she took her place—beside Cambrian, thankfully—at the king's table. Madame Karan had produced sketch after sketch of appealingly simple gowns, until a page arrived with an official schedule for the rest of Constance's week. Using the interruption as an excuse, Constance had returned swiftly to her borrowed chambers, where she had remained, reviewing the logbook that had mysteriously been transported there during her absence.

"Was it alright?" Cambrian asked Constance quietly, thinking of her fitting. It was more than a mere pleasantry, of course. He was concerned by how distant she had been since they sat down.

"Hmm?" she asked, looking at him directly. She knew he had asked a question more by his tone and facial expression than the words, which she had only dimly heard. The conversation up to that point had been unremarkably general, to the point that she had allowed her thoughts to drift back to the dress shop despite knowing better. "I am sorry," she apologized as quietly as he had spoken. "I should have been listening."

Cambrian drowned the flash of annoyance he felt with a spoonful of consommé. It was unreasonable to expect others to be as intensely interested in the minute details of his life as he was.

Constance tore off a small bite of the crisp roll and conveyed it to her mouth, chewing slowly. She had promised herself to give Cambrian time to think while they were speaking, hoping to be a sort of emotional refuge for him.

"I was just saying that I hoped your visit to the dress shop went well," Cambrian said at last, discarding the idea of turning the conversation to trivialities with the story of the disaster that had been his sisters' first fitting.

"Oh," she smiled. "Yes, it was wonderful." She smiled a little at the way Cambrian let his spoon rest on the side of his bowl for a moment while he studied her face. Yes, she really meant it. What she had expected to be an ordeal had proven quite pleasant. "Madame Karan has the most delightful verse on her wall."

"She does?" Cambrian asked, surprised that he had never heard of it. "What does it say?"

She blushed lightly, wondering if the quote was quite appropriate for mixed company. Deciding that he would understand, and approve, she ventured to quote it.

"A dress should never hug you tighter than a friend, a neckline descend below your dignity, or a hemline rise above your modesty." She popped some more roll into her mouth while she waited for his reaction.

Cambrian ate some more consommé before nodding. "I think I finally, truly understand why she is Mother's favorite designer."

"And how was your fitting?" she asked, deciding they were on a safe topic.

He smiled wryly. "Mark was horrified when he heard what Bane dared to do with his creations." He maintained a serious tone mostly out of respect for the tailor's feelings, "and then promised me a new wardrobe so fabulous that even he would be glad my old one got thrown over the side of a windship."

Constance laughed softly, delighted to see him feeling so well.

"Of course," Cambrian shrugged with his left hand, then dropped it below table level and reached for her right hand, which she had been using to straighten her tunic, "he was a little disappointed when I explained to him that my new wardrobe should be more like Oliver's."

"Is Oliver so staid?" Constance asked, glancing at his brother to cover her confusion at his touch. As usual, Gemma and Oliver wore clothes that had been carefully coordinated, not to the extreme of matching but so that their outfits complimented each other. The burnt orange accessories of her ivory gown were at once complimented and contrasted by his bark brown suit with its frost white embroidery lacing the lapels and sleeves.

"Not really," Cambrian acknowledged. "But he does get irritated when his clothes make more of an impression than he does." Also, as much as his brother enjoyed pomp and circumstance, he preferred to be taken seriously.

They chuckled together at that, and he released her hand with a gentle squeeze before the servers reached them with the next course. Between the salad and the entrée, he came to the conclusion that perhaps he was not the clumsiest suitor in the kingdom. Granted, their relationship was due in some small part to the unusual circumstances they had experienced together. Still, some of those circumstances conspired to rip them apart as surely as others had drawn them closer to each other. Therein lay the mystery; therein lay the answer. After learning of his delirium, he might have allowed embarrassment and fear to consume him—if Constance had let him. And how she could even look at him without remembering the damage she had been called upon to do, to her own windship, her *home!* Silently he resolved that she should never regret the sacrifice she had made.

"Cambrian," Constance repeated, aware that the server was willing to wait until the mousse fell.

He started, surprised to find that he had been staring at her. "Chocolate mousse," he smiled and moved so the server could reach past him. "Excellent!"

Constance had a strange feeling that he had been lost in thoughts about her, an idea that sent a squadron of dragonflies spiraling through her stomach. She almost declined the mousse on account of them, then decided it would be impolite. Feigning absorption in the frothy mousse, she tried to imagine herself explaining their relationship to her mother. She had been home on vacation when her younger sister had announced that she was 'in love.' It had seemed so *simple*. Her young man-fairy was someone the whole family, including their father, had known for quite a while and approved of. Agreeing that he should become a full-fledged member of the family had required less discussion than the wedding menu! Now that she was, quite irrevocably, 'in love,' what was she supposed to do about it? She had always supposed that the burden of courtship lay primarily with the man-fairy, but now that hardly seemed fair.

"Captain?" King Jasper was not accustomed to repeating himself, though he was quite capable when circumstances required it.

"Sire." Constance straightened in her chair, coming as much to attention as she could without rising.

"At ease, Captain," he smiled. He looked forward to the day that she would regard him as a father first and a king second, but was willing to admit that would take some time. "Did you receive your copy of tomorrow's schedule?" Unfortunately, questions like this would only make that process take longer.

"Aye, sir," she nodded. "A thought had

occurred to me," she hazarded, "that I might request Master Twain's services as guide during my stay?" She watched the king slowly set his spoon down and saw, from the corner of her eye, Prince Oliver glance quickly toward, then away from, her right side. Perhaps she should have discussed it with Cambrian first, she thought, it not having struck her before how the request might sound.

"A grand idea," Edgar volunteered from where he sat, on the far side of the triplets from Constance. "It has already been my pleasure to help the captain find a few things," he added. A sure sign that I have been here too long, he sighed to himself, is that I have begun talking like them.

"Well," King Jasper said slowly. "Perhaps that would be wise, for now." He had just given Cambrian an assignment, he told himself. Edgar very definitely needed something to keep busy with, before he lost himself to this style of life. Perhaps she had struck upon the best solution, after all.

"Mind you keep an ear on the bells, cap'n," Cambrian teased as he stirred his mousse. "I am told Master Twain struggles with punctuality."

Constance hid her dismay behind a perfunctory smile. It was a small insult, at least to someone from a world where days were measured by what got accomplished instead of breaking them up into chunks of time that folks scurried about in obedience to. Nevertheless, it was unlike Cambrian to choose to insult anyone.

Edgar laughed good-naturedly. "Never fear, Highness," he said as he raised a large scoop of the mousse. "I will take good care of her."

Constance turned sharply towards Cambrian while Edgar occupied himself with the mousse. Catching Cambrian's eye, she held his gaze for a few breaths. When she saw him stop stirring the mousse, she felt better. Looking at her own dish, she found that her appetite was completely gone. Taking a deep breath, she began dipping her spoon and lifting it to her mouth. A taste at a time, with occasional pauses for conversation with Gemma, who seemed determined to keep the table from falling completely silent, she made her way through a respectable percentage of it before the servers returned.

Cambrian watched unhappily as his own partially eaten dish of mousse was replaced with a generous portion of pecan pie, still warm from the oven. It was small comfort to know that he had not voiced his true concern, that Constance would find she enjoyed Edgar's company more than his own. A small error was not really better than a large one; it was just different. Besides, he had been on the verge of humiliating himself further when Constance intervened by capturing his attention.

Lesley watched her brother curiously during the rest of the dessert course. While it was quite true that Master Twain was given to tardiness, she had not mentioned it to Cambrian so that he could throw it in their guest's face at the first opportunity. Looking back at the few minutes she had gotten to spend with Cambrian at breakfast, she wondered now that she had even brought it up when there were so many other, more important, things they could have discussed. She accepted it as a painful lesson on manners—her own included, she never should have criticized Master Twain—and let her thoughts move with her eyes to the subject of the captain. Her mother seemed of the opinion that Cambrian and she were a twosome. It was probably true, her mother had a sixth sense when it came to that sort of thing, but Lesley could not help wondering if they were well matched. After all, if the captain preferred the company of someone other than Cambrian, how interested could she really be?

Laura sat to Lesley's right and was, predictably, thinking along the same lines. According to her information, the captain and Edgar had spent most of the day together. She had not yet spoken to her sisters about it, but it seemed to her that Cambrian would find someone with a little more polish much more suited to his life at court.

Lila, who was sitting between Laura and Constance, was not sure what to make of things. From her vantage point she had been able to see the faint changes of color that Constance suffered while the rest of the table was busy not-reacting to her request. And, if Lila was not mistaken, Cambrian had been holding hands with Constance earlier in the meal. Lila chewed a bite of pecan pie without really tasting it. Cambrian might be 'back,' as Lesley had happily observed after breakfast, but it would be illogical to expect him to be exactly the same as she remembered him before his great loss. At length she decided she should get to know this new Cambrian before trying to help him too much.

"Ah," King Jasper smiled as a server arrived with goblets of nectar. "What flavor have we tonight?" he asked his wife with a fond smile.

"Kiwi," she smiled back. "It will soon be time for mulled apple cider and sweetened chocolate, but as long as this marvelously warm weather lasts, I thought we might enjoy a few of our more exotic nectars." She was disturbed to see her husband's features stiffen slightly, telling her that his mind was no longer on the subject of sweet after-dinner drinks, but on something infinitely more important. She had not meant to trouble him.

Finding himself with his goblet halfway to his lips, Jasper finished the motion. *Would the good weather last long enough for him to bring in representatives from the other tribes? Or would Kuntza be doomed to spending the entire winter with his nose in dusty old history books, catching up on the last hundred thousand or so years?* Those questions were beginning to haunt him. He swallowed.

"Lovely," he assured his wife. "A delicate, refreshing flavor."

Pleased but still concerned, she raised her own glass so that their guests, who were patiently waiting, might also drink their nectars. She had learned centuries ago that Jasper preferred to keep some aspects of ruling separate from his family life, and wondered as she had so many times before how she could best support him without knowing exactly what was troubling him. Was there a new development regarding the Water Fairies?

Lesley dabbed at her mouth and set her folded napkin down by her plate, a signal to her sisters that she had something to discuss with them as soon as possible. Laura responded almost immediately with the same gesture. Only Lila hesitated, reluctant to leave her half-full glass of delicious kiwi nectar.

"Lila," Constance turned to the triplet beside her, "can you tell me if there are any perfume shops still open in Regalis?" All that had happened today was making her homesick. It was a long shot, of course. By now most of the satellite shops around Regalis would have closed so as to not trap their keepers away from family over the long winter months—including the perfume shop her family had opened here a few decades ago. It required very little effort for her to imagine her brothers and sisters greeting each other as though the spring and summer months they spent at their satellite stores were at least a lifetime long. Resolutely, she swallowed the lump in her throat and asserted her practical side. Odds were that her youngest brother had left Regalis for the family hub days or even weeks ago. Wisely, of course. Trusting the weather this late in the year was a fool's game.

"I," Lila glanced automatically at her sisters, who signaled that they did not know, either. "I do not know." Seeing Constance's disappointment she asked, "Were you wanting something special? My sisters and I have quite a collection." She suffered a sharp kick to her left leg for her generous offer, but Constance's grateful smile was worth it.

"No, thank you. I just…wondered." While she might have explained her reasons to this agreeable young woman-fairy, she knew from having a twin of her own what a cruel thing even the most innocent secret could be, when one had to *keep* it a secret.

Lila, hearing a chair slide back and realizing it was probably Lesley's, hastily drank the rest of her nectar.

"Your Majesties," Lesley curtsied politely, a stark contrast to the captain's stiff, unfeminine bows, "I thank you for an exquisite meal." She curtsied again. "I beg your pardon, for my sisters and myself."

"What, all three of you?" Jasper teased her. It was not like them to leave before the real socializing had begun.

"Time grows short, my liege," she smiled, not minding his teasing, "and we have still so much to discuss."

"The winter festival, my dear," Queen Marta reminded him quietly. "This is only their third year planning it."

"Very well," Jasper relented. "But I expect an update at breakfast."

"Of course, sire," they answered together, curtseying as a unit.

Constance watched them fly away, waving back when Lila gestured shyly.

"You have a new friend," Cambrian observed quietly.

"Oh?" she asked, turning in her seat to face him, her knee brushing his under the table.

"Definitely. But you must be careful. Lila is by far the most tender of the three, which makes Lesley and Laura quite protective."

Protective, thought Constance, turning over in her mind some of the looks she had gotten after openly asking for Edgar's company. Yes, that was a good word for them, though she doubted that Marta, Lesley, and Laura had been thinking of Lila at the time.

"Walk with me?" Cambrian invited her abruptly. The table would be overrun by good-natured, well-intentioned guests in a moment, come to thank their hosts and arrange audiences with his father and brother. He really should stay to shoulder his share of the burden, but... "In the gardens?"

Constance tried to take a deep breath without looking like she was taking a deep breath.

"Of course," she smiled. Her stomach did summersaults as Cambrian made their excuses. She felt Edgar's eyes on her as she followed Cambrian from the dining room, using the ramp to descend to the ground floor and stepping at last into the moonlight.

"I am sorry," she told him as soon as she believed they were out of earshot.

"So am I," he responded after his amazement faded. "I should never have brought up Edgar's failing. But what are you sorry for?"

"For not being at breakfast. For not being at lunch. For not talking to you first about Edgar." She bit her lip when she realized she had used his first name.

"And I am sorry for reacting so badly to your simple request." In his eagerness to apologize, some of his theory as to her reasoning tumbled out. "Of course you will need a guide. Regalis is a very large city, with many military buildings, and a confusing array of shops." When Regalis had originally been settled, the intention had been to house the bulk of their military there, in close reach of the Royal Family. The original structures had been spaced accordingly, with room for each branch of the military to grow and build as necessary. "I should like to volunteer myself, though," he tried to grin, "for any visits you might make to the city..."

Constance stepped forward and put her fingers over his mouth before he could rattle on any further. Kuntza had told her that Cambrian would go through many phases as he wrestled with his emotions, including nervous speaking that he might find difficult to stop on his own.

"I asked for Edgar," she said in the sudden silence, "because I want to keep an eye on him." Looking about, she dropped her hand to his arm and led him further into the gardens. "There is something you need to know about him, something you should probably tell your father and brother."

Distracted from his own situation, Cambrian allowed her to seat him on a convenient bench and leaned closer so he could hear her whispers. It was such an extraordinary tale that he forgot the moonlight for a moment.

"You mean he actually showed you a way to leave the castle grounds *without* going through a gate?" he asked, incredulous.

"Yes. And he did not find it on his own. It was shown to him by," she broke off suddenly at the sound of someone approaching. Recognizing the voice, she pressed herself deeper into the shadow of the sculpted flower bush they were sitting under. Thankfully, Cambrian followed suit. She half-smiled when he slid closer to her, as if having his arm about her waist would make them more difficult to see.

"Nonsense, my dear," Arnold's voice was at its most soothing as he addressed the woman-fairy on his arm. "Just because she was wearing a larger necklace than yours, it does not mean that it is more expensive."

"Perhaps not," returned the woman-fairy, "but you will have to admit that she got a lot more attention than I did wearing this old thing." She disdainfully flicked the antique necklace, a matched set of three flawless fire sapphires, that hung about her neck.

Arnold looked at her appraisingly, the effect of her physical beauty dulled by two weeks of constant exposure to her petty nature. She seemed quite oblivious to the fact that she had just told him his company, his attention, was not enough for her.

"Well, never mind," he told her, smiling. "If you really do not like it, you do not have to keep it."

"I should think not," she answered sulkily. "You just tell your jeweler friend that I want something with more sparkle."

"Oh, I shall," Arnold agreed immediately, relieved that he would not have to work any harder than that to get the necklace back. As for the jeweler, well, it probably would come up in conversation the next time he went in to pick out a gift—for her successor.

Chapter XII

Cambrian watched them fly over the hedge and fade into the night. His mind was racing along the lines of his investigation. Who was that woman-fairy? He was sure he had seen her before, but not with Mosley.

"Odd," Constance mused aloud. She did not just mean having the subject of their discussion appear unexpectedly, either. "She does not seem his type."

Startled, Cambrian looked down at her. "Really?" An open-ended question, usually, gained him far more information than any line of direct questioning.

"No. That is, I do not think so," she corrected herself, wondering if he disagreed and if it was even important. "I only talked with him for a short while. Edgar introduced me to him at lunch today." She felt a vague sense of triumph as she explained, "*He* showed Edgar the gap in the wall."

"A gap he probably engineered," Cambrian muttered darkly, more than one illegal use for such a thing having occurred to him. "He has more connections than..." He abruptly left that thought and returned to Constance's previous statement. "What is his type?"

"Oh." Constance hesitated, flustered. "Someone gracious, dignified. And beautiful.

Someone that would make him look good." She suppressed a shiver. What a cynical assessment of a man-fairy she had barely met. She had met some few that aspired to be like him, unfortunately.

"Which she was not?" Cambrian raised an eyebrow, not liking where his thoughts were going.

"Beautiful? You know she was." Constance blushed before her words had faded from her ears. Would she like his response to that? "But surely you did not think she was gracious? Or dignified?"

"No, she was neither of those things," Cambrian agreed. "And compared to true beauty," he pressed a kiss to her forehead, "I am not sure I would even call her attractive."

Constance stayed where she was, close enough to feel his breath stir her hair. Someday, she hoped, they would have a moonlight walk that was not invaded by pirates or conversations about business.

"I appreciate your concern for Edgar," Cambrian told her. "Mosley surely has no good reason for cultivating his friendship." He took a few deep breaths to clear his mind and had to lean back from the delightful distraction of her daffodil-scented hair. He wanted to be sure he had thought through what he was about to say. "It seems he agrees with you. I doubt we will see her in his company again."

"No, I suppose not," Constance agreed, remembering the exquisite necklace and the woman-fairy's tone of voice.

"He will be looking for someone to replace her. Someone," he closed his eyes, "beautiful, gracious, dignified." Unable to continue, he let the idea settle. He felt like he had swallowed an icicle and it had lodged in his throat.

"Someone with an established position at court?" she offered, afraid she was following his line of thinking correctly. "That you would trust to report back to you?"

"Never mind," he pulled her close, fiercely angry with himself for even considering it.

"Cambrian," she pushed against his chest until he was forced to release her. "I will do it."

"Out of the question," he answered firmly. Luckily his ribs were responding well to the doctor's potions.

"There is no question. I am the perfect fairy for the job. Anyway, he seemed quite interested in me at lunch." She rubbed her right hand, which she had already washed a few times, against the back of her jacket.

"Really." His flat tone invited no response. "I suppose you plan to just fly over and tell him how perfect you are for him?"

"That might work," she teased, leaning close again. "But actually I thought I would let him tell me. According to my sisters, that is the simplest way to deal with men-fairies." She slid her hands up to his shoulders and asked, "Shall I go test their theory?" She had no intention of chasing after Arnold right then, of course; she just wanted to hear Cambrian tell her to stay.

"Morning will be soon enough," he admonished her, tightening his hands on her waist. "And do *not*," he stressed the negative word, "try to find anything out. Just listen to what he says, remember to whom he says it, and tell me everything."

"Aye, aye." Glancing up at the night sky, she realized how late it was. "I must go. Early morning, you know." She chuckled softly and leaned in for a kiss.

Reluctantly, Cambrian released her. Rather than watch her fly away over the same hedge Mosley had, he began walking slowly back down the garden path towards the castle. He had effectively drawn the woman-fairy he loved into danger yet again. All that remained to be seen was whether Mosley was more or less dangerous than a pirate king.

Once she reached her rooms, Constance changed with military efficiency and tumbled into bed. Years of practice permitted her to sleep despite the anxiety she felt, though a confusion of dreams left her feeling barely rested when Natalie gently shook her awake.

"The inquiries start today," Natalie reminded the groggy captain.

"Right." Constance sat bolt upright and

began struggling to free herself from the bedclothes.

"Here," Natalie whipped the top sheet and comforter back, laying them on the chest at the foot of the bed. It was part of making a tidy bed, anyway.

"Thank you," Constance grinned in relief as she rolled out on the other side. Automatically she set to making the bed, but Natalie shooed her away.

"I will tend to this," Natalie took the pillows from her. "You get yourself ready."

Constance smiled a little at being ordered about by a maid, but had to admit that it would take more concentration than she cared to spend to get the bed shipshape. Whistling a little, she completed a brief toilette and made short work of the light breakfast Natalie had brought up. When she had brushed her hair thoroughly, she twisted it up in her second-favorite regulation hairstyle— a sort of crisscross-bun that started with two tightly wound strands brought up from the base of the head, pinned to the opposite sides of the back of the head, looped at the top, then twisted into a single rope back down the center. It could be a nightmare to fasten, but at least it got it out of the way.

"Are you nervous?" Natalie asked, plumping the pillows.

"At least," acknowledged Constance as she flew over to the dressing screen. The outfitters had delivered a perfectly tailored dress uniform that morning sometime, thank goodness. "They have our official reports by now." As per regulations, she had left a signed, sealed copy of hers in the lockbox on the *Nadauld* to be retrieved at the admiralty's pleasure. There was no proper logbook of the trip to the island, but she had done her best to make an accurate accounting on the blank paper Bane had been kind enough to leave them. "Today the questions begin." She came out from behind the screen, fingers trembling as she struggled to tie her sash.

"Let me," Natalie gave the comforter a final, smoothing pat and hurried over to assist the captain. The sash properly tied, she smiled. "Good luck."

"Thanks." Constance smiled. She stood a moment before the mirror, one hand over the spot on the sash where a sword should have hung. Her father's sword had been in her cabin aboard the *Nadauld* when Bane attacked. She had no idea where it was now.

A rap on the window by her bed brought her out of her reverie. Edgar. Retrieving her bicorn from where she had dropped it on the vanity, she zipped over to the window.

"Good morning," Edgar greeted her, offering her a handful of blue dawn flowers he had borrowed from one of the castle's humbler gardens.

"Oh, Edgar," Constance accepted the loose

bouquet and inhaled deeply. "Thank you!" Reluctantly handing them off to Natalie, who nodded that she would take care of them, Constance exited through the window, which Natalie closed behind her. "Blue dawn flowers covered the fence by the back door at the home where we lived while I was in school," she told Edgar as she took his arm. "I always sat there while I was peeling thips with my mother or puzzling something out."

"A bit of home for you," he smiled, well able to empathize with the wistful tone in her voice.

"I am sorry, Edgar," she squeezed his arm gently. "Now I have gone and made you homesick, too."

"Nah," he tried to brush it off. Then an idea struck him. "But since you bring up the subject, I was hoping you might share your secrets with me."

Surprise overrode the homesickness, throwing up walls of defense as she waited breathlessly for him to continue. Was he actively working for Mosley, then?

"You spend so much time away from your home and family. How do you stand it?" Edgar attributed the tension on her face to the fact that the admiralty's office had just come into view.

"It was worse when I was younger," she admitted after taking a moment to collect and redirect her thoughts. "I had only simple tasks to perform and a fair amount of free time, which could have been miserable if my father had not taught me to keep my mind busy with other things."

"True, that helps," Edgar agreed. "Alas, there is little here to be done by a man-fairy like myself."

"The castle has no smithies?" she asked, teasing.

"The castle has a very fine smithy," he corrected, easing them towards the ground. "With a very fine smith who is more possessive and jealous than a school child!"

She laughed at his comparison even while she worried. How easy it was to get into mischief when there was nothing else interesting to do.

"Will you stay and watch?" she asked him as they landed. "It would be nice to see a friendly face," she added, unhappily aware how the remark might be misunderstood.

"Sure," Edgar agreed. "Sure," he said again, with more enthusiasm.

"Constance!"

She looked around, startled to see Cambrian approaching from the direction of the admiralty building.

"It occurred to me this morning that you would need a sword to complete your outfit," he grinned, holding up his dressiest sword. The hilt was gilded silver and topped with a thumb-sized diamond, the grip wrapped with soft coorelum leather. The razor-sharp steel blade was encased in a leather scabbard that was finely tanned and elaborately decorated.

Constance was glad she had both feet on the ground, because the prospect of wearing his sword, clearly emblazoned with the crest of the royal house, might have knocked her right out of the sky.

"Cambrian, are you sure?" she asked, doubtful as to the appropriateness of the idea. And there was no turning the scabbard to hide the decorations, for its sash clasp was fixed in position.

Cambrian, following her gaze, saw what he had hoped others would see. He was still several days away from a proposal, there were some technicalities to sort out, but even if Mosley was the only one who noticed what she was wearing it should be worth it. If there had been time, he would have warned her about the flurry of excitement that would surely result from her being seen wearing it. Unfortunately, the bell tower was already striking the hour.

"Quickly now," he stepped forward and hooked the clasp about her sash. While it was hard for him to step back without embracing her, he reminded himself that they were partners in an investigation now. That would have to come first. In public, anyway. "Good luck, Captain," he told her gravely.

"Thank you, Your Highness." She had heard the bells, of course. She was almost grateful when Cambrian nodded to Edgar and walked into the building.

"Shall we?" Edgar asked. His smile was strained and who could blame him? He was not so blind that he could not see how it was between them. Ah well, he could do with a friend, and a friend she seemed willing to be. Time to count his lucks instead of his misfortunes.

"Thank you," she smiled tremulously.

They barely had time to seat themselves, Edgar in the tightly-packed visitors' gallery and Constance beside the other captains, before the gavel struck.

"Hear ye, hear ye," a lieutenant intoned from where he stood by the scribes' table. "The admiralty's investigation into the return of the *Talon*, the loss of the *Kimuxwe*, and the deaths of His Majesty's windfairies is begun on this the twelfth…"

Constance stopped listening, for she had seen a familiar face on the far end of a row of military personnel. Braxton? What was he doing there? When had he arrived? Why had she not been told? She puzzled over those questions while the lieutenant read the official account of the loss of the *Talon* during the pirate offensive.

"Calling Captain Andrew Trevaille, of the *Talon*, to testify."

Her attention snapped back to the proceedings as Trevaille flew forward to take the stand. *Who was with Kuntza?* She gripped the soft hilt of Cambrian's sword while Trevaille drew his newly issued sword and offered it to the lieutenant. It was such an act of trust, standing there weaponless while one's superior officers reviewed in relative comfort decisions that had been made under completely different circumstances.

"I, Andrew Trevaille of the King's Fleet, do solemnly swear to tell the truth and will be heard to tell the whole truth by this inquiry." Without his sword or windship, he stood bravely, waiting for the questions to begin.

"Captain Trevaille," a white-haired admiral leaned forward, bracing himself on his elbows, one on each side of the papers before him on the table. "Your report indicates that during the pirate offensive your silver mirror, which was changed by fairy dust into a magic mirror, was damaged beyond use." He continued without pausing, "That circumstance resulted in your disorientation and eventual clearing of the Mists by good fortune rather than skill. As you exited the Mists, you encountered a windship flying the Sky Fairy flag."

Constance reminded herself that the recounting was for the sake of the gallery, which was populated by quite a few faces familiar to her after dining at court. Kept alert by an awareness that she would soon be answering similar questions, she waited patiently while the three admirals assigned to this investigation took turns interrogating Trevaille. Despite their pointed questions, she was relieved that he was able to avoid all allusion to the Water Fairy Tribe. When had he become aware that the other windships were pirate vessels? How many of his lads had survived? What were the conditions of their imprisonment? Had they tried to escape? Did he regret choosing not to fight?

Trevaille stood ramrod straight, white-knuckled fists clenched at his sides. "Aye," he ground out at last. "I regret it. We would have lost," there was no doubt in his mind of that and he had spent weeks considering it during his captivity, "but we would have taken some of them with us. Instead, I watched my lads die in cold blood at Bane's hand." For the first time in the interrogation, his shoulders sagged a little.

"That is all." The admiral who spoke gestured for Trevaille to take his seat.

The lieutenant returned Trevaille's sword and called, "Port Captain Michael Braxton."

Constance eagerly watched Michael take the stand, wondering if she would learn more about the file he had been keeping, to which time had permitted her only limited access.

"Port Captain Braxton," a younger admiral started this time, "it was your command that discovered the *Talon* beached near Port Herio. How did you know it was the *Talon* and what steps did you take?"

"I first spotted her on her approach to the

beach," Michael corrected, as he had told Prince Cambrian. "When she was safely grounded, I sent a squad to investigate. Finding her crewless and with no logbook, I sent a communique to Major Layton at Fort Bakarti on the *Dispatch*."

Constance would never forget the day the *Dispatch* arrived at Bakarti. It was the first time that she and Cambrian had worked together. Their efforts to save the *Dispatch* had failed, but they had at least prevented it from crashing into the dock at full speed, saving quite a few lives in the process. That had been the first time Cambrian held her in his arms, too. Amused at herself, she steered her thoughts back to the interrogation.

"By tracking her approach, and having some knowledge of the water currents in the area, we were able to determine that there was an island along her back path," Michael explained. "When they arrived at Port Herio, I made this information available to Prince Cambrian, Major Layton, and Captain Kimberlite." He nodded at Cambrian and then Constance, noticing for the first time the royal crest on her scabbard. The prince was a fast worker, apparently.

"What other actions did you take?"

Michael considered the question in relation to his oath. He had sworn to tell the truth, with the understanding that in order to tell the whole truth he might answer a question quite differently from how the asker anticipated. Answering this question with the whole truth, however, meant revealing that he had given to Edgar a copy of the complete file he had shown to Cambrian. And that Edgar had brought that file directly to the king, who must have decided to keep it confidential for the time being.

"After making the shipyard available to the *Nadauld* and the *Kimuxwe*, I submitted detailed reports to my superiors of what had taken place," he answered. Surely the king was his superior.

"That is all."

Michael took his seat, sparing a half-smile for Constance as he passed her. He was a little surprised that there had been no questions in regard to the survivors he had brought with him from Herio, but decided the admirals were waiting to question them directly.

"Captain Constance Kimberlite."

Constance took the stand and tried to draw her sword. She was so accustomed to the specialized grip of her father's sword that it was a surprise to feel her fingers sink fractionally into the coorelum leather. She could feel the heat rising in her cheeks as she surrendered the crest-bearing sword and took the oath. An unusual silence fell over the room after the oath, the members of the panel exchanging discretely questioning glances while the gallery waited with baited breath after the initial flurry of whispers.

"Captain Kimberlite," the admiral in the middle leaned forward, her braid slipping over her shoulder and brushing the papers before her. "You were in command of both the *Nadauld* and the *Kimuxwe* during this voyage." Her eyes flicked to the empty scabbard then rose immediately to meet Constance's eyes again. "When did you first come to believe that Major Layton was a traitor and a pirate?"

"I had no suspicion of that until we had almost reached the island," she answered, thinking wryly of how completely he had fooled them. "I was on the quarterdeck when a sideboat filled with pirates tried to board us."

"Tried?" This question came from the admiral who had led Trevaille's questioning. "You defeated them?"

"We defeated that sideboat, yes," she nodded. "But," she stopped speaking rather than try to speak over the admiral.

"We?" The one-word question, asked by the third (and up until now mostly silent) admiral, hung in the air between them.

"I was not alone on the quarterdeck," she answered vaguely. Cambrian had been with her, but she would like to avoid making that public for as long as possible.

"Who sounded the alarm? I assume," the third panel member lounged back in his chair, as much as one could without slouching, "that an alarm *was* sounded."

"I called for the alarm and the beacons."

"You called for the alarm. You defeated the

sideboat—with help, of course." He waved dismissively as if to indicate the help was negligible. "And then you abandoned your windship, your crew." He shook his head and folded his arms across his chest while the gallery gasped. "Brilliant strategy."

Despite the anger, embarrassment, and other emotions roiling about in her chest, Constance smiled. She could either remain calm or expect Cambrian to spring to her defense—which, even if it turned out as well as possible would be a bad thing for them both.

"Your skill at summarizing leaves something to be desired, sir." She heard the gallery members hushing each other, then whispering, presumably passing her words on to those that had not heard them. "But I cannot deny those things did happen, and in that order." She left it at that for a moment, watching the questioning admiral begin to squirm a little as the silence reached the far corners of the room.

"In the interests of the whole truth," the admiral in the middle brushed her braid back over her shoulder, "would you care to share your own summary of the events of that night?" She did not know what game the captain and the admiral were playing, but she was annoyed with them both for behavior that would only serve to prolong the inquiry.

"Yes, thank you," Constance nodded. "I sounded the alarm as soon as I realized we were under attack. But it was not until after repelling the sideboat and its pirates that I became aware we had been boarded amidships as well. Because the alarm had been sounded and the beacons lit, I was able to see the fighting quite clearly. I was also able to see Major Layton come aboard. He casually remarked that he wanted as many of the crew alive as possible and ordered Roberts, the prince's valet at the time, to fetch him Prince Cambrian's crown."

"You heard him?" The summarizing admiral fairly pounced on the idea. "Over the fighting?"

"Major Layton was possessed of a strong, clear voice, sir," she added the title to distance herself from the dislike she was developing for the admiral. "And he was speaking loudly enough to be heard by his pirates. That was when I realized what must have happened. The *Kimuxwe* was nearby but neither responded to our alarm nor offered assistance. The major had been aboard the *Kimuxwe*. Having nowhere to turn for aid, I piped for my lads to abandon ship and used an aft pebble-thrower to damage the mainmast."

"Yes, that is in the report," the admiral who had led Michael's questioning leaned forward again. "I will confess, I have been wondering since I read that what you were hoping to accomplish by your action."

"I hoped that the pirates would become more invested in keeping the *Nadauld* flying than they were in fighting," she answered quietly. "To give my lads, the prince, myself," she paused to take a deep breath, "a fair chance at escaping."

"Your report indicates that your strategy was at least partially successful," the older man-fairy leafed through the papers before him. Finding the one he wanted, he read directly from the report, "After navigating our way to a small, outlying island, we took shelter in a dormant lava tube until morning." Setting the page aside, he folded his hands and looked at her directly. "You took quite a risk, Captain. You then compounded it by deciding to attack the pirate fort with a minimum force. Explain, please, why you did not attempt to secure reinforcements and make a proper attack?"

Cambrian leaned back in his chair, aware of how close he had come to making a fool of himself by rushing to confront the admiral who dared accuse Constance, however cunningly, of being a coward. He had done far more good by not interfering, for she had shown wisdom and courage in her response. She had even sounded convinced that she had done the right thing in sabotaging the *Nadauld*, which made him not hate himself quite so much as he had that night when he had held her, sobbing, in his arms while they escaped. Feeling a bit more in control of his emotions, he refocused on the inquiry, which had by this time moved on to Constance's summing up.

"So, rather than risking the pirates' departing to another hideaway or giving them time to prepare, we infiltrated the fort, rescued the few prisoners Bane had kept alive, and escaped aboard the *Nadauld*."

"Destroying the *Kimuxwe* in the process." This time the third admiral spoke with almost a sneer. "How did that tragedy come about, Captain?"

Constance heard more than the question, more even than his mocking tone of voice. She did not actually know the man-fairy, but it seemed to her that he was making this very personal. Why was he attacking her—to provoke Cambrian, perhaps? It was a wild guess, to be sure, yet she could think of no other reason for his continued, blatant animosity towards her.

"Tragedy it was," she agreed soberly. Choosing her words carefully, she explained, "Our original intent was to recapture the *Kimuxwe*, which was in good repair as far as we knew. Unfortunately, Bane outguessed us and was waiting aboard the *Kimuxwe*." She hesitated, but the admiral seemed to have lost his stomach for the game. He looked quite miserable, in fact. "Those who boarded her first were made prisoners. The prince, an officer, and myself were the only ones to avoid that fate." Again she paused. Again there was no challenge made. "While Prince Cambrian distracted the pirates, the officer and I began quietly freeing our lads, who secured the *Nadauld*."

"The prince distracted them." The female admiral looked at her narrowly. "It is the duty of every member of the Sky Fairy Armed Forces to defend and protect the Royal Family. You, on the other hand, permitted the prince to engage in a duel with a pirate, in the course of which," she raised her voice to be heard over excited whispers from the gallery, "he was badly injured."

Constance shivered, the memories that rushed over her of that night almost overpowering her. The sound of steel on steel, the reek of the kerosene she had spilled on herself while rigging the *Kimuxwe*, trying to control her breathing as she aimed the flaming crossbow bolt—the cold night air sucking the life out her, out of Cambrian, while they waited on the mizzenwing of the *Nadauld* until they could be brought safely aboard. Making eye contact with the admiral who had asked the question, she almost told her just how stubborn Cambrian could be.

"Yes, I did." A poor beginning to her defense. "Because Bane chose to fight him. If I or my officer had challenged Bane, he would have laughed in our faces and ordered his lads to take us prisoner. Only Prince Cambrian's challenge was taken seriously, because it struck Bane as worthwhile, made him feel powerful."

"Made?" All eyes turned to the older admiral, who repeated himself. "You said 'made him.'

Are you so sure Bane is dead?"

"Yes."

The admiral waited, but when she did not move to speak further, he pointed out, "We have had his death reported to us once before."

"Yes," she answered heavily. "Pirate prisoners confirmed that Bane was aboard one of the windships pursued and destroyed by the combined Fairy Forces at the pirate offensive." Shaking her head, she voiced a dreadful thought. "If *that* was a lie; if Layton was *not* a liar; and *if* he was actually the pirate called Bane, then Bane is dead. Dead by my hand."

Chapter XIII

Lesley stared out of the sitting room window, thinking hard. The inquiry had broken for lunch hours ago, sending the gallery scurrying off to be the first ones to tell somebody the news that Bane was dead. And how he had died. Lesley shivered involuntarily at the thought of having Captain Kimberlite as a sister-in-law. For the signs were unmistakable. Cambrian, impervious to the romantic darts women-fairies had been flinging at him for half a century, had succumbed to the dubious attractions of this stranger.

"Do you suppose she even understands what she is getting into?" she wondered aloud.

Laura looked at her blankly, her mind more on the upcoming festival than on the latest gossip. "Do I suppose who understands what?" she asked after unsuccessfully trying to figure out what Lesley meant.

"Constance," Lila supplied, tapping a pile of papers into a tidy stack and setting them by the inkwell. "Lesley thinks she is not good enough for Cambrian."

"Oh." Laura nodded that she understood, then cocked an inquisitive eyebrow at Lesley. "Do *we* get a vote?" she asked mischievously.

Lesley tilted her chin imperiously before answering, "The last vote may be his, but we may have time to open his eyes before he makes the mistake of his life."

Lila began inspecting a cupful of quills to make sure their tips were still correctly shaped.

Lesley watched her briefly before prompting, "Yes, Lila?"

"I know you are trying to help," Lila began timidly, setting the cup aside, "and yet I find myself wondering if we know enough about such things to do more than make a mess of it."

Lesley blinked, surprised. The eldest of the triplets, she had assumed her natural role of leading them at the tender age of twelve. They had gotten in a fair amount of trouble, it was true, but they had never yet failed to accomplish what they set out to do, with the general exception of changing rules such as bedtimes.

"You like her."

Lila stared at her hands, feeling strangely guilty. She struggled with the guilt, reminding herself that she was at liberty to like whom she chose.

Laura frowned at Lesley's accusing tone and sprang into the breach.

"I cannot say that *I* like or dislike her." She smiled, faintly amused at how definite her tone made the ambiguous statement sound. "But I am willing to listen if you have someone else to suggest for Cambrian. He deserves to be happy."

Lesley, feeling badly for making little Lila, as she thought of her youngest sister, feel badly, nodded, admitting Laura had a valid point.

Brilliant, in fact. But whom could she suggest?

"Historian Janet. She has almost as much experience at court as we do. And Cambrian has always liked her." Lesley smiled, pleased at how rapidly she had come up with an answer.

"She was Joanna's best friend," Lila protested quickly.

"True." Lesley frowned. "Though that may mean she is perfectly suited to him in nature as well." She smiled triumphantly. "Best friends are usually alike, are they not?"

Lila twitched, upsetting the inkwell. "Oh no!" she cried, rescuing the papers that were in the ink's direct path.

"Careful," Laura caught Lila's hand just as she was about to try shaking the ink off the papers. "That will splatter everywhere." Looking for a joke to ease the embarrassed pink of Lila's complexion she added, "And I look horrible in polka dot." With a wink at her younger sister, she caught up the can of sandarac mixed with chalk and shook its contents liberally over the damp pages.

In the meantime, Lesley had snatched several pieces of scratch paper which she used to soak up the remaining ink. She had to bite her tongue to keep from reprimanding Lila. Disappointed in herself that she had not made more progress at not being bossy since she had resolved to do so almost fourteen years ago, she said nothing at all.

Righting the ink well before it could quite

finish emptying itself, Lila stared at the mess she had made. It might have been simpler to champion Constance after all.

"I am sorry," she murmured. When neither of her sisters replied, she looked for something useful to do. Drying her black-tipped fingers thoroughly on a used piece of paper that she rescued from the wastebasket, she glumly fetched a pair of gloves. "I will get some ink remover in town," she announced in a subdued tone. They had all managed to get ink on them somewhere, though she had gotten the worst of it.

Looking up from the guest list she was holding, Laura managed a smile. It would take an hour or more to recopy some of the ruined papers and she hated copying.

"If you pass the sweet shop," she spoke in time to keep Lesley from embarrassing herself with a querulous remark, "would you bring me some rock candy?"

Lila blinked, surprised. Rock candy was *her* favorite, not Laura's.

"I," she paused, understanding dawning. "Yes, of course." She smiled gratefully. She would also bring back an éclair for Lesley and a packet of tarts for Laura. Midday sweets were a rare indulgence for them, but would probably go a long way towards sweetening tempers, including her own injured one.

Ducking out the window, she zipped across the yard towards the vine-covered southwest wall.

She would normally have used the front gate, if only because it was closer to the shopping district of Regalis, except that she was upset enough to like the idea of a longer flight. However short her absence, Lesley would think it too long anyway. Tucking up, she dove feet first through the hole in the wall. Landing softly, she grinned to herself while she waited for the patrol, which never looked towards the castle, to pass. That hole had only been the size of a fist when she had first found it. With a little time and effort, she had enlarged it to the point of being useful. It was almost her only real secret, one that not even her sisters knew about.

Safe from the eyes of the patrol, she zipped towards town, feeling better already for her little adventure. Here again she chose an indirect route, deciding to pass by the perfume shops to see if there were any still open. It was a pity she had not been able to find out what scent Constance was looking for; she might have picked up a bottle of it for her.

When she reached the line of perfume shops, she slowed enough to study them. Not surprisingly, she was the only fairy on that street. The few shops that were not closed were not worth recommending…except she had never been in the little shop furthest from the castle. As a rule, the shops nearest the castle were the most prestigious, leaving the others to compete by providing unusual wares or less expensive ones, the sort of thing a visiting villager would be able to purchase and parade around when they returned home. But this did not look like a curiousity shop.

Landing nearby, she debated with herself briefly before peering through the heavily tinted glass window. Rows of plain-looking bottles adorned the shelves. Three tables with graduated displays in the shape of three familiar mountain peaks were evenly spaced about the room and she was pleasantly surprised to find she had been standing there for several seconds without having the shopkeeper come out to try to persuade her inside. In fact, where was the shopkeeper? There was no one at the counter. Looking up, she saw that there was no bell on the outside of the door. She was about to turn away when she heard laughter. From *inside* the shop.

Captivated, she opened the door a little. What was so funny? Papa had not laughed like that for months, and Momma never laughed so unreservedly. Preparing for the winter festival had certainly made her own life more serious than she liked it. She was halfway across the floor to the counter before she realized it. Had she missed laughter so much?

"Hold that thought," a cheerful voice said from the back of the shop. "While I tend to this customer."

Stunned, Lila just stood there when she should have fled. She had not come to town to buy perfume. Oh, this would take forever! He would want her to sample this or that, pump her for the latest gossip, and... Her agitation faded when a clean-cut young man-fairy came around the corner.

"Good day, miss," he greeted her pleasantly, placing long-fingered hands flat on the counter. "How may I serve you?"

"I was just passing by," she began to explain, "when I remembered that a friend of mine had asked me if any of the perfumeries were still open."

"Oh?" The young man-fairy grinned pleasantly. "Yes, Uniquely Yours will be open all winter." It had taken him weeks to convince his mother, who owned and managed the Kimberlite Perfumeries, to allow him to remain at the shop, but he was convinced it would prove worthwhile. If nothing else, it would get him out of the dreary work of processing the hundreds of pebble-weight of petals, seeds, roots, bark, and who knew what else the harvesting crews had brought in. Not that they would miss one pair of hands among so many. Four of his older siblings were married.

"All winter?" Lila repeated, certain she had heard wrong. "Is that customary?" That was a delicate way of asking if it was wise. Few fairies would risk the tunnels beneath Regalis for something so trivial as perfume.

"No," he shook his head. "But like the best

flowers, we are hardy, if small. So Uniquely Yours will be offering customized perfumes, made to suit the tastes and natures of our clientele, all winter long." He congratulated himself on delivering the speech his mother had written without sounding like he had been practicing it for weeks. Which he had. While he did not much enjoy processing raw materiel or making the perfumes, he knew they only offered the best.

"Customized perfumes?" she repeated, intrigued. It was traditional for the king and queen to be presented a gift at the winter festival, but even with their collective knowledge of their mother neither she nor her sisters had been able to decide what it should be that year.

"Yes." He smiled again. "May I?" Holding out his hand, he nodded at hers. When she had placed her hand in his, he was about to remove her glove when she snatched her hand back.

"Sorry," she apologized, holding both hands behind her back. "I…" At a loss for words, she was backing out of the shop when she bumped into a table.

"Wait, please," he held up both hands in apology. "I did not mean to startle you." He was in no hurry to have her leave, and not just for business reasons. She was really quite pleasant to look at. "Perhaps," he glanced over his shoulder and nodded. "Wait there." Zipping into the back, he engaged someone in a low-toned conversation.

Lila, who had turned to steady the display of glass perfume bottles, found herself alone again in the front of the shop. *What* was she doing? Toppling inkwells, bumping into tables, acting like a ninny in front of an attractive young man-fairy. Strangers they might be to each other, but surely by now he thought she was stranger than he was! Though not half as strange as he would think her if she removed her gloves.

"Thanks to my amazing powers of persuasion," he came back around the corner, "my sister is going to help us."

Lila stared in complete consternation as Captain Constance Kimberlite came around the corner.

Constance stared right back at her.

"Lila?" she asked as if she doubted her eyes. Or perhaps she just doubted her identification, for the triplets were nearly identical.

Lila debated the merits of playing herself off as one of her sisters, something she did occasionally to get herself out of trouble. Lesley was so quick-witted, she always knew what to say. And Laura was so self-possessed, so confident. Somehow she felt more capable when playing either of them than she did as herself.

"Yes," she said at last, deciding that she would rather be honest with her brother's flame.

Constance quickly set aside her surprise and said, "Welcome to Uniquely Yours." Swept back years to the times she had spent helping in one of her mother's early perfume shops, Constance smiled. "Todd tells me you have a question about the customized perfumes."

Todd. Constance had a brother named Todd. Of course, Lila might have supposed that Constance would have siblings, but how could she have guessed some of them would be in Regalis?

"I did not realize you two knew each other," Todd remarked, puzzled by the bit of stiffness between them at first.

"We only just met the other night," Constance replied, automatically reaching for several vials of liquid. When she had decided to seek out her family after the inquiry closed for the day, she had not anticipated this overlapping of worlds! "We barely know each other." She smiled at Lila to remove any sting from her observation even as she wondered how Todd could be as ignorant of the royal family as he had to be. As part of his plea for her help, he had mentioned that Lila was the first really refined client he had seen since reopening the shop that spring. And yet, underlying his argument that making a regular patron of her would help business, she had sensed a personal interest. Now that she knew who the client-to-be was, Constance wondered if she should enlighten him as to her rank?

"May I see your hand, please?" she asked Lila,

the bottles at last arranged satisfactorily before her.

"Oh," Lila blushed. "I cannot remove my gloves."

Constance leaned her waist against the counter, thinking fast.

"Lila," she had learned years ago that addressing someone by name added import to what one said next, "what is wrong?"

Shyly, Lila glanced at Todd. Then she gave in to the consistent friendliness that marked Constance's behavior toward her.

"I have ink stains on my fingers," she admitted with a small sigh. Removing first one glove, then the other, she displayed them to her startled audience.

"No problem," Todd smiled. Zipping to the back of the shop again, he procured two small bottles and quickly returned. Taking a large clump of soft cotton from the bag of it that he kept under the counter to use for samples, he poured a little of each of the bottles' contents on it and held out his hand once again to the enchanting visitor. Somehow, and he could not have explained it, the ink on her fingers made her all the more endearing to him.

"What do you mean to do?" Lila asked as she approached him warily.

"This will remove the ink," he explained and rubbed the damp side of the cotton against the back of his hand. "It does not hurt," he promised.

Constance watched in surprise as Lila surrendered her hands to Todd. Feeling almost as though she were intruding on their familiar, yet innocent, interaction, she looked down at the bottles she had chosen. Lila. Remembering the apologetic look Lila had given her the other night when Lesley had somewhat authoritatively announced that all three of them were leaving after dinner, she mixed a few drops of high grade grapefruit oil in with the clear alcohol base, enough for a refreshing, fortifying whiff.

"Tell me about yourself, Lila," she encouraged, breaking the silence that she attributed to youthful infatuation.

"Me?" Lila shook her head. "There is not much to tell."

"Do you prefer the morning or the evening star?" Constance asked, her hand poised over two bottles.

"Morning," Lila answered promptly, wishing that court events permitted her to see it more often.

"Hot or cold?" she asked as she added a carefully measured amount of bergamot.

"Hot." Lila did not have to think about that, either. She hated shivering through an evening's entertainment.

"Suppose you are having a new dress made. Do you choose bottled sunlight or lavender for the fabric color?"

Lila hesitated. She loved to look at vivid colors, they seemed to fill her with energy—but to wear them?

"Sapphire blue," she answered, not realizing how much her alternate answer revealed about herself.

Constance reached for a bottle in the back, amused and pleased by Lila's choice. Blue was the traditional color of the Royal Family, but not one of the options she had given. As for it being sapphire blue, that was a so-called 'cool' color, not flamboyant and yet its own distinctive shade, which seemed to be the balance Lila was struggling to find. Constance mixed in minute amounts of jasmine and rose oils, a little less of the first as it was a heavier scent.

Todd, having finished removing the ink, handed Lila a soft towel to dry her hands with. He was glad she knew his sister. Instead of wasting days hunting her down or hoping she would return to his shop, he could get right into spending time with her.

"Ah," he held up his hand when it looked like Constance was about to give Lila the bottle. "One of the main reasons women-fairies wear perfume is to capture the attention of a likely man-fairy." He grinned to take most of the seriousness out of his generalization. "That being the case, I had better test that first."

Constance almost laughed out loud at seeing her youngest brother trying to act grown up and suave by holding a perfume bottle under his nose. Stifling it somehow, she instead raised her eyebrows as though intensely interested in his verdict. It was his shop, after all. And he must be doing something right, or their mother would never have agreed to his addlepated scheme of keeping the shop open all winter.

"Missing something," Todd proclaimed, his lofty air vanishing as he rummaged through the bottles on the counter. He eventually stooped down and brought a box up from the lower shelf. "I put it away," he smiled, dusting a bottle off with the cloth Lila had just dropped on the counter.

"Be careful," Constance warned without thinking. Myrrh was a heady base note, the sort that could overpower a perfume. Added in the correct proportions, of course, it made the best better, warming and enriching the other fragrances while adding its own special spice. She felt a bit dubious about adding it to such a fruity, floral mix, but…it *was* his shop.

"Of course," Todd agreed, too aware of the costliness of what he was handling to be irked by her admonition. They combined their myrrh with a hint of amber, but he would still go easy on it. Constance had mixed only a minute amount of perfume, intentionally as he knew, in keeping with Uniquely Yours' philosophy.

Lila watched Todd carefully unscrew the top of the dark glass bottle, wondering what was inside. A miniature pipet was fastened to the bottom of the lid and from that two drops of golden liquid were squeezed into the mixture Constance had made for her.

Todd exhaled in relief when he had replaced the bottle safely in the box. Myrrh was getting more and more difficult to find in the wild.

"There." Taking up her bottle and lidding it, he swirled its contents ever so gently. Holding out his hand, a habit from dealing with giddy tourists that he would rather not trust with glass bottles, he was gratified when Lila put her hand in his without hesitation. "A little of this," he transferred a dab of the mixed perfume to her wrist, "will go a long way. Now, rub your wrists together."

Lila obediently rubbed her wrists together, as she had thousands of times over the years, and cautiously raised them toward her nose.

"That is incredible." She looked up, first at Constance, then at Todd. "What is in it?"

Todd folded his arms across his chest, a slow smile spreading across his face.

"A secret." Looking her in the eyes, Todd felt his heart leap into his throat. Whatever suave platitudes he might have palmed off on a tourist faded from his mind, leaving it almost blank. "When you have used it up," he pressed the bottle into her willing palm, "come back and we will see if you have a new secret to add to the formula."

"I do not understand," Lila admitted, completely charmed out of herself by the cozy little shop and its friendly occupants.

"Perfume is a very individual thing and should reflect the nature of the fairy wearing it," Todd told her seriously. "Instead most fairies wear the same perfume for centuries without even noticing that it no longer suits them."

"So you see," Constance intervened before Todd, who truly enjoyed his job, began sharing some of his humorous experiences with overly-perfumed patrons, "the reason we only mixed a little is because by the time that is used up, you will probably need a slightly different blend."

Lila nodded. "Yes, I see." She was not sure yet if she completely agreed, she was hardly a dynamic fairy, but there was no need to mention that here and now. "How much do I owe you?"

Todd shook his head. "Nothing. No," he shook his head again when she opened her mouth to protest. "I never charge my first customer on the last day of the third week of the tenth month of every other year."

Constance did laugh aloud at that, which prompted Todd to join her. Lila was glad to laugh with them, for that had been about as silly an answer as she ever hoped to hear!

"Oh dear!" Lila stopped laughing suddenly. "I almost forgot, I have to get back." She started to set the bottle on the counter, then remembered it was hers. Tucking it into her handbag, she looked at the two bottles Todd had used to remove the ink from her fingers.

"More ink at home?" Constance guessed, following her gaze. "Go ahead," she smiled, handing them to her. "We have plenty more."

"Thank you." Lila was sincere in her gratitude. She was about to leave yet again when she remembered the sweet shop. Looking down at her full hands, she despaired of getting it all back to the castle safely.

"What is it?" Todd asked.

"I have to make another stop," she explained without thinking.

"Too many bundles to carry?" Todd was delighted. "I know just the thing. If Constance will mind the shop, that is." He turned hopeful eyes towards his sister.

Constance barely kept from rolling her own eyes—it was just like him to find a way to leave her doing his job—while she nodded. Lila deserved a good friend and Todd was a cheery lad.

"You had better hurry," she told them. "The shops will be closing soon and," she turned her mock fierce gaze on Todd, "I have to be back at the castle before their dinner hour."

Deflated, Todd said, "But I was going to make us dinner here. We have so much to catch up on!" It had been years since they had spent any real time together. He would have liked her advice on a few things around the shop, too.

"Well," Lila began to speak, then hesitated before venturing, "perhaps Todd could join us at the castle."

Constance liked the idea, for it relieved her of the responsibility of telling her brother that Lila was a princess.

"Me?" Todd stared at them both. "Eat at the castle?"

"Why not?" Constance teased. "It would be good for business." As she had expected, Todd gave her an exasperated look. He had been dropping subtle hints about how slow business was since she arrived but had never taken advice well.

"Wearing what?" he retorted. "Even my best suit," he stopped, glancing sideways at Lila. If he had been thinking, he would have come up with some smooth excuse instead of revealing his lack of suitable attire.

"You must not let that worry you," Lila protested, undeterred. "We have visitors from all over the kingdom, many of whom eat in their travelling clothes."

"I wish you would come," Constance added, a little wistfulness entering her tone.

"Then I shall," Todd agreed, smiling despite his inner misgivings. If they could invite him, he supposed he could go.

Chapter XIV

Constance turned away from watching the two of them zip away down the street. There was plenty to be done and she relished the thought of an hour or so in the familiar duties of her childhood. She had little enough skill at salesmanship, she admitted as she began dusting one of the displays, but somehow she had always found herself stationed at the perfume shop while home on leave. When the door opened behind her light poured in from outside, striking the mirror painstakingly positioned on the far wall and from there transferring down the hall to the kitchen, the same means that had alerted her brother to the presence of a customer earlier.

"Good day," she turned, smiling. She almost dropped the bottle in her hands when she realized she was facing Arnold Mosley.

"Good day," he smiled back. He leaned on his silver-tipped cane for a moment, taking in the picture of a windship captain polishing a bottle of perfume in her shirtsleeves, rolled up to the elbows, uniform trousers and boots. It was deliciously incongruous. "I just stopped in," he lied, unless having her followed and her location reported to him could be interpreted so harmlessly, and reminded himself to proceed carefully. She could be very valuable to him. "Looking for a present," he continued. That was safe, so long as he did not mention a recipient. "Do you know if the proprietor is available?"

"No, he," she stopped, not wanting to admit they were there alone. Then she gave herself a mental shake and reminded herself that she was *supposed* to find her way into his company. "He has gone out to help a valued patroness with her other errands. I am in charge for the moment." She tried to sound calm and collected while she combed her memories for clues as to how she should act. Her younger sisters used to practice flirting with the mirror in their shared room at home. There had been eye batting and side-smiles—but she was reluctant to act ninety now when she had not even acted that way at the time.

"Is it a gift for a lady-fairy?" Constance kicked herself for asking the automatic question. It made perfect sense, from a business perspective. A woman-fairy would hardly appreciate a gift of spicy, woodsy scent, for example. But somehow it seemed intrusive when speaking to him. Perhaps that was because she believed he was seeking a new companion. Or because she was angling for the position herself.

"Yes." He agreed quickly, intrigued to see a frown flicker across her face. "Alas, I do not often buy perfume." Tucking his cane under his arm, he tried his hand at a helpless shrug and was gratified at her response.

"I think I can help with that." Replacing the bottle she had been polishing, Constance folded her arms across her chest. "What is she like?"

"Let me see." Arnold drew his eyebrows together and rubbed his chin with his hand. "She loves to travel and to be outdoors." At least, he assumed windfairy captains loved those things. "Confident, a strong personality." That was clearly true of her.

Constance began mentally picking through the shop's stock. That certainly did not sound like the woman-fairy he had been with last night. Had he found someone new already? A man-fairy like him probably had a whole string of women-fairies that he rotated through the way other men-fairies rotated through their suits.

"Perhaps this one," she picked a bottle of the most expensive perfume and held it up.

"Perhaps," he smiled, coming closer. "Would you try some on?" he asked.

"Me?" she asked, startled.

"Oh yes." He nodded, thoroughly enjoying himself as he used her position against her. She had thought herself in control of the situation, but now she would have to decide whether or not to comply with a customer's request. "I learned long ago that perfume smells different in the bottle than it does while being worn," he told her, his face and tone the perfect masks of innocence.

She knew that was true. However, she found it odd that someone who did not often buy perfume knew that. Deciding there was minimal chance of harm, she put a drop on her wrist and held it out to him. She had to grit her teeth to keep from reacting when he took her hand in his, his thumb placed squarely in her palm, his fingertips resting lightly on the back of her hand.

"Yes." He held his nose right next to her wrist without quite touching it. "Yes, that is very pleasant." Releasing her hand because he did not want to make her too uncomfortable, he asked, "Do you like it?" He set his cane tip back on the ground, leaning on it out of habit.

"Oh, yes." She smiled, relieved to have her hand back.

"Then I will take it." He put the thumb and forefinger of his free hand into the money pocket sewn on the inside of his sash, raised his eyebrows expectantly.

"Seven granules of silver," she told him, raising the price just a little. It was already outrageous, but as Todd had pointed out, they *were* in Regalis.

Arnold did not hesitate. Producing a pinch of silver, he sprinkled the granules across her waiting palm. He knew it was proper form to place it in a neat pile in the center, but he did it this way so that she would remember him.

"Thank you," she closed her right fist hard around the silver, annoyed at his trick. With her other hand she slipped the bottle of perfume into a decorative paper bag and held it out to him. "I hope she enjoys it."

"Thank you," he smiled as he took it, then

held it back out to her. "I hope you will, too."

Confused, she stared at him.

"I know it is a bit forward of me," he bowed slightly, "as we have scarcely more than met. However, I hope you will accept it as a gift of gratitude?"

"Gratitude?" she repeated, more confused than ever.

"Oh yes." He gestured slightly with the tip of his cane. "This whole pirate affair could have gone quite differently without brave captains such as yourself." Not that he would have been disappointed if it had. He was first and foremost a business-fairy, interested in selling his goods to the highest bidder, never mind who they were or how they procured the money he was paid with.

"Yes," Constance nodded slowly. "Very differently." Had she seen a glint of silver in his eyes, or was it just that his tone of voice rang a bit false? "Thank you." As she accepted the bag, she wondered what Cambrian would say when she told him that Arnold had given her a gift.

"Since you have been so gracious as to accept my poor gift," he leaned forward on his cane when he saw that she was about to turn away, "I am tempted to ask an even bigger favor." Certain that he had her whole attention, and deciding to mix business with pleasure as he often did, he invited, "Would you do me the honor of joining me for dinner one night this week?" He left the night open, aware that she had inquiries every morning.

"I," Constance paused, managed a smile. The thought of having dinner with him was repugnant at best. Not that that mattered, all things considered. "Perhaps tomorrow?" That gave her enough time to coordinate with Cambrian without having to dread it very long.

"Marvelous." He straightened by bringing his feet forward, which significantly reduced the space between himself and the captain. Was something amiss? Or was it merely that he was accustomed to greedy, grasping women-fairies? Playing with them was much simpler than making the effort to remember and respect any one woman-fairy. "I shall call for you at dusk, then, milady." Forgetting that she had both hands full, he held out his hand. To his delight, she placed her right fist in his palm. Yes, he told himself as he raised her hand to his lips, this would be a pleasant challenge.

He was turning to leave when a thought struck him. "Are you sure tomorrow night will be convenient for you? I understood that the other survivors would be testifying in the inquiries the next morning." He watched her closely for some clue as to what she was hiding. Her response was completely unexpected.

"*Other* survivors?" In her excitement she almost forgot her loathing of the man-fairy and leaned toward him. Given that Bane had kept most of Trevaille's officers alive, for the first few weeks at least, she had been horribly disappointed not to find her first officer, Watts, amongst the prisoners they found alive at the pirate stronghold. Had he been moved? Were there other, better hidden strongholds? She barely suppressed a shudder at *that* thought.

"You had not heard?" His surprise was not feigned this time.

"No, I," she caught herself in time to keep from admitting that her homesickness had brought her to Todd's shop immediately after the inquiry had closed for the day. *Did Cambrian know?* Stupid question. "I wish I knew who it was." She looked at him hopefully.

"Alas," he shook his head, "I know no more than that Braxton, of Port Herio, brought some windfairies who are reported to be members of the crew of the *Nadauld*." Deciding he had told much in exchange for nothing, he nodded at the bag of perfume in her hand. "Be sure to wear that tomorrow." Smiling broadly, he let himself out of the shop.

His smile froze into a scowl when he saw who was waiting for him across the street. An angry flick of his silver-tipped cane kept the fool from joining him right there. It had been expedient to deal with that one himself at first, but the further he got from the decision the more he regretted not using the messenger system he ordinarily used when dabbling in less than legal ventures. Lifting off, he began making his way at a leisurely speed toward a small eatery. While it was hardly the sort of place he voluntarily frequented, it had a sufficiently high ratio of well-to-do clientele to permit him to blend satisfactorily.

A glance in the darkened, reflective window of a shop across the street confirmed to him that his contact was meekly following. It did not, however, reveal the fact that Constance, who had moved swiftly forward to lock the door behind him, had seen the whole thing, from his signal not to be approached to the other man-fairy's not-so-casual glance up and down the street before moving off after Arnold.

Dropping the silver granules into her own pouch, she locked the front door and zipped to the back of the shop. Seizing her uniform jacket on her way to the back door, she exited the shop as quietly as possible. An officer might attract some attention zipping through back streets and hiding in doorways, but an officer in her shirtsleeves would attract far more, far *worse*, attention. To save time, she zipped up and over a row of shops, pausing on an obliging roof until she caught a glimpse of Arnold's shadow. Shifting her gaze forward in the direction that the diminutive man-fairy was flying, she was surprised to see Arnold entering a middle-class eatery.

Cautiously she flew close enough, hiding among the rooftops, to get a better look at the sign. The Raven's Beak. From what she could see through the windows it was a mixed crowd, mostly travelers she judged by the style of their clothes, and a few that looked like wealthy local merchants. As soon as his shadow had followed Arnold inside, Constance dropped to the ground. She was debating following them further when someone behind her cleared their throat.

"Fancy meeting you here," Edgar said, wearing a frown that went clear to his heart.

"Edgar!" She could not keep the surprise out of her voice.

"I thought we were to meet at your brother's shop," he observed, his months at Regalis manifesting themselves in his restraint. He was deeply disappointed to find her following his friend Arnold, having completely missed seeing the other man-fairy. He had been willing to understand when it became clear that she preferred Cambrian to him—that made sense. But the idea that she was playing them both while secretly meeting with Arnold! It was enough to make him wonder about his ability to judge character.

"Yes, except," she stopped. How could she explain? Did she have the right to?

"Yeah, sure." Catching her by the shoulders, he spun her about so that they were facing the castle. "Tell it to the prince."

Stunned, Constance complied when he took her by the arm and began flying her to…well, she supposed he was taking her to Cambrian. Edgar had probably kept her from being discovered by Arnold, for if she had gotten close enough to get a very good look at the other man-fairy, she would have been close enough to be recognized herself. The irony of it all made her start to laugh.

"What is so funny?" Edgar asked gruffly, his own mood dipping sharply.

She shook her head. "I cannot tell you," she apologized, the laughter fading in the face of his obvious disapproval. "Only please believe me, dear Edgar," she made him hover long enough to look directly at her, "I have done nothing wrong."

Edgar resumed flying, the now-quiet captain in tow. He could not quite decide what to believe—his own eyes? Or the sincerity in hers? He waved away the protests of the gate guards as they zipped past and took her straight to the set of windows in the royal suites that were no longer dark. Rapping on them firmly, he squared his shoulders.

"No, I will get it." Cambrian's voice preceded him to the window by only a few seconds. "Oh," he remarked after recovering from the first moment of surprise, "will you come in?"

Constance entered first, with Edgar close on her heels.

"Pardon our intrusion, Your Highness,"

Edgar barely noticed the smoothness of his own speech in his earnestness, "but the captain has something to tell you."

"Yes, I have," Constance nodded her agreement. She had seen Jennings slip into the inner chamber as they entered and she called him out now. "Jennings, front and center." When he had obeyed, she moved to where she could see all of their faces. "I think I have stumbled onto a connection between Arnold and the Royal Record Keepers."

Cambrian shot a hard glance at Edgar, then took a deep breath. Trust her, he told himself. She might be an amateur, but she is not a fool.

"Go on," he nodded.

"Edgar took me out to the city after the inquiry," she began at the beginning, "to see if my family's shop was still open. When we found that it was, I stayed to talk to my brother while Edgar ran some errands." She paused, only just noticing that Edgar had no bundles or packages. Had he said errands or that he had someone to see? "Then he found me following Arnold to an eatery and assumed I was meeting him." She plunged forward with her explanation, suddenly unsure of Edgar.

"I see," Cambrian said, though that was only partially true. If he *had* detected a subtle change in her attitude toward Edgar, it only served to alarm him further. "Well," he attempted a smoke screen, "that makes sense in a way. Being friendly with a recorder would make tax evasion much easier." He refrained from bringing up the altered maps, which he hoped was information still restricted to the *Nadauld*'s crew and a few of the senior military personnel.

"Tax evasion?" Edgar parroted. "Arnold?" He frowned, several things he had noticed subconsciously now surfacing and clicking together like pieces to a puzzle he had not even known he was working on. "That explains a lot!"

Constance said nothing, determined to try listening for a change. She might have just upset the entire investigation by being willing to trust someone on a hunch. If Cambrian had successfully distracted Edgar—if Edgar was innocent of collusion with Arnold in the first place—she could do the most good by not doing any more harm.

"How so?" Cambrian asked the question easily, lifting an eyebrow in a friendly, interested manner.

"Arnold is a slick operator." Edgar felt no disloyalty in making that remark, for tax evaders usually were. "I have spent enough time with him to know that he never pays full price for anything, can tell you where to get anything you want, and quite a few fairies around here are scared of him." He shoved his hat back on his head. "At first I thought he was like Braxton, a decent fellow who just happened to have ready money. Now that I think about it," he shook his head decisively, almost dislodging his hat, "he has a long, lean look to 'im, like a coorelum after a hard winter."

Cambrian thought over what he knew about Braxton, who had hand-picked Edgar for the delicate task of bringing a confidential file to the king. He had almost forgotten about that. If not for Constance's change of heart just now, he would have taken Edgar into his full confidence right there.

"Jennings," he spoke abruptly, "would you and Edgar mind giving the captain and me a few moments?"

"Aye," Jennings agreed affably. He had years of experience with fairies at every dock in Fairydom and figured that was reason enough to trust Edgar, but the captain and her prince had their reasons for being cautious.

When Jennings had closed the door behind them, Cambrian flew close to Constance.

"What is wrong?" he asked her directly. "When you first came in, you trusted Edgar enough to begin speaking before him."

"Yes," she agreed. "Then I realized he had no packages. And then I could not remember if he said he had errands to run or someone to see."

Seeing her in confusion forced Cambrian to search in himself for the steadiness they both needed.

"Excellent," he nodded, finding a smile for her. "Such a small discrepancy might easily have gone overlooked." Wrapping his arm about her shoulders, he gave her a gentle squeeze. "He comes pretty highly recommended, though." Answering her raised eyebrows, he reviewed for her his thoughts of just minutes ago. "Braxton chose him for a sensitive mission. Oliver and my father both like him. Jennings was telling me only yesterday that he liked the cut of Edgar's jib." They were both smiling as he led her to the window. "Let me talk to him privately, see if I can sort out what happened after he left you this afternoon. If I am satisfied, I may invite him to join the investigation. Until then," he kissed her gently, "promise me you will be more careful. Following Arnold is not what we agreed you would do," he hurried before she could protest, "and worrying about you is not what I am supposed to be doing."

Constance swallowed what she had been going to say about being able to take care of herself. And whatever she might have said about the survivors Mosley had mentioned. There just was not enough time.

"Alright," she promised at last. Hastily she described what she had seen of the man-fairy, which amounted to very little besides the fact that he had been wearing a record keeper's robe. Then she bit her lip. "You should probably know that I am having dinner with Arnold tomorrow." Feeling his arm tighten about her shoulders she quickly added, "Let me know if you identify the man-fairy I saw him with." Kissing him on the cheek, she zipped out the window.

Chapter XV

The king's dinner guests were arriving already, in groups of twos and threes, by the time Constance finally made it to the gate. Constance waited at the main gate, trying not to betray how self-conscious she felt. Natalie had been busy assisting Gemma when Constance arrived at her suite, so Constance had done what she could while she waited, including the obligatory face powder. Now, as she curtsied to passing dignitaries and travelers, she was enormously grateful that she had not given in to the temptation to do her own hair. Natalie's gifts were many, and hair styling was not least among them.

Four tower clocks struck the quarter hour with impressive precision, making her smile and fret at the same time. Where was Todd?

"Your pardon, Captain." A guard landed beside her, saluting even though as a marine he had no obligation to do so.

Constance returned the salute reflexively. "Yes, Captain?" She smiled at the situation despite her preoccupation. To her relief, he visibly relaxed.

"I noticed you seem to be waiting for someone," he began. "As the time draws near for dinner to begin, I thought I might offer my services in watching for you."

Constance held back her surprise even as she curtsied back to the young couple entering the castle gates.

"I would have you answer a question for me first," she decided aloud.

"Of course, if I can," he answered immediately.

His response only made her more certain that she was being singled out for special service.

"I am not the only one from the castle awaiting guests." She paused to curtsy again, reflecting wryly that she was getting much better at it. "Can you tell me why nearly all of the arriving guests are offering me, a stranger, the formality of their salutes?" Perhaps that was the wrong way to word it, referring to a bow or a curtsy as a salute, but she felt reasonably sure that he, as a fellow member of the royal military, would know what she meant.

A faint smile played at his lips, but only for an instant. When he answered her question, his demeanor was perfectly serious.

"Has the captain forgotten that she appeared in public wearing the prince's sword?"

Under the pretense of checking for her brother amongst a new group of guests, Constance looked away from the captain's intense gaze. Every prince served ten years in the Royal Marines; the law required it. But how many generations had it been since a royal had married someone with an actual military career? She felt a little dizzy as she curtsied for what felt like the hundredth time.

"Constance!" Todd hailed her from where he stood, a wing's breadth inside the gate. He was staring at her. "You…" Suddenly aware that he was shouting across a goodly distance, he flew to her side at once. "You look beautiful."

Constance blushed furiously. She was furious with herself for blushing, too. And she was a little upset with Todd for acting so surprised. Not that her uniform was terribly feminine, but still…

"Captain," she did not have to look at him to know he had snapped to attention. "May I present my brother, Todd Kimberlite, a merchant on your own perfume row?"

"An honor." The captain unbent enough to shake Todd's extended hand. "Your pardon, m'lady," he turned his attention back to Constance, "you must hurry if you do not wish to be tardy."

Constance nodded acknowledgement of his warning and took Todd by his near hand. They had not gone far before he smilingly put her hand on his arm instead. She had to smile back at that. He might be her youngest sibling, but he was not a child-fairy to be led by the hand.

They entered the dining room just as the guards were beginning to open the large, double doors that separated the royal family from their guests long enough for both groups to settle themselves. Silently, Constance steered Todd over to their table, grateful that she had taken the time to check with Lila on her way to the gate. They had just taken their places by their chairs when Constance noticed that the right elbow of Todd's brown barkcloth suit was shiny, as though worn smooth. His white cravat was a little lopsided as well, but an oddly colored shadow inside the knot convinced her that her brother had chosen lopsided over visibly stained.

The royal family began entering the room before she could even think what to ask him, though a dozen questions instantly came to mind. *This is your best suit? Are you too busy or too poor to buy yourself a new cravat? Were you late on purpose so I could not ask you these questions?*

"Captain."

Constance blinked away the questions to smile at Lila, who had arrived on Cambrian's arm. She looked on as Cambrian and Todd sized each other up. She had not thought to be concerned about them meeting until they both smiled and shook hands, their mutual approval implicit in the gesture. Todd was not Craig, her twin, but he was her brother. It felt wonderful to finally begin introducing Cambrian to her family.

Lila was seated between Todd and Cambrian, which left Constance with the prospect of eating in silence or trying to engage the man-fairy seated at her left in conversation. She saw at a glance that he was well-groomed, not overdressed, and had a complexion of almost the same color as their off-white tablecloth.

"So," he leaned a little towards her while the waiter on his left arranged the first course at his place. "Are you Miss Kimberlite or Captain Kimberlite this evening?"

Constance had to wait while a second waiter performed the same service for her, which gave her a chance to glance at his name card. *Doctor Reginald Dubois.*

"To you, I am simply Constance," she answered, making up her mind in an instant. Doctor Dubois was one of those rare individuals who served the military and medical communities with equal effectiveness. Initially, his fame had been tied to a laboratory accident that resulted in a new solution which almost indefinitely extended the life of the thin fabric that covered a windship's wings. By now, however, the bards were singing his praises for his many improvements to potions and cures.

"I am honored." Doctor Dubois bowed slightly and tasted his soup. "Perfection," he announced.

Between spoonsful of soup and swallows, they chatted companionably. The doctor shared a story about his one trip aboard a windship—a perfectly dreadful experience, he assured her— and she teased him back with a tale of her early days at the academy, deliberately sprinkling the story with dark and gloomy accounts of her trips to the library. They kept up their banter through the first four courses, when he winked at her and turned to rescue Cambrian from the garrulous fellow on Dubois' left.

Constance made eye contact with Cambrian and smiled when he returned the slightest of nods. The table was just small enough to be seat six cozily, without knocking knees, and she imagined that if she reached for the small shaker of salt in the center of the table at the same time that Cambrian did, their fingers would touch. Unhappily, she also imagined the buzz of conversation at the neighboring tables should they attempt it. She had known being at Regalis would complicate their courtship, but it had never occurred to her to wonder if she could take the pressure. And if wearing his sword in public caused a stir sufficient that strangers recognized her on sight and bowed as though she was already a member of the royal family, she could only hope they never learned it had been a ploy to draw out a possible traitor. Her thoughts slipped sideways like a sideboard caught in an unexpected crosswind as she remembered what that traitor had said about survivors.

"Constance," Todd leaned towards her. "Are you alright?" He watched in mild concern as she smoothed her face before facing him.

"Fine," she smiled. She did not bother to ask him why he was worried. She had probably been frowning. "Are *you* alright?" Todd spent quite a bit of time in the shop, of course, but he still seemed unusually pale just now.

He hesitated, then said softly. "You should have warned me."

"Warned you?" she asked blankly. His dark, heavy eyebrows drew so tightly together that they resembled one of the more dangerous caterpillars found in the Deep Woods. "Oh." She took a deep breath and risked a look at the king's table, where Lesley and Laura just happened to be looking at her. "If she had wanted you to know, she would have told you herself."

"She did," Todd muttered. "Tell me, I mean." He nodded past Constance, who realized the waiters were replacing empty dishes with full ones. They had only a moment more. "I…I just…"

Constance impulsively put her hand on his where it rested on the table. Squeezing it gently, she leaned closer, ignoring the waiter temporarily.

"She likes you," Constance whispered. "Believe that." Withdrawing quickly so that the waiter could continue before the rest of the table became too curious, she watched her brother consider her words.

Dubois was not able to free himself from his new conversational partner, though he sent Constance an apologetic smile. Todd bravely recaptured Lila and they quickly became absorbed in whatever they were talking about. And that left Constance and Cambrian not staring at each other while they ate. The sixth course went largely uneaten, even though it was dessert. Constance chose the dark chocolate cake, Cambrian selected a slice of chilled lemon pie, Lila shyly recommended a strawberry gelatin, and Dubois found himself robbed of a choice when the heavyset fellow to his left told the waiter they both wanted the crème brullè.

When the waiters came to remove the last course, the cloud blue curtain which had been hanging against the east wall was suddenly pulled back to reveal a small orchestra. The cake lurched in Constance's stomach when she made eye contact with Cambrian. Firsts were always important. A first date, a first kiss, a first dance … But what made tonight different was that they had an audience.

King Jasper rose and offered his hand to his queen. Oliver rose and offered his hand to Gemma, who was still mostly successfully hiding her condition. The glow that surrounded her as she took her husband's arm would soon make those nearest her suspicious, however.

Cambrian rose and Constance nearly dropped the napkin she had been twisting in her lap. She was relieved, disappointed, and pleased when he bowed to his youngest sister, offering her his arm with a smile.

"Would you like to dance?" Todd asked Constance, his tone revealing little besides the fact that he was still a bit on edge after finding out that his date was a princess.

"Please," Constance surprised herself by accepting. Together they found a place on the dance floor.

Todd started on the conductor's downbeat, waltzing them past a few couples that were still trying to catch the rhythm. "Do you still dislike the flying waltz?" he asked, cocking his head to one side.

"Not if you promise not to dip me," she winked back. The incident might be a hundred years old, but it was still worth an occasional tease.

"I never *dropped* you," he insisted even as he lifted off.

She chuckled as she matched her ascent rate to his. "Then how did I end up in Craig's arms?"

Todd chuckled back, confident enough to let the teasing pass. "This much I will admit," he told her, trying to sound stern and failing. "I do not blame you for preferring Craig as your dancing partner."

Constance laughed and shook her head. It was true that she danced with her twin as she never danced with anyone. They had been together always during their first fifty years. Reading his mind came as naturally to her as breathing. And the fluid coordination that they enjoyed when dancing together was merely an extension of that relationship.

Realizing that the waltz was nearly over,

which meant Todd would claim Lila, Constance gently tugged on his cravat. It took a little effort and two hands, but she was finally able to straighten it sufficiently. Todd never said a word, though he did drop his free hand to her waist while she worked.

"Have you considered raising your prices?" she asked softly, resting her hands against his chest. "I made a sale after you left," she tried not to wince at the sharp look he gave her, "and that was just of a popular blend. Surely customized perfumes could be sold for even more."

Todd drew her closer, holding her to him so that she could not flap while he lowered them to the floor.

"You will not tell our mother," he told her firmly. "I can run this shop just as well as Richard runs his and Sandy runs hers."

"Of course you can." The final strains of the waltz were still playing when she felt the floor under her feet. Todd had placed them neatly at the edge of the still-spinning group. "And I will promise not to worry…if you will promise to write to Sandy and ask her how to increase your customer base." She watched him consider the proposal. Relief washed over her when he nodded.

"Todd?" They looked around to see a young woman-fairy smiling up at Todd. "I believe this is our dance."

Constance frowned and did not remove her

hands from her brother's chest. *Now I know why Lesley is wearing a gown that is nearly identical to Lila's tonight.* Constance opened her mouth to warn her brother, but he spoke first.

"You flatter me, Your Highness," Todd bowed and removed his sister's hands at the same time, holding them gently in his own. "However, I must regretfully decline." He nodded to where Laura was trying—and failing—to coax Lila away from Cambrian. "I have already promised this dance to Lila."

With effort, Constance kept her jaw from sagging in surprise. Lesley was less prepared and stood there, visibly shaken by the refusal.

"By your leave." Todd bowed again and turned away, his grip on Constance's hands bringing her with him. The dance floor was somewhere between empty and crowded, a few couples from the last dance lingering there even as new couples came forward. He was determined, however, to reach Lila's side.

"Your Highnesses." Todd bowed and Constance curtsied, the flame-colored bottom of her dress standing up on its own for a moment when she dropped as low as she dared. When they had straightened, Todd looked Cambrian in the eyes. "May I ask the princess to dance?"

"Most definitely," Cambrian smiled.

Todd looked wordlessly at the blushing Lila. She nodded and he swept her into his arms, leaving Laura staring after them wide-eyed.

Cambrian stepped closed to Constance. Something about the way he was looking at her made her pulse race. She stood barely breathing as his right hand settled on her waist. Her heart began doing summersaults when his left hand slipped under her right elbow and ran, palm down, along the bottom of her arm until he reached her right wrist.

"Dance with me?" he invited huskily.

Her eyes fluttered closed as his words softly caressed her face. She was having trouble just standing. How could she dance? Then he swayed once, bringing his right hand up to her shoulder blade. Her left hand automatically came to rest on his right bicep. Her feet never left the ground, yet she felt as though she were soaring high above Regalis, looking down at the stars.

"You look enchanting tonight," Cambrian murmured for her ears alone. There were other things he wished he could say—like explaining about the closed inquiry, the survivors—but did not dare. He had been ordered not to. Besides, right they were attracting too much attention. Even a whisper of gossip about additional survivors could ruin their best chance for wiping the organization of pirate collaborators out.

"Thank you." She could feel herself blushing. "Madame Karan calls it my sunset dress." Suddenly she was spinning away from Cambrian, the dress's full skirt flaring out from her in a gradual scale of colors, from the flame red bottom to the deep pink of the waist. Then she was wrapped tightly in his arms, barely able to breathe as he tightened his hold on her at about where the layer of dark grey-blue started. She was pressed against him so that if she had looked down, all she could have seen was the very top band of color, which was the same as her three quarter sleeves—a blue so pale that it was almost white.

"You may tell Madame Karan that I like it," Cambrian murmured, stopping them abruptly just outside one of the doors. He had waited until almost the last note of music to whisk her off the dance floor, and wondered for a moment if anyone had seen them go?

The hem of her dress, flung to one side by the suddenness of their stop, slowly slipped down off his highly polished boots. He held her for as long as he dared, enjoying the color in her cheeks, the light in her eyes, the inviting tilt of her head. Releasing her hand, he slid his own behind the nape of her neck. Her eyes fluttered closed as slowly, deliberately, he accepted the invitation.

Chapter XVI

Late the next morning, Constance twisted slightly in her seat, her back aching from sitting at attention for the last four hours. Worse than that was the ache around her heart as she wondered which of her lads had survived. There had been too many fairies about last night to risk Cambrian about something that was clearly meant to be kept confidential; and in the few private moments they managed to steal, they had spoken very little. So when she arrived this morning, with only a few minutes to discreetly ask around before the inquiry started, she had been acutely disappointed to learn that no one else knew anything at all. Braxton did, obviously, but he appeared just as the gavel struck.

"Hear ye, hear ye," the lieutenant called for all wandering attention to return to the bench. "We will now hear testimony from Prince Cambrian, acting royal investigator into Major Layton's command capacity."

Cambrian smiled a little sourly as he took the stand. Given the opportunity, he would gladly testify that his failure in this investigation had cost the lives of over a hundred windfairies. He doubted it would happen that way, though, and not just because his parents were present in today's gallery. When the lieutenant approached him, he removed his crown and surrendered it.

"I, Cambrian Bijou, prince of the royal house of the Sky Fairy Tribe, do solemnly swear to tell the truth and will be heard to tell the whole truth by this investigation." In the silence that followed, the sound of the scribes' quills could be heard clearly as they recorded his oath. Idly Cambrian wondered how the admirals had decided who would ask the first question. By seniority? Or by drawing straws?

"Prince Cambrian." The female admiral was glad she had chosen to do her hair in a crossover bun that morning as it eliminated the distraction of her braid. "Why did you agree to accompany Major Layton and Captain Kimberlite to Port Herio?"

Cambrian considered the question carefully. Up until then, the panel had been trying to piece together what happened when, and if what happened could reasonably have been avoided. Telling himself this question could not be as personal as it seemed, he worked out a detached answer as quickly as he could.

"For several reasons, not the least of which was a desire to see Major Layton operating under pressure." That was, in fact, one of the reasons he had expressed to his brother when Oliver protested his getting involved in a potentially dangerous reconnaissance. "But also because I was the royal investigator in that area. Solving the mystery of the return of the *Talon* seemed a worthy endeavor."

"I see." She scratched some ink onto the paper before her to give herself time to collect her thoughts. At least the admiral on her right, who had behaved so abominably yesterday, seemed disposed to be quiet today. "Port Captain Braxton testified that he submitted a report to you and to his superiors. Yet you persisted in this investigation instead of waiting for the proper authorities to hand down a decision."

Cambrian fought to take in air and still felt like he was suffocating. Her line of summarizing was coming dangerously close to the guilt he felt each time he thought of how his overconfidence—nay, his arrogance—had cost so many windfairies their lives.

"Yes," he spoke before she could formulate a question. "I not only did that, I was the driving force behind the decision to attack the pirate fortress. I take full responsibility for my actions." While he waited for the admirals to stop looking back and forth at each other, he told himself that he had known this might happen. He had stayed up half the night last night reliving what he had done, asking himself what he could have done differently—dragging himself back from the precipice of madness more than once. He would abide by their decision.

"Then you agree," the eldest admiral leaned forward, "with the reports that you led the attack on the pirate fortress yourself, freed dozens of fleet windfairies who would have otherwise been executed by the pirates, and successfully challenged the pirate king Bane, formerly known to us as Major Layton, enabling the survivors to escape?" When the prince said nothing for several seconds, the admiral held up the files he had read and reread since receiving them. "The reports are all quite clear on the matter." True, the youngest captain had an interestingly self-absorbed approach to telling what had happened, lots of personal pronoun usage, but they all boiled down to the same story.

"What?" Cambrian asked blankly. Then he stopped speaking, for he could not think what to say. Mercifully, the scribes did not record his stunned question for history. Digging down, way down, past the elation he felt when he heard the admiral recount the good that had come from his actions, Cambrian slowly grouped his thoughts. "I had thought only of the lives that were lost because of my involvement. Those lives have weighed upon me as nothing else in my life has ever done." It was completely different from when Joanna died, for then he had disconnected himself from his emotions, unable to otherwise cope with the pain. Now, older and more mature, he had forced himself to fight the man-fairy in the mirror for the right to hold his head up, the right to keep living instead of dying emotionally a second time. "It now occurs to me," he continued, taking hold of the railing with both hands, "that my actions also benefitted some few lives. And that, while none of us take lightly those lives that were lost, those who died to defeat the great evil that is piracy, were proud to die that others might live."

He looked up, startled when someone in the gallery began to clap. Frowning, he waited for silence. "I participated in the attack on the fortress and aided the very capable windfairies of our king's fleet, it is true. But I did nothing alone." Stepping off the stand, he gestured with both hands to the rows of windfairies assembled to testify. This time when the clapping began, he joined in, applauding the courageous fairies to whom they all owed so much. Though he had eyes only for Constance, who was blushing adorably, his father must have risen because the admirals came to their feet, prompting the rows of officers to stand as well.

Cambrian was vaguely aware that the inquiry had been unofficially ended by the enthusiastic response of the gallery. Oliver and his father appeared, one on either side of him, retrieving his crown and steering him towards the door despite his efforts to reach Constance's side. With the help of some junior officers, a path was cleared for his escape from the crush of well-wishers. The last glimpse he caught of Constance before being whisked back to his chambers was of her with Arnold at her side, talking earnestly about something.

"Have you really?" she asked, a little disturbed that a civilian had been able to breach military security so thoroughly as to have obtained a list of the newly arrived survivors.

"I have." It took real effort for him not to sound as smug as he felt. This was his way in with her. A tiny favor to him, a huge favor for her. She would feel indebted and… His thoughts ground to a halt when Braxton spoke to him over her shoulder.

"Mosley!" Braxton was more surprised than pleased at finding the patronizing bully of the mines talking to Constance, but he flattered himself that he covered the disparity of emotions well. "Fancy meeting you here." He slid between the two of them deftly, gripping Mosley's arm with his near hand. "This is perfect. I am finally in a position to take advantage of all the times that you have offered to show me Regalis." He emphasized the city's name, gesturing with his free hand as if pointing to a vast something on a far horizon.

"Not tonight," Constance interrupted, taking Mosley by his other arm before Braxton could ruin her plans. While she was confident that she understood Michael's intentions, she was not about to postpone her dinner with Mosley. She had already made plans for a quiet dinner with her brother the next night and was expected back at the king's table the night after that.

"No?" Braxton asked. He had definitely

thought she had better sense than to get involved with a man-fairy like Mosley. So much so that he had been willing to sacrifice his free evening in an effort to allow her to escape Mosley's attentions. She was still wearing the sword with the royal crest, it was true, which only made her behavior seem even more peculiar.

"No," Mosley agreed, tentatively jubilant at how adamantly Constance had spoken. He could use some good news after yesterday's public encounter with the recorder. Even after wasting an hour with the nervous man-fairy Arnold failed to see how the cessation of bribe money that the recorder had been getting paid was his problem. "The captain and I are dining together this evening."

"Which reminds me," Constance withdrew her hand from Arnold's arm before he got any ideas, "I still have to change." Arnold had made a point of telling her how much he looked forward to seeing her in a dress again before Michael interrupted.

"I shall see you at dusk, then," Mosley smiled. He would have kissed her hand, but the press of fairies about them—including Mister Dixby and Captain Trevaille—jostled him just at the wrong moment and she was away before he could recover his balance.

Braxton watched her fly off, reassuring himself that she could not possibly have passed over him for a man-fairy with more money than friends. There must be something else going on.

"Dinner with the captain, eh?" he murmured just loud enough for Mosley to hear. "I hope you know what you are getting yourself into."

Mosley shot Braxton an amused glance. His experience with the port captain had been limited partly by expedience but mostly by choice. During the few days each season that he spent at Feo'lyn, the nearest colony to Port Herio, he starved for decent company, so endured the stuffy fellow as a break in the tedium. Braxton's deeply ingrained integrity, which Mosley found positively nauseating, kept them from becoming friends or eventually from being partners when he had made a deal to sell his ore for twice what their government was offering.

"You know the captain?" he asked, not trying to keep the disbelief out of his voice.

"A bit," Braxton answered tersely. "Frankly, I think she is more woman-fairy than you can handle." He did not move a muscle when Mosley reached for his sword hilt. Having seen what Constance's lads did to cover her exit, he was prepared when their previous collision with Mosley reoccurred. Side-flapping neatly to allow Mosley to lurch past him unimpeded, he joined Mister Dixby and Captain Trevaille. "Who will join me for a nectar?" he asked cheerfully.

Mosley stopped himself just short of crashing into the row of benches where the officers sat during the inquiry. Furious with how casually he had been dismissed, literally shoved out of the way, he spun about and glared after the departing officers. In a matter of seconds, his anger iced over. He could wait to return their contempt. In fact, it would take time to prepare the perfect penalty for their insolence. Straightening his jacket, he began forcing his way through the crowd. He had already arranged for a carriage to bring Constance to the restaurant, but it would hardly do for him to arrive looking rumpled. He allowed himself to smile as he wondered what Constance would be wearing.

Constance, meanwhile, had followed a direct course to Cambrian's rooms. She was a little worried by the hasty exit his father and brother had made with him. Were they worried about the exuberant crowd? Possibly. Even the best intentions could get out of hand when there were that many hands to bring to bear. She continued pondering as she zipped along, almost forgetting the list Mosley had given her. Reaching Cambrian's window at last, she rapped on it sharply.

"Told you," Jennings chuckled from the other side of it. He stuck his head out a moment later. "Come in, cap'n," he invited, swinging the window open wide.

Cambrian looked over from where he stood by his fireplace, his attention arrested by the site of her. She was beautiful. She must have flown quickly to get that pink in her cheeks—or was it the result of finding that his parents were present? Smiling, he stepped towards her.

It had been a matter of minutes since he had arrived back at his rooms, but already the idea had begun settling into his mind. He was not solely responsible for anything that had happened. Layton chose to become Bane. The pirates followed him by their own choice. Jennings and the lads chose to fight, to follow not just him, but Constance. The list went on. Already he felt himself beginning to find a balance between being responsible for his choices and allowing others the right to be responsible for their own choices.

"I am glad you came," he said reassuringly as he took her hand in his.

Pleasantly surprised at the change in him, she paused, trying to put her finger on what was different. He seemed completely relaxed, his shoulders at their normal pitch for his princely carriage. His warm blue eyes were not narrowed as if in reflection, as they so often had been since their escape. His whole demeanor seemed calmer, more like his old self than she had seen in days.

"Then I am glad as well." It was no answer at all, but she felt she must say something. And the vaguer the better, with his parents looking on.

He took another step towards her, grateful when his mother turned and spoke to his father. They were gracious enough to at least pretend they were not watching.

"I wish you were available for dinner tonight," he murmured. "I wish you had the faintest of ink smudges right there," he reached up to touch a finger to the exact spot on her cheek that had accidentally sported ink the night he surprised her with dinner aboard the *Nadauld*. "And after dinner we could take a walk around the palace roof."

The tenderness Constance felt in her heart seeped out in a blush that warmed her cheeks thoroughly. Jennings and the others might as well have been paintings on the wall for all they mattered. She tilted her head, pressing her cheek into the palm of his hand.

"I could make myself available," she whispered.

"And I would ask you to do just that," he turned her neatly, wrapping one arm about her waist and starting towards the window. When they were at its ledge, he paused, looking down at her.

She found that she could hardly breathe for the thrill of wondering what in Fairydom he was thinking.

"Except that we gain far more by getting tonight over with." He watched some of the light go out of her face as her eyes narrowed in confusion. "After tonight," he promised, "Mosley will be my problem." Bending, he gently kissed her eyelids, her lips. "But you will, always and forever, be my love."

Her eyes flared open. He had just told her he loved her. She was more confused than before. She raised her hand to touch his chest, beginning to wonder if the whole thing was a dream—and poked him with the list.

"What is this?" he laughed, capturing her wrist and turning it so that he could examine the rolled-up paper she was holding.

She hesitated. She was still confused as to why she had not been told, officially, that there were more survivors.

"A list of names," she said at last. And waited.

His amusement faded with her words. "Where did you…?" he began to ask, then stopped. Answered his own question. "Mosley."

She nodded.

"I wanted to tell you," he sighed, correctly deducing the source of pain in her eyes. "But since you know this much already…the inquiry shifts its focus to interviewing them tomorrow, in a closed session."

She nodded, accepting his words and implied apology. When she had received a schedule of weapons training for early tomorrow, she knew tomorrow's inquiry would be different.

"We were hoping to find something out about Bane's informants tomorrow, without them finding out, but if Mosley is that well connected…" He nodded at the paper she held, then shook his head doubtfully.

Constance hesitated, her grip tightening on the roll of paper until she crushed it. Bane's death was merely a stopgap measure, she knew that as well as any member of the military. Unless or until his civilian collaborators were located and dealt with, the pirates needed to do little more than elect a new leader. And, of course, with her assignment to be Mosley's companion, the less she knew, the less she could accidentally let slip. The struggle between what she wanted and what she knew was not long. Exhaling slowly, she offered the paper to Cambrian.

"I doubt Arnold wrote this out himself," she smiled wryly. "Perhaps if you examine it you can find some clue as to how he procured it."

Cambrian blinked, surprised at the offer. She could not have had time to read it. Accepting it humbly, he managed a small smile.

"Thank you. I am sure it will prove useful." After glancing back his parents, Cambrian leaned down and whispered three names in her ear. "I do not think you know the others personally," he added, "and the full list will be publicly available soon."

In her excitement at hearing that more of her lads had returned safely, she caught him in a hug. "Oh," she drew back, blushing as she remembered his ribs.

"Stay," he invited, cradling her in his arms.

He had been faithfully taking his potions and results like these made it well worth the effort.

"As you say," she demurely smoothed his cravat. "I had better go." She neatly removed herself from Cambrian's hold. "Mosley told me to wear a dress," she shrugged, her playful mood deflating as she wondered just what to expect from this evening, "and I am sure Natalie is waiting for me."

Cambrian stopped her with a look. "Meet me at our bench when you are done," he told her, still speaking softly.

She surprised herself by nodding. Her weapons training would begin at the 'gray bell' tomorrow, as her father had fondly called the hour of dawn. As she hastily exited, she was sure of only one thing. This was going to be an interesting evening.

Chapter XVII

"You are sure?" Natalie asked. The repetition of the question said all that her tone and face politely refused to say.

"Absolutely positive," Constance reassured her for the third time. She had no intention of going any further in complying with Mosley's request for a dress than to wear *a dress*. This was the plainest dress available to her and that made it the dress of choice. It would have been easier if she could have just explained to Natalie that tonight's engagement was purely business, but once she had mentioned, '*he* asked me to wear a dress,' the maid had become quite single-minded.

"Very well." Resigned to her fate, Natalie obediently did up the nine obsidian buttons that ran down the captain's very straight spine. How any woman-fairy could pick a grey and periwinkle dress with heather blue accents for a dinner with Prince Cambrian was beyond her! She secretly planned to stay up so she could help Constance change afterwards. It was unlikely that she would say much about her evening, but it might prove interesting anyway. What would it be like to be romanced by a poet? The very thought sent pleasant chills up and down Natalie's own spine.

"I will do the powders tonight," Constance smiled as Natalie moved towards the vanity. "That will be all." As the door closed behind

Natalie, Constance wondered vaguely what had gotten into her. During the few days she had known her, the maid had been much easier to deal with.

"Oh dear!" The windows in her sitting room had begun to rattle ever so slightly, a deeper hum resonating so that the tinier bottles of perfume on the vanity toppled over. Her carriage was arriving! Snatching up a bottle of face powder, she hastily brushed it on, then added a faint blue eye shadow. Dabbing the expensive perfume on the inside of her right wrist, she pressed it to the left side of her throat. As a final touch, a fingertip's worth of pink gloss lent the illusion of color to the white lips of her reflection, which nodded sharply at her. Ready or not, it was time.

Responding to the rap on the far windows, she exited her sleeping chamber, crossed to them and flung one open.

"You look lovely," Mosley lied, amused at the stunned expression on her face. "Shall we?" He offered her his hand.

Gloves. She had forgotten gloves. The only pair she knew of in her rooms was her military dress gloves, which were relatively thick and distinctly undainty in design.

"My wrap," she offered tremulously, turning away for a moment of collection. Darting back into the other room, she picked up the wrap Natalie had laid out for her. Cream with colorful embroidered blue and scarlet flowers, it added a splash of color to an otherwise somber outfit. Throwing it around her shoulders, she turned to rejoin him.

"These rooms are lovely," Mosley observed from where he stood a twig's distance in from the window inside her sitting room.

She almost slammed the door to her sleeping chamber behind her. However tidy Natalie kept things, he had no business entering her rooms without her express invitation.

"I am ready." She forced a smile. She even accepted his hand while she transferred to the carriage, though she extracted it promptly under the guise of arranging her skirt comfortably.

"I am so please you were able to join me this evening," Mosley offered a neutral topic to her. "Your schedule is so hectic these days."

"Yes." She found a genuine smile tugging at her lips as she thought of the reason for her rush to be ready in time tonight. "It has been a bit crowded." The smile eased the tension and she paused to look at him. Tonight he looked the consummate business man, at ease somehow in his coal black, pressed-until-it-cried-for-mercy three piece suit. The silver tipped cane was missing, but he wore a small court dagger at his waist and it glistened when he moved. "No more than yours, I am sure."

"Bother my schedule." He waved it off with a flick of his hand. "I always have time for a pleasant diversion." He was annoyed at how difficult it was to see her face in the dimly lit carriage until he heard her grave response.

"It is rare to find someone so confident in their power." She all but held her breath, hoping she had chosen the right tone, the right words. She needed him to be unwary, wanted him to feel he was impressing her. She hoped he would let something slip that Cambrian could use.

"Yes." He paused, taken completely by surprise. "I suppose it is."

The rest of the flight passed in silence. Constance struggled for something witty to say, but could think of nothing that would lead into an open confession of guilt from him.

On the other side of the carriage, Mosley was deep in thought, considering his empire in a new light and feeling excessively pleased with himself. Why had he not seen this before? She chose a career that put her at the head of between two and four hundred windfairies at a time. Her romantic interest was none other than a prince of the realm. She liked power. Armed with this new information, he plotted the evening out as he would a high stakes game of Stratagem. He would have her in his pocket before the night was through!

He had but finished the thought when the carriage settled softly on the roof of the restaurant. "Here we are," he announced, smiling though he doubted she could see it.

In an instant the carriage door sprang open, a

white gloved hand darting in to lower the built-in step.

"Welcome to the Do'tore," a rich tenor voice accompanied a proffered hand, again in a white glove, which assisted Constance as she exited the carriage.

"Thank you." She allowed her hand to linger on the maître d's, grateful for the warmth of his smile. If she could just relax a little…

"Ah, Mister Mosley, a pleasure to see you tonight, as always." The maître d' took a half step back, more or less surrendering her hand in the process. Common sense told him to increase the distance between himself and the companion of one of his more prominent patron's. Relieved when the lady allowed the transfer of her hand to Mosley's, Terrance cocked an inquisitive eyebrow at Mosley. "We had heard you arrived in Regalis some days ago."

Mosley chuckled at the implied question. This restaurant was usually one of his first appointments.

"That is true, Terrance." Tucking Constance's hand under his arm, he used his now free hand to pat the dejected-looking maître d' on the shoulder. "But I could hardly have come alone, could I?" He winked with the eye that Constance could not see, a long-standing signal between the two men-fairies that tonight was to be more than special. It was to be perfect.

Terrance's injured pride instantly recovered.

"Of course you are right!" he agreed, modulating his voice to match the dignified air that surrounded Mosley's companion. She was not the type, he knew by instinct, to want undue attention drawn to their arrival. "It is truly a compliment to Do'tore to have such a lovely guest."

Constance nodded acknowledgement of the pretty phrase, idly wondering how much practice it took for words like that to get tossed around so casually. Her liking of the man-fairy had faded somewhat, though she retained her respect for such a skilled professional.

"Permit me to escort you to your table." Beaming, Terrance led the way. Just under his cheerful surface, the mind of a brigadier general snapped away, noting who was where and doing what in his dining room. The new waiter was going to work out, but oh how he wished the waitress across the room would remember to serve side dishes from the *left*. Not that the couple visiting from Arrotz was likely to know the difference. His sweeping gaze paused for a fraction of a second on the water clock cunningly hidden in the statue in the middle of the room and he knew he would soon have to visit the kitchen to make sure that the soufflé Baron Eddington always ordered was put in on time.

As Constance flew silently beside Mosley, she observed that he was well known here. From her brief time at court, she recognized most of the fairies who nodded, waved at, or otherwise acknowledged him. Many held positions of power in the various ministries; all of them would be useful to a schemer like Mosley.

"Forgive me, my dear," Mosley smiled apologetically as they reached the table, something he was surprised to find he could still do, "I must take a moment to greet the Minister of Weather." Squeezing her hand familiarly, he left her for Terrance to seat.

Stunned, she watched him go before responding to Terrance's invitation to accept the padded, straight-backed chair he was dutifully waiting to push in. She waved him sharply away when he asked if there was anything she needed, then changed her mind.

"Wait." Her one-word command arrested his motion, though he had already begun turning away. For a split second he looked ridiculous, and she almost laughed. "Is that really the Minister of Weather?" she asked, working hard to temper the intensity of her tone. It should not surprise her that Mosley was the type to walk away when it suited him, as though she were a chair and would obediently wait for him where he left her.

"Oh, yes." Terrance swelled with pride. "He often brings his entire family here, sometimes for celebrations and other times simply because it is the best restaurant in all of Regalis."

An amused smile tugging at her lips,

Constance nodded his dismissal. Sitting back against the chair, she ran one finger lightly over the table cloth on one side of her plate. Pressing her fingertip into the fabric briefly left a dent. Yet when the waitress appeared and began pouring an ice cold nectar for them, the condensation that ran down the side of the crystal decanter left a pattern of glistening water beads that the waitress promptly mopped up with a towel that magically appeared in and disappeared from her hand.

Constance felt the energy of her reaction to his discourtesy fading as she discreetly observed Mosley, whose smile had slipped after his first few words with the minister. The smile had been restored before he turned away from her, but if she knew anything at all about men-fairies, the short flicks of his wings meant he was angry about something.

"It must be fascinating to work at such a splendid restaurant," she sighed to the waitress, who was waiting silently, having sent the decanter off with a passing attendant. "All sorts of fairies come here. Travelers," she nodded at the couple she had seen Terrance eyeing on their way in, "ministers, powerful business moguls..." She let her voice trail off, as if awed by the wonder of it.

"Yes, we do see a variety here," the waitress smiled, having come closer to imply a confidentiality to their conversation. She was glad the guest had chosen to speak to her, for she was curious as to her identity. It was unlike Mosley to pick a woman-fairy no one had heard of and the kitchen was abuzz with speculation. Over the years that she had worked there, he had been accompanied by several famous performers, a few daughters of industry, and even the queen's second cousin. He seemed to prefer women-fairies that he had to take from someone else, in fact.

"I suppose Arnold knows them all." Constance forced a low laugh, hoping that the color she could feel rising in her cheeks would be mistaken for pride or something.

"Mister Mosley is well-connected," the waitress agreed, further intrigued by the apparent innocence of the remark. Now she wanted to know not just who the mystery guest was but *where* Mosley had found her. Under a rock?

Before Constance could pursue her clumsy questioning any further, Mosley appeared.

"Ah, Michelle," he greeted the waitress by name as he seated himself. "I am surprised to find you still here." He turned towards her, placing one hand casually on the arm of Constance's chair. He was disappointed when Constance did not respond. At all.

"Oh?" Michelle felt a sick knot beginning to form in her stomach. Had she bungled something at his last visit? That had been over a year ago, though, and disappointed patrons rarely left silver nuggets for tips. "Why is that, sir?"

Mosley shifted slightly, hiding his amusement at her distress. "I thought you would still be counting all that you had earned after your windfall."

Frantically Michelle combed through her memory. She relaxed as it came to her. Mosley had advised her to purchase an interest in a small touring company.

"I could never leave the Do'tore," she dodged the question with a calculated shrug.

Constance almost winced under the impact of Mosley's sudden shout of laughter.

"You ungrateful lass," Mosley shook a finger at her, completely disregarding the interest he had attracted from the tables around them. "You did not take my advice."

"Your pardon, sir," Michelle bowed her head slightly. "I did not." His nugget had been added to the pile of them she was collecting at the local bank. Tips were just barely above and beyond her living expenses, and she was no fool. When she eventually wanted to retire, she was going to live comfortably.

"Well, never mind." Mosley shrugged it off. Her loss. "What are we having for dinner tonight?"

Startled by his question, Constance almost turned to look at him. But finding that he was closer than she had thought, she satisfied herself with a sidelong glance in his direction. Where she had been expecting a demand for this meal or that, or perhaps a casual reference to having his 'usual' meal, he suddenly switched tactics, placing Michelle in control. She barely listened as Michelle smoothly shifted into her professional role, listing off half a dozen dishes with appropriately descriptive adjectives. In her mind there was room for only one adjective at the moment, and it was meant to describe Mosley— *manipulative*.

"Perfection," Mosley slapped one hand lightly on the table, the thick tablecloth reducing the sound to a muffled thump. "If that is acceptable to you, Constance?"

She smiled at his familiarity, having begun to wonder how long it would take him. "Perfectly." Her smile remained exactly the same width and warmth as she watched him watch her. She was no master manipulator, it was true. However, she had not reached her age and rank without dealing with a few. She knew when Michelle left without taking her eyes off Mosley.

"I really do not know how to…" she let her eyes drop self-consciously, lowered her chin fractionally, then brought her gaze back up to his so that she was looking at him through the screen of her lashes, "convey my gratitude for the list you gave me earlier."

Astonished, Mosley stared at her.

"You must promise me," she put her hand on his, where it lingered on the arm of her chair, "that if there is ever anything I can do to repay you, you will come to me at once." She leaned forward marginally to further impress her earnestness on him. If she leaned much closer it would only take an exhalation on one of their parts for them to kiss, and she guarded her expression carefully lest she should give herself away.

"I," Arnold began. "Nonsense." He leaned back abruptly. "You must think no more of it, my dear." He drew his hand from under hers to wave it airily.

"But it meant so much to me." She did not press her luck by reaching for him or leaning any closer. "You have no idea." It meant far more than he would ever guess, for now it was in Cambrian's hands as another piece of evidence.

Michelle blinked in surprise and almost dropped the tray she was carrying. Someone had finally figured out where they had seen the lady before, and this was not what she had been expecting when she returned from the kitchen.

"First course," she announced as calmly as she could while she flipped out the brace she would set the tray on.

Constance ignored Michelle beyond a small smile, the bulk of her attention on Mosley even as she appreciated the weight of the spoon she picked up from beside her bowl. To her delight, Mosley waved Michelle away as soon as she had delivered the dishes, but rather than trying to engage in conversation, brought his full concentration to bear on the soup. Satisfied, she tasted her own. Delicious!

Most of the meal passed in silence, for she watched him just closely enough to look him in the eyes every time he tried to speak, smiling slowly without giving any explanation for her behavior. And her smiles were real. She read an increasing agitation in him that had her struggling not to laugh. This might not be the best way to get a steady stream of information out of him. It was however, almost certain that when he did manage to say something, it would not be what he had planned.

"Oh," she gasped in delight as a charming sound rippled through the dining room. Far above them, immaculately garbed waiters were opening large windows, letting out the heat, which had been building as more and more candles were lit to supplement the setting sun. As the fresh air surged in, it caressed the strings by which dozens of wind chimes were hung, setting them in motion.

"My favorite part of eating here," Mosley said, his eyes on Constance. There was something so…enchanting about her tonight. He met her gaze steadily this time, able to keep his thoughts in order for the first time since she had put her hand on his earlier. "I was raised in Ventus, the city of wind chimes. The first time I came to Regalis, a few hundred years ago," he smiled wryly at the unnecessary reference to his age, "I was approached by a chef at my favorite restaurant."

Spellbound, she waited in silence as he took a sip from his water glass.

"He had a dream. A dream of a restaurant with the finest silver, the finest linen," he tossed his napkin onto the table beside his mostly-full plate, "the finest crystal." He continued the forward motion of his hand, gently flicking his now-empty water glass, which rang as only the rarest crystal could. "The silver lining on his dream was all the financing that he had."

Constance sat back, feeling anew the padding in her chair and looking about the dining room with a fresh sense of awe. The marble walls, so intricately carved with flowers, birds, a young couple permanently trapped in the act of smiling at each other on the far wall. The high, domed ceiling, painted in delicate hues that somehow caught the flickering candlelight and flung it back at the diners with added color.

"You own the Do'tore?" she asked, her tone hushed in surprise.

"Not anymore." Arnold shook his head, feeling again the regret he thought he had purged from his system decades ago. "Anton is every bit the chef he thought he was. This," he looked about the room, up at the wind chimes. "This would be empty if not for his skill. Part of our original agreement," he straightened slightly, the change of subject as good as clearing his throat for shifting his mood, "was that he could buy it from me, a little at a time."

"I see." She had seen too much, into his soul as it were. Even as she watched him draw the veil of sophistication back around himself, nodding stiffly to a lower minister of the court who was just arriving with his wife, she knew he would never quite be able to shut her out as he had before. She did not even flinch when he put his hand lightly on hers.

"Would you care for dessert?" he asked, maintaining a respectful distance by his posture.

She shook her head. "Even one of Anton's creations would pale in comparison to the pleasure of your story."

He looked at her sharply, confused by the sincerity in her tone, the friendly light in her eyes which did not waiver from his. Removing his hand from hers, he summoned Michelle to the table. He cursed himself for a fool as he fumbled the tip, dropping twice what he had intended to on the tablecloth. The hope in Michelle's face, though she carefully kept her eyes averted, humbled him still further and he pushed his chair back, leaving the silver where it lay. He could afford it, after all.

"Come," he growled peremptorily at Constance. Even that did not remove the gentle smile from her face. As they left, he fancied he could feel the warmth of her hand through his tailored sleeve. He found it highly disturbing.

"Where are we going?" Constance ventured to ask as they turned away from the carriage and began flying slowly into the night.

Arnold considered the question, considered her tone, which had been only vaguely curious, a moment longer, then shrugged.

"Nowhere in particular." When had he last flown with a woman-fairy just to prolong his time with her?

"Alright." Feeling his gaze on her, Constance turned to smile at him. She was no longer repulsed by him. Someday, with a lot of effort on both their parts, they might even become friends.

"Do you not worry about the prince?" Arnold asked, turning sharply forward again.

"No." She did not elaborate, content with the honest, one-word answer. Cambrian would have to complete his investigation, of course. There was no doubt in her mind that Arnold was guilty of breaking many laws for many years. Neither was there any question about whether she would report the entire evening as it had occurred, including her embarrassing attempt at manipulation at the beginning of the meal. She simply had more hope for Arnold's future now than she had had since their first meeting.

"Oh look," she smiled, glancing around the empty street, lit only by a few lamps and starlight. "This *must* be the promenade."

Entertained by the certainty with which she spoke, Arnold could not resist teasing her.

"What makes you think so?" he asked, hovering in place for a moment.

"Edgar's description of it the other day," she answered, unperturbed by his teasing. "He told me he used to lean against the posts," she pointed at the decorative sign posts that marked each shop on the street, "while he waited for the triplets. And," laughing, she pulled Arnold along with her to a shop now closed for the winter, "this chocolate shop is where he had so many samples that he made himself ill."

Caught in the charm of her at ease, Arnold willingly flew with her further down the street, chuckling at her recounting of Edgar's misadventures during his first two weeks in Regalis.

"Ah, Edgar," he shook his head. "For having as much good sense as he does, he certainly has a knack for getting into difficulties."

"It is well that he has you for a friend," Constance said without thinking. She watched in concern as Arnold's face changed, his smile struggling with a frown before he pulled away from her. "Arnold?"

She waited a moment before following him. They had reached the far edge of the promenade, and she settled beside him on the smooth rock pathway. From where they stood at the overlook, they could see out over the valley, the green tops of pine trees gilded by moonlight, the small stream that wove its way through the forest glistening like a path strewn with perfect diamonds. She took her time enjoying the view, imagining that she could taste a hint of salt in the breeze that tugged playfully at her escape-artist curls, then sighed. Tucking her hand under his arm, she leaned her head against his shoulder.

"Will you not tell me what is troubling you?" she invited.

Chapter XVIII

Stifling a yawn, Constance fluttered in the general direction of 'their' bench, as Cambrian had called the place where they retired to talk a few nights before. If she were at all smart, she told herself as she bumped into a bush, she would write a note and have a page meet him instead. Weapons training was hardly an appointment she could sleep through, after all. At last she reached what she thought was the right place and landed clumsily on the path.

"Captain?"

She snapped awake, searching the shadows for the speaker.

"Here, Captain." A man-fairy detached himself from the shadows to her left, landed beside her, and saluted.

"Mister Watts!" In her drowsy state, she acted on her excitement at seeing him without really thinking. It was only as his arms came slowly to embrace her, returning her hug, that she realized what she had done. "I am so glad you are here." Feeling his arms tighten about her, she gave him a final squeeze before drawing back.

"Thank you," he studied her even as he released her, "Captain."

"Forgive me, Mister Watts," she stifled another yawn. "I *am* glad to see you, but that is no excuse for my behavior."

"Do you need an excuse?" he asked, reaching out to tuck her curl safely back into her braid, as he had wanted to do a thousand times before. When she did not object, he slipped two fingers under her chin.

Shocked, Constance stumbled backwards. How *could* she have just stood there while he kissed her?

"Mister Watts!" There was no mistaking the command in her tone. She was fully awake now.

"Captain." He snapped to attention, not regretting the kiss in the least.

"I find it difficult to believe it is a coincidence that you are here where I was to meet," she bit back Cambrian's name, not quite ready to think about him yet, "someone."

"The captain was not informed with whom she would be meeting?" Mister Watts adopted the strictest, most formal tone he could in an effort to distract himself from the lingering sensation of his lips on hers. And what *was* that perfume she was wearing? It was a far cry from the military soap they all used on the wind.

"She was not," Constance barked her response, distancing herself still further from her officer by using the third person.

"My apologies, Captain. Mister Watts, first officer of the *Nadauld*, reporting as ordered." He kept his gaze firmly fixed on the statue to her right.

"As ordered by whom?"

"Prince Cambrian."

Her eyes closed and she wished she were standing closer to the bench. Of course. Cambrian had known how glad she would be to see for herself that her lads had been returned, safe and sound. She dragged her thoughts away from how thin Mister Watts had felt when she had enthusiastically flung her arms around him. Something her father used to say about 'the best intentions' flitted through her mind.

"Permission to catch the captain if she falls over?" Mister Watts spoke in earnest. He had seen her tired too many times not to be worried. She pushed herself to the brink of exhaustion when she thought it was at all warranted.

"Permission granted." She opened her eyes again. Meeting his gaze directly, she shook her head. "But that is all."

He nodded slowly, relaxing enough to clasp his hands behind his back. Decades of working together, trusting each other with their lives, restored a semi-sort of balance between them more quickly than otherwise could have happened.

"Tell me about it."

He hesitated, recognizing a request where there might have been a command. "There was a windship waiting at the fort," he reported quietly. "The officers were transferred there immediately upon arrival. I heard Layton," his voice took on a noticeably bitter note as he experienced again the shock of betrayal by a fellow officer, "give the order for her to take off." He shrugged. "We were dumped into the hold, still bound and gagged. They left us there until well after the sun had reached her zenith the next day."

Constance nodded slowly, encouraging him when he paused.

"They were careless when they came to release us." He smiled grimly, unconsciously bringing his hands forward and rubbing one wrist. "Once we had some weapons, we took her over by degrees, flew her to Herio." After another pause, he shrugged eloquently.

Constance watched her first officer for the space of several breaths. He had told her the highlights of the story only, sparing her the dark details, much as she would have done had their roles been reversed. There was, however, one point on which she could not bear for him to remain silent.

"David." That brought his eyes to hers. She rarely used his first name. "Tell me the worst of it."

"The worst of it, Constance?" His head lowered so that his chin nearly touched his chest. "The worst was thinking that you had betrayed us."

She flinched as if he had slapped her, even though she had suspected the blow was coming.

"Have you forgiven me so quickly?" she asked, her voice small in the silence of the night.

"The first thing Prince Cambrian did when we arrived was explain to us all that had happened."

Their eyes met again. He yearned for the right to wipe away the tear that slipped down her cheek, but stayed where he was as though he had become a statue, too. He did not tell her that despite his doubting her, his fiercest regret on finding himself heading, as he believed, to a slow death in a pirate stronghold, had been not advancing sufficiently in rank so that he might have courted her. His reluctance to be separated from her for the long tours, his rationalization that her first love was her windship, had combined to rob him of his chance. For he knew from even their small time together that she belonged to someone else. The kiss, which he still did not regret, was part of how he knew.

"Mister Watts," she blinked back her tears and coughed to clear the ones lodged in her throat, "you have been my first officer for too long."

His shoulders slumped. Had she kicked him in the stomach, he could not have been more surprised.

"I should have recommended your advancement to captain long ago." She waited until her meaning seeped past his shock and he looked at her. "Can you forgive me for my selfishness in not wanting to give up my best friend, even when it was the best thing for him?"

He stared at her hard, his emotions twisting this way and that while he tried to decide what to do with the future she seemed to be offering.

"With your permission, I will formally recommend you for the captaincy of the *Nadauld*."

"The *Nadauld*?" The very idea of taking her windship stung a response from him. "I could never…"

She interrupted him gently. "I am withdrawing from the service. If I could leave her in your hands, I would be very grateful."

Her words seemed to hang in the still night air, to echo in Cambrian's ears. He had left a page on watch with instructions to fetch him as soon as Constance arrived, then returned to his own chambers and worn a pathway in the plush carpet while he tried not to think about how her date with Mosley was going. Now he wondered if he had been worried about the wrong encounter. There was considerable tension between Constance and Watts, more than he would have expected given his careful explanation of her involvement in the attack on the *Nadauld*. He was hesitating, caught between interrupting something important and not wanting to eavesdrop when he started in surprise at Watts' next words.

"The prince." Watts' tone was flatter than a smashed piece of ship's bread. "You are leaving the service for the prince."

"I love him."

Cambrian stared back and forth between them in consternation. She had said nothing to him about retiring. And why was she discussing her private affairs with her first officer, anyway?

Constance waited, her concern growing with each passing moment of silence. One of many things that had made Mister Watts her valued advisor was his ability to think before speaking, but this—this was different. He looked as if he might explode from not saying all the things he wanted to.

"Permission to speak freely." She reverted to the tone of command and shrank before the look in his eyes. Then the look changed, melting from wild anger to a deep sorrow.

"My time for speaking freely has passed, Captain." Watts squared his shoulders out of habit. "Permission to retire?"

"David," Constance stepped forward as he moved to take off. "I did not know." She held perfectly still as he reached up to run the back of his hand lightly down her cheek.

"How could you when I concealed it so carefully?" he asked, his sorrow reaching his tone.

Stepping back, she gestured quickly for him to leave. She was going to start crying in a moment and suspected that he was not as far from tears as he would like to appear. Turning so that she would not have to watch him fly away, she covered her mouth with first one hand, then two. It was not enough. If Cambrian had not appeared, drawing her into the shelter of the shadows and pressing her face to his chest, the sound of her sobs would surely have reached David's ears, with unknown consequences.

She cried a little, until her internal water level had reached manageable proportions, then rested against Cambrian's soggy shirt.

"How long have you been here?"

He rubbed her back, avoiding the row of buttons, knowing he would have to tell her the truth. But not just yet. She was so tired she could barely stand. He was not convinced that he was thinking straight at the moment, either.

"Later." Lifting her in his arms, he turns towards the castle. She stirred before he reached the door.

"Your shoulder," she protested, trying to squirm free.

"Be still." It was a command, no question about it. "I am well enough to want to take care of you," he added a moment later, hoping she would accept that until he could find a better way to apologize.

Subdued as much by the weight of her own thoughts as by his admonishment, she wrapped her arms about his neck and snuggled close.

"That will take getting used to," she whispered as he carried her through the not-quite empty hallways. He could have handed her off to a half dozen guards if ensuring her safe arrival at her rooms was his only concern. She was saved from pointing that out only because she was too tired to think of it.

"We will both have to adjust," he agreed aloud as he turned the corner towards his brother's hallway. "I am confident that we will manage."

She smiled, realizing more fully what they were discussing. "I love you."

He had to lean a little closer to hear her murmured words and almost stopped to kiss her right there, regardless of who might pass by unexpectedly. Instead he pressed his cheek to her forehead and kept walking. Reaching her door at last, he leaned her against it.

"Shall I knock for you?" he offered, looking for any excuse to stay longer.

"Knock?" She was so tired that she giggled. "Have I acquired a roommate?"

He chuckled with her, then explained, "I should be very surprised to find that Natalie is not in there somewhere."

"Natalie?" Constance blinked several times but could not quite clear her vision. Closing her eyes, she leaned against Cambrian again. "I sent her away."

"Maids are notorious for coming back when they sense there is gossip to be had." Cambrian chuckled again as he smoothed her hair, then kissed it. "Hey, sleepyhead," he shook her gently. She was asleep standing up. "Time to go to bed."

She tensed when he bent to kiss her. Hiding her face against his chest, she had a sudden fear of what he would say when she told him what had happened before he arrived in the garden.

"Darling?" Cambrian whispered the question into her hair. "Darling, look at me." He gently lifted her away from him when she would not. A thought had occurred to him. "Did Watts kiss you?" He waited until she nodded. That had been the easy question. "Do you not want me to kiss you?" It was almost more than he could do to articulate that fear.

"Oh no." She looked up at that, her hands coming up to rest on his biceps. She took a moment to ponder the rapidity of his physical recovery, then expressed her own fear. "I was afraid that you would not want to kiss me once you knew."

Cambrian drew her close, nudging her elbows so that her arms slid up around his neck. He took his time tenderly relieving her mind on that score, then reached past her to open the door to her rooms.

Reluctantly, she backed out of his arms and into her sitting room. She wanted to stay in his arms forever, for her date with Arnold to be a thing of the future, not the past. Things had been so much simpler when she woke up that morning! But now? In a weak moment she had promised Arnold she would not reveal what she learned to the king until tomorrow and already regret was rearing its ugly head. Granted, Arnold had promised her hard evidence in return for her patience—incriminating letters, official documents, and other things that Cambrian could use to track down the mastermind of the dastardly plot Arnold was involved in up to his neatly manicured eyebrows. All Constance had to do was meet him at his lawyer's the next morning.

Cambrian, blissfully unaware of the her turmoil, softly closed the door between them, his eyes glued to hers until she was blocked from his view. He waited a moment, his hand on the knob, then laughed silently at the sound of Natalie's voice greeting Constance.

"You should not have waited up," Constance protested as Natalie expertly removed her from the dress.

"I do not mind." Natalie shook out the clean night things she had laid out earlier and stepped back to let the captain find her own way into them, as was her expressed preference. "Though I did not expect you to return quite so late."

Constance almost laughed at the poorly concealed curiousity, but did not dare. She was too tired, too…everything.

"We can talk in the morning." Not that she expected a few hours to make *much* difference in her ability to coherently relate the events of her evening. She just hoped to be better able to censor what she said. It was all running through her head at the same time as she crawled under the layers of soft, thick blankets, tucking her wings and curling into a comfortable position. Everything was so soft in Regalis, from sheets to tablecloths.

"Of course." Natalie bobbed a disappointed curtsy before leaving, taking the one lit candle with her. She did not sigh until she reached the servants' hallway. She supposed she should be grateful that Constance seemed willing to talk at all.

As soon as Natalie had gone, Constance forced herself to sit up. What was she forgetting? Oh yes. Reaching under the collar of her nightshirt, she fumbled for the thin silver chain Arnold had slipped about her neck a little over an hour ago. Finding it at last, she pulled it out and stared at the heavy, masculine ring dangling inches below her hand. Its stone, a nearly flawless diamond, seemed to absorb all available light before giving it back in a painfully brilliant flash. She had no idea what or whom she was supposed to be keeping it 'safe' from, but Arnold had been very clear on the point that no one find out she had it. Groaning, Constance dragged herself out of bed and stumbled towards her boots. Shaking it down to the very toe of her right boot, Constance focused her energies on setting the boot back exactly where she had gotten it from. Natalie noticed almost everything, and she was bound to spot something out of place when she returned in the morning.

Finally back in bed, she curled up and tucked herself in again. Slipping one hand under her cheek, she touched the spot on her cheek where Arnold had kissed her goodnight. She was still in that position when sleep finally overcame her, carrying her off swiftly to a place where even dreams could not reach her.

Cambrian smiled wearily as he dropped a report on his father's heavy mahogany desk. It was a perfectly ordinary report, the type of thing royal record keepers submitted weekly. He had had the idea during breakfast and followed it to the hilt, as much to keep himself from attending Constance's weapons training as anything else. A few hours and hundreds of reports later, the handwriting from Mosley's list had finally stared back at him from a recounting of the Minister of Trade's official visit to Castlemain last year.

"Harold Scroggins," he announced. "I need as much information on him as possible."

King Jasper glanced over at the report, up at his son, and back down at the letter he was writing. Deciding the letter could wait a bit longer, he set his quill down beside the letter, leaned back in his chair.

"What have you found?" he asked Cambrian. He did not ask how long it had taken.

"The handwriting on that report exactly matches the list of survivors that Mosley gave to Constance."

"And?" King Jasper did not hesitate to press his son for details. It was no small thing to ask for a man-fairy's supervisors, possibly even friends, to be questioned.

Cambrian rubbed the back of his neck while

he ordered his thoughts. Blasted starched collars, why had he never before noticed how itchy they were?

"Scroggins has close ties to the royal record keepers as well as the import and export industry. I believe," Cambrian paused, troubled that he had so little on which to base his next statement, "that he is a pivotal figure in Mosley's plans."

"What is Mosley planning?" Oliver spoke this time, from where he stood to one side of their great-grandfather's portrait. He had managed, inadvertently, to wear a suit of royal blue with burgundy trimming into his father's office and had just been pondering his resemblance to the portrait when Cambrian joined them.

"I am not sure," Cambrian admitted. "That is part of why I must find leverage with Scroggins."

A profound silence settled over the occupants of the room as they considered how to proceed. Eventually, Constance decided to break it. Even if that meant entering without invitation.

"In the future you should probably shut these before having confidential meetings," she suggested as she flew lightly through the windows. She was aware of varying degrees of consternation in the reactions of the king and his sons. Taking her own advice, she locked the windows behind her. "I can answer any questions you have about Mosley." As she felt her cheeks warming, she wondered how long it would be until she could think of Arnold without blushing.

Cambrian frowned. He was only guessing, but he did not think he was going to like what came next.

"He has authorized me to act as his agent in negotiating his full cooperation with the crown—in exchange for a royal guarantee that he will not be formally charged for his actions prior to this conversation." The ring she wore under her blouse seemed to grow heavier by the second as she waited for them to respond.

"Cooperation?" King Jasper straightened in his chair and reached for his quill. When Cambrian made no move to intervene, he continued, "I was not aware that we had solicited—or require—his assistance."

Constance watched the king dip his quill in the inkwell, knock off the extra drops of ink, and resume writing. She waited, needing the opening that only patience could grant her.

"Constance," Cambrian stepped towards her, catching her hands in his and turning her to face him. "Is this about last night?"

She nodded, her heart pounding as she carefully withdrew her hands. She simply could not think while they were that close.

"Constance?" Cambrian fought against the fear that leapt into his throat, cutting off further speech when she turned away from him.

"Please," she could wait no longer. "I must have your word."

King Jasper's writing paused. Did she know what she was asking? Arnold Mosley was easily guilty of a dozen crimes against the crown, including endangering their millennia old treaty with the Water Fairy Tribe. Assuming that she *did* know what she was asking, how well did they know her? He studied her for several seconds, contrasting her meticulously pinned hair and starched collar against the dark circles under her eyes and the white knuckles on her hands where she gripped the chair that stood between them. Setting aside the letter he was writing, he scribbled a note generally agreeing to her request, signed it, and slid it across the desk towards her.

Coming around the chair, she took the note, her hands shaking as she folded it. She did not even glance at it to confirm what the king had written before she stored it in the inside pocket of her jacket, next to another recently acquired legal document.

"You two should sit down." She gestured for Oliver and Cambrian to seat themselves. She had the benefit of a few hours breathing space between herself and the news she had to share, yet she still felt as though Mosley had smacked her with a sailboard. In a way, he had, and less than an hour ago at that. But that was a different story. "Ian?" she asked the shadows.

Much to King Jasper's surprise, Ian stepped out from where he had stationed himself.

"Ian." Constance relaxed a little. She could

explain this to him. Protecting the crown was the thread that bound them together, something she could use to breach protocol. The others in the room could listen in, but she would be talking to Ian. "Our kingdom is in grave danger." She held up her hand to stop him when he reached for his dagger. "In less than two days, a handful of merchants and bankers will shut down all traffic to Regalis. All guests who wish to leave Regalis may do so. The royal family, military personnel, and any others who choose to remain will be doomed to winter here without hope of supplies from outside."

The quill in King Jasper's hand snapped, the sound seeming to echo in the otherwise silent room. All of his vigilance, his careful preparation against a violent enemy would be turned against him. The extra marines and soldiers stationed there for protection would become nothing more than extra mouths to feed during the long, bitterly cold winter months where the only travel that could take place was via tunnels, including supply tunnels, carved through their mountains. There was usually a final shipment of goods, but it was already overdue. It seemed almost impossible to comprehend.

"Arnold assures me that there will be no armed attacks," she continued, keeping her eyes glued to Ian's. "In the spring, there will simply be a new capitol—Aureus, the city of wealth." She started when King Jasper sprang to his feet, somehow overturning his heavy mahogany chair.

"Who is coordinating this?" he hissed, the mangled remnants of the quill crushed in his hand.

"Arnold swore that he does not know," she answered haltingly. Then, remembering that she was not there on her own behalf, she squared her shoulders. It was always easier to fight for someone else. "Confident in your majesties' wishes, he has already begun pulling the teeth of this plan."

"How?" This time it was Oliver who spoke. His voice did not tremble, which surprised him, for he was trembling on the inside. An entire winter without additional supplies? Even via the tunnel network? Would anyone survive to protest this usurpation…or would spring simply find their tribe locked into its fate, the kingdom having already shifted hands?

Her wings fluttered slightly in frustration. "There was no time for him to share that with me." Taking a deep breath, she steeled herself. The worst was still to come. "Steps had to be taken so that I might have the authority to act in his behalf without anyone being able to question it." She had just come from completing those steps, in fact; was still reeling from the shock of learning how Arnold had decided to make that come about. She focused on her task as she took the silver chain between two fingers and drew out Arnold's signet ring. It was made of pure gold, a thick, heavy band with his family's crest inscribed in the metal that surrounded the diamond in the center. With that ring, documents pledging Arnold's loyalty to the crown, papers altering previous orders, even sales up to the full limits of his business empire could be duly authorized. Any court in the tribe would uphold her right to use the ring in his behalf because… "We were married just a few minutes ago."

Cambrian lunged to his feet. Finding himself with nowhere to go and no action that he could conceivably take, he picked up the chair he had been sitting in and hurled it against the wall.

"Once the kingdom is safe," Constance resumed, each breath coming painfully, "our marriage contract will be dissolved." Her stomach twisted, whether with hunger or nausea she did not know. It had been hours since breakfast, which she had barely been able to touch given what she had learned last night of the cold-blooded coup. She had nearly been skewered during training practice, thanks to her distraction.

Jasper leaned against his desk, suddenly feeling much older than his seven hundred and fifty years.

"What can we do?" Oliver asked. He had to ask. He had to know—there *had* to be something that they could do to protect the kingdom from this calamity.

"This was meant as a sudden, crushing blow,"

she answered, pleased at the question. "You must send guards to shut down all means of transportation out of the city. Most of your enemies have been guests here for the last few weeks. Arnold considers it likely that the ringleader is here as well. Faced with the same fate as the rest of Regalis, they will capitulate."

"Your husband is very insightful," Cambrian muttered through clenched teeth from where he stood, still staring at the broken wood and cushion that he had sat in since childhood. "And I agree." He swung to face his father, avoiding eye contact with anyone else. "Anyone callous enough to plot the kingdom's demise in such a manner would take great pleasure in watching from the front row."

Ian flew forward, catching Constance as she swayed. Drawing her towards a chair, he urged her into it.

She smiled wanly up at him, too embarrassed to make excuses.

"Ian," Jasper spoke quietly. "You know what to do."

Ian bowed, squeezed Constance's hand reassuringly, and vanished through yet another hidden panel. The plan he was about to implement had originally been intended to protect the citizen's in Regalis against invasion, but could easily be altered to fit the current situation. The first thing to do was shut down all forms of air travel... He reviewed what needed to be done as he hurried through the dark corridor, finding his way by memory alone.

"Perhaps this would be a good time for a storm."

They all looked at Oliver. He was watching his father, a strange expression on his face.

"The first storm of winter is long overdue." A storm would trap them all here, loyal citizens and dissenters alike, for a while at least. It would certainly accomplish Mosley's suggested strategy of convincing the dissenters to arrange for supplies to be brought in.

Jasper drummed his fingers on his desk, something he never did.

"Yes," he agreed, his eyes half closing as he focused on something none of the rest of them could see. "Yes," he repeated himself, speaking more loudly as he rose. "Oliver, come with me." He stopped to look at Cambrian and Constance, who were deliberately ignoring each other. "Constance."

She looked around, hardly daring to meet his eyes. Arnold's case was made, his future fairly secure. She had only her own actions to defend at the moment.

"Thanks to you things will work out." He swallowed hard at the thought of how miserably they had all failed to correctly determine the threat Mosley posed. "Eat something. We will require further assistance from you." The plural pronoun had never weighed so heavily on him as it did at that moment. Hundreds of fairies were in Regalis at that moment, blissfully ignorant of their intended fate. Expecting the royal family to keep them safe.

Despite herself, she smiled. "I am yours to command, sire." She watched Jasper and Oliver disappear through the window, shutting it behind them. That left her with Cambrian. Alone.

Cambrian stared at her, not saying a word as what he knew warred with how he felt. He loved her. She was married. She had no choice. To someone else. It was temporary. *She had married Arnold Mosley.* He glared at Mosley's signet ring. He could almost feel it between his fingers as he imagined himself breaking the flimsy chain about her neck and throwing the ring out the windows, closed or not.

"Smash something else." She sank wearily back into her chair. The unreality of it all was starting to catch up with her. "It might help." In the wildest stories she had told her younger siblings, her father had never faced the situation of helping to save the kingdom by marrying a relative stranger—who just might be executed for betrayal by his former partners before the sun could set on their wedding day. And of course, he was somehow the only one who could possibly undo the carefully laid plans to leave them all bereft of food and fuel through the long winter. She shook her head. Totally unbelievable.

When Cambrian made no reply, she risked looking at him. "I should have told you what I knew last night." Her voice sounded small, even in her own ears. And anyway, she had only learned of the most outrageous bit—their marriage—that morning. Arnold had presented it as a dire necessity, the only way to be absolutely sure no one could question her right to act in his behalf.

Cambrian bit back a retort that he was ashamed of even having thought. Shifting his focus to her white face, he stopped to ponder. Then he clasped both hands behind his back, comprehending that his shame had ripped a jagged hole in the self-righteous anger that had been building inside him. It was not a perfect cure, but it at least allowed him to think rationally for the moment. This was not her fault. If he knew Mosley's type half as well as he thought, Constance had flown right into a spider's web of neatly framed, highly compelling, reasons as to why she should agree to even the temporary legal alliance that she had.

"Last night was too short for all that might have been done, and what time we had together was nearly perfect. I suppose," he managed a half-laugh, "that is part of what makes all of this so shocking." His heart softened even more when she raised hopeful eyes to his. "I will order a late lunch," he offered. "For two, um, *three*." He doubted Jennings would turn down extra rations and he wanted a third present, either as referee or chaperone, as needed. His emotions were still fighting amongst themselves, despite his outward calm.

"Thank you." Constance whispered.

Cambrian took a step towards her, then took a very disciplined step back. The depth of feeling in her voice reached his heart, salving some of the surface scratches. After dispatching a page to the kitchen and warning the guard not to let others enter, Cambrian went personally in search of Jennings.

Chapter XX

Constance forked a piece of acorn bread and plunged it into the brown gravy and mashed thips that she had meticulously stirred together. When she was sure the bread was thoroughly coated, she carefully conveyed it to her mouth. It probably would have set the kitchen staff on its ear to see her abuse the feather-light bread in such a fashion, but the day had been challenging enough without trying to conform to stiff palace etiquette. It was all she had been able to do to choke down the perfectly cooked coorelum and vegetables, what with the way her throat tightened every time she looked over at Cambrian. Just now he was sitting across from her, very properly alternating bites of this with bites of that, so that she felt positively boorish as she considered soaking another piece of bread. And that made her cross on top of the vexation she was already feeling.

"More thips?" Cambrian offered her the silver serving bowl. His mother often referred to mashed thips as comfort food, something he had never properly understood until now. When Constance refused with a sharp shake of her head and a scowl, he raised an eyebrow at Jennings before scraping the rest onto his own plate. As there was plenty of roasted coorelum left, he just helped himself to that. He was prolonging the

~ 302 ~

meal as an excuse to delay the inevitable. Unless he was sadly mistaken, they were about to have their first official argument. He winced at the thought that one good thing about how abruptly his relationship with Princess Joanna had ended was that they never really had the chance to argue.

Noticing his wince, Constance froze, wondering what she had done. A few hundred years on the wind was enough to make anyone relax a bit when it came to eating, though she flattered herself her manners were not *that* bad.

"What?" she asked at last.

"Hmm?" Cambrian looked up from where he was ruthlessly cutting his meat into bite-sized portions as an outlet for his anxiety. "What?"

"What did I do?" she asked. When he just blinked at her, she set her fork down. "You winced just now. What did I do to make you wince?"

He winced again, then wished he had not. "Nothing." He shook his head and slowly set his utensils down. "I was not thinking about you." Well... "Exactly."

"Oh." Constance stuffed some bread into her mouth to keep from expanding on that word. She knew better. She was not thinking clearly. Even without being physically exhausted, her head and her heart were as mixed up as her gravy and thips right now, which made her chances of asking the right question about one in a few thousand.

Jennings cleared his throat when he saw Cambrian opening his mouth. The youngest of nine siblings, he figured he knew a fight brewing when he saw one.

"Could someone pass the bread and butter?" he asked hopefully. It was the first time he had eaten with them, and he had yet to figure out why they wanted company, but it felt good to watch them both simmer down while he spread butter on the loaf heel he selected. "It ain't quite like at home," he ventured after swallowing most of his first bite. "Good, though."

Constance had to smile at that. "Your mother is a baker, if I remember correctly?"

"Aye." Jennings grinned. "That was the worst part of my first fifty years on the wind," he offered. "Hard bread after the first week. Sometimes months on hardtack when the flour ran out. I used to lie in my hammock and drool at the memory of fresh baked bread with wild honey."

"Yes, I know what you mean." Constance slid her plate away from her, set her napkin on the table. "While my mother was no professional, she baked when she had the time."

"Had her hands full of young'uns, eh?" Jennings guessed, having heard her speak of her family a time or two.

"Most of the time," Constance agreed with a laugh. It felt so good that she tried another chuckle and felt her heart unknot itself, sort of like a muscle loosening in a hot soak. "I spent a lot of time listening to stories or telling them. The best ones were about my dad," she remembered. "Whether they were completely true or not."

"Had himself adventures every night, I s'pose," Jennings chuckled.

"Oh yes, he was always rescuing a merchant or diverting a storm cloud, doing something heroic."

Cambrian's smile dimmed slightly at her reference to the weather. Technically, Oliver was correct and they were well past the time when the first winter storm should have arrived. Frankly Cambrian had no wish to try interpreting the expression on his father's face when he and Oliver had left together. Every member of the Sky Fairy Tribe was taught from infancy that they had a responsibility the size of Fairydom. Of all the tribes, theirs alone possessed a talent for directing the weather. Sometimes that meant delaying or dispersing storm clouds; other times it meant rerouting them to cover a crop specified in their contract with the Plant Fairy Tribe. But intentionally delaying winter? That was unheard of!

Constance leaned forward, staring at Cambrian until he blinked and looked back at her.

"Do you want any more of the nectar?" she repeated the question so Jennings would not have to.

Cambrian shook his head. When Jennings happily poured what was left into his own cup, Cambrian realized what had happened.

"My mind wandered," he admitted, setting his own napkin on the table. "Forgive me?"

The words hung in the air between them, their eyes meeting and locking.

Jennings wished he could melt into his chair or escape out a window, but they had both made it quite clear when he arrived that he was to stay with them *no matter what*. If he had known this would be part of his valet duties, he never would have agreed to take the job. But he had. So, he did his best to hide behind his goblet, drinking slowly, and feeling quite uncomfortable.

"I should be the one saying that," Constance ventured when she got her breath back. "What I did…"

Cambrian lifted his hand to interrupt her. "I am the guilty one," he contradicted her. "If I had not suggested that you pursue…"

"You needed my help," she protested, unwilling to let him shoulder the blame. "And I bungled it."

"You brought us critical information while there was still time to act on it," he shot back, retaining just enough self-awareness to be amused at what they were arguing about. "I will not let you apologize for that."

She was silent for several seconds, working

up the courage to whisper, "And the way I got the information?"

He leaned forward, grateful for the table separating them. "You agreed to an expediency." He could not bring himself to speak of her situation as a 'marriage.' "I know of nothing that you have done for which you need feel ashamed."

She blinked back tears. "You do not know it all." Rising abruptly, she flew over to the window.

"Then tell me the rest," Cambrian invited, gripping the arms of his chair to anchor himself in place.

Jennings started to stand, then sank back, pinned to his chair by the intensity of the gaze Cambrian fixed upon him. Unhappy about it all, Jennings filled the silence with the sound of his noisily stacking empty dishes on the serving tray.

"After we left the restaurant, we walked down to the overlook." Constance rubbed her upper arms with her hands, feeling colder now than she had when last night's breezes had carried the sounds of a sleepy forest up to her from the valley below. "Arnold changed during supper; or at least, how I saw him changed," she corrected herself. "I think his perception of me changed, as well." It seemed the most logical explanation for the genuine friendship he had offered her in place of the aloof, taunting man-fairy who had maneuvered her into eating supper with him. "We talked for over an hour without saying anything important. Then he asked me about the list he had given me and I let it slip that you had it."

Cambrian gripped the arms of the chair so tightly that the flow of blood to his fingers was completely cut off. If Mosley knew that before he began volunteering information to her, how sure could they be that the information was accurate? The man-fairy was just short of a professional manipulator and would derive enormous amounts of pleasure from drawing them all into a game where he pulled the strings. Was it all a clever ruse?

"That was a strange moment," she confessed, staring out the window and into the past. "He looked so angry that I was actually afraid. Then he laughed and said it served him right for being sloppy." Her best guess was that the list could, somehow, be used to implicate him in a legal charge, though he had never gone so far as to say so. "After that, things moved very swiftly. I scarcely had time to realize that he was confessing to his involvement in a plot to overthrow the monarchy before he was inviting me to share in his gains."

Cambrian's right hand twitched and the wood he was gripping snapped free from the rest of the chair. Rising abruptly, he tossed the broken piece into the pile of rubbish from his earlier display of temper.

From where he still sat at the table, Jennings

stared at them both, so engrossed in the story by now that he forgot to be embarrassed.

"What did you say?" Cambrian asked, his back to her. He had been days away from proposing to her himself, so close that it could have been spoken of in hours. And the suave, charismatic Arnold, whom he had not even considered as a rival, had beaten him to it.

"I told him no." Constance had turned at the sound of snapping wood and now she leaned back against the window, watching Cambrian closely. This was more like the Cambrian she remembered from before his duel with Bane. A bit more forceful, perhaps, but still more self-assured than he had been for the last ten days. He had yet to *say* a single thing without thinking it over carefully first. Given time, she expected him to balance back out, different but ultimately still himself. "He seemed surprised."

Cambrian grimaced. From what Edgar and others told him, Arnold was not the type to take rejection from anyone. Which made him question again the way things were playing out.

"Then I asked him to come tell you what was going on." Reflecting back, it was just as well that Arnold had declined that invitation. There was really no telling how things might have turned out when they found Watts at the bench instead of Cambrian. "He countered my offer with another of his own." She paused, trying to mentally sum it all up. "He has suspected for some time that he was under investigation by the crown. Naturally he felt some reluctance to change his allegiance from a group promising to reward him to a group threatening to punish him."

"So he asked you to intervene on his behalf?" Cambrian's dislike for the situation heightened. Arnold, knowing of Cambrian's feelings for Constance, had either truly entrusted his future to her, believing Cambrian would give her what she asked for—or he had used her to buy himself time to escape. Somehow the second scenario seemed more likely. Arnold reportedly had a selfish streak as wide as the sea and as long as winter.

"That was my idea." When Cambrian turned to face her, she met his gaze directly. Oh, she understood the frustration evident on his face. How had she *dared*? Cambrian had only grudgingly agreed to accept her help, for though the idea originally came from him, he had dismissed it as soon as he thought it through. She had no authority in the investigation whatsoever. "He tried to dissuade me, but really there was nothing for it. I was the best fairy for the job."

Cambrian cringed inwardly. That was the same argument she had used to convince him to accept her help.

"Things went fairly well until I got to the garden," she continued. "After my interview with

Mister Watts, I completely forgot to tell you what I had learned from Mosley." She shrugged that off fairly easily, for her main self-assigned task last night had been to assure Cambrian that Arnold had behaved himself towards her. Since details of the investigation had not exactly come up, she was willing to excuse herself the omission.

"Understandable," Cambrian agreed. According to his recollection, it had been his idea to bundle her off to bed as soon as he could. He would have liked to go back in time and keep her up a few minutes longer, but since he could not...

"Mosley claimed it would be dangerous for him to alter any of his plans so close to time and insisted I accept his signet ring. We were to meet after weapons training, when he would provide me with a list of names, letters, and other documents to be used as evidence during the trials."

Cambrian stepped eagerly towards her, his hopes rising.

"Yes," she nodded. "He gave them to me. I even looked a few of them over." She felt enormously pleased with herself for taking that precaution, and had to laugh at how smug she sounded, even to herself. "I hid them because I was worried about negotiating with your father, but you can find them at the south end of Gemma's herb garden. The ground was recently plowed for winter, so that was the first place I thought of."

Cambrian nodded sharply and was about to go fetch them when he suddenly remembered what they had originally been talking about.

"Is that what worried you?" he asked her quietly. "That you had not trusted your king?"

Her cheeks flamed at his question and she slowly shook her head. Folding her arms across her chest, she reflected uneasily that she still had no idea how to tell him.

"It is significantly more," her words came slowly as if she were using the utmost care in selecting them, "personal." She started to turn towards the window again, forced herself to continue facing him. "I told you how Arnold convinced me to marry him." Her eyes dipped to Cambrian's suddenly clenched hands, then lifted only as far as his top vest button. "The wedding ceremony was…brief." Abrupt was more accurate. Arnold had handed her some papers and a quill pen. A few of his associates, assembled especially to act as witnesses, looked on as she scribbled her name on the appropriate lines. It had been about as romantic as doing ship's inventory. Until… "He sealed it with a kiss." At first, the kiss had been a rather formal contact, in keeping with the tone of the proceedings to that point. That she had been taken by surprise by Watts was bad enough—it was almost ridiculous that she, who had never kissed anyone before Cambrian had now been kissed by three men-fairies in a single day's time—but while being kissed by Arnold had not been entirely unpleasant, she reproached herself for her failure to retreat, thus avoiding it altogether.

Cambrian narrowly avoided adding the rest of his second chair to the pile of rubble against the wall.

"You enjoyed it."

Constance rubbed her left hand meditatively for a few heartbeats before responding. Where she had initially melted at Arnold's touch, she now froze at the memory of it. It had been nothing like kissing Cambrian. For one thing, of the three of them, Arnold clearly was the most experienced. For another, when Cambrian kissed her, it was by mutual consent, however tacit. *They* kissed.

"He had a certain…traditional right to kiss me," she began, frowning in concentration. While she readily admitted that Cambrian did deserve an apology, she was not in a position to give the one she ached to give him. "And he claimed that right."

Cambrian's hands slowly reformed into fists as he watched her struggle to finish the thought.

"When this is all over and my marriage to Arnold is dissolved," she could feel herself blushing again, "I would very much prefer marrying someone else."

At just that moment, Jennings knocked the

serving tray off the table, sending dishes and utensils clattering through the room. "Blast," he muttered loudly and dove after the serving bowl that was spilling its contents as it wobbled uncertainly away from him on the plush carpet. He had come to himself about the time that his captain admitted to being kissed by Mosley. Worried at the level of tension building in the room, he waited just until she had given a satisfactory answer, then deliberately created a diversion. Unless he missed his guess, those two needed time to cool down before moving forward.

Cambrian, who had reflexively lifted off when from the corner of his eye he saw something hurtling towards him, was stopped by the ceiling. "Ouch," he grunted, rubbing his head.

Constance stared up at him from where she stood, stock still, by the window. "Are you hurt?" she asked, deciding that was fractionally better than asking if he was alright.

"What is going on in here?" demanded King Jasper as he entered the room through the hallway door.

Queen Marta, who was directly behind him, stifled a horrified exclamation at the sight of Jennings kneeling on the expensive carpet, using a white cloth napkin to sop up the trail of vegetable juice the rolling bowl had left in its wake.

"Oh, nothing." Cambrian rubbed his head one more time, then began descending gradually, straightening his shirtfront and so forth as he neared the floor. "Nothing at all," he added, stooping to pick up the goblet at his feet.

"Hmm." Frowning, Jasper shot a look from his son to where Constance had dropped to her knees and begun picking up utensils. He wondered briefly at his own foolishness in leaving the two of them alone together, and was glad to notice Jennings—despite the noise the man-fairy made as he rammed a serving tray into the side of the table where they had apparently eaten a late lunch.

Marta saw the pile of broken wood and cushions heaped against one wall but closed her eyes and looked away. Any doubts she might have entertained as to the importance of Jasper's news had permanently fled.

"Constance." Jasper addressed her familiarly, beckoned for her to leave the dishes and join them. "Come here."

She obeyed at once, blinking back the tears that threatened her when she heard him call her by name.

Jasper closed the door behind him in the moment it took her to cross the room.

"Oliver and I," he paused, made eye contact with Jennings, and resumed speaking, "have just made a terrible discovery. Winter has been deliberately delayed."

Marta gasped and covered her mouth with her hand. Rerouting a storm cloud here and there was one thing. Tampering with the seasons was a far more dangerous business.

"By Mosley?" Cambrian asked, taking Constance gently by the arm in case his support was needed. She clearly had believed in Mosley's change of heart.

"I can hardly believe it, but no." Jasper shook his head. "I went to accuse him of it myself and am convinced that he had nothing to do with this. In fact," Jasper continued heavily, "it was he who pointed out that this bears a fiendish similarity to the master coup planned by our pirate friends this past summer. And unless we act quickly," King Jasper drew a map from inside his vest, "Regalis will be buried under enough snow for three winters."

Constance paled at the thought. Earlier that year (before their coronation), Queen Rebecca and King Hugh of the Silver Fairy Tribe had discovered a pirate buildup that threatened all of Fairydom. For the first time in a dozen generations, the four tribes had pooled their military resources for the express purpose of defeating those pirates. Later, she and Cambrian had come face to face with Bane-Layton, the pirate leader and a traitor from their own tribe. *How could delaying winter threaten Regalis? Was Bane merely a highly-trained puppet after all? Who is pulling the strings?*

Constance allowed herself to lean on Cambrian's arm for a moment as they followed the king to his desk. She had a horrible feeling she knew what the king was going to ask her to do. She caught her breath when she got her first glimpse of the map he was spreading out. *It was a twin to the map they had taken from Bane's cabin.*

"Here," Jasper indicated an upper mountain valley. "Cloud chasers have been illegally stormpiling all of the winter clouds in this area for the last month." He saw the color fade a second time from Constance's cheeks and quite agreed. "According to Mosley's informant, the sheer power of the storm has driven the chasers to the edge of the valley, where they are doing their best to hold it."

"However it gets past them," she had no illusions that it might somehow remain safely bottled up there, "it will come down this pass." She traced the route with her finger.

Jasper nodded. "All villages, settlements, outposts, everything between here and there will be destroyed. Even Regalis will fall before its onslaught."

Cambrian caught his mother about the waist and helped her over to the nearest couch. Had his father told her nothing before they flitted in?

"They lied to Arnold." Constance barely realized she had spoken aloud. "They were just using him." Shock rendered her speechless as she tried to realize that none of Arnold's reasons for insisting on their 'marriage' was even faintly valid in light of this new revelation. The crux of his argument had been based on the idea that his new enemies (former friends) would try to eliminate him and use his business ties to lock down Regalis. As his wife, she could have stepped in and prevented that. She narrowly resisted the urge to join the queen on the couch. If she survived, she could mourn her stupidity later.

Jasper nodded again, the irony of Mosley's situation being of minimal importance to him at the moment. If that storm struck as intended, whether supplies arrived or not was irrelevant. There would be no one left alive to use them.

"That storm must be dispersed before it intersects with the Liviano." He rapped on the map as if he could knock the storm apart that way. The Liviano was a swiftly moving air current that travelled in from the sea and up, over the northernmost mountain peaks, dropping its accumulated moisture as it rose. But this time, when it came in contact with the heavy snow clouds the updraft would drastically alter the kind of weather they were dealing with, turning relatively harmless storm clouds into the most fearsome kind of weather a fairy could encounter—thundersnow.

"Permission to act, Your Majesty?" Constance had snapped back to the here and now by sheer force of habit. There was work to be done. She had done her time on a cloud chaser, every windfairy in the fleet had. Windship launching had to begin now if they were to stand the faintest of chances.

"What are you saying?" Cambrian spoke through stiff lips. Leaving his mother, he flew to Constance's side, looked back and forth between his father and the woman-fairy he loved. They could not be seriously thinking of... "If we send cloud chasers to intercept and *if* they survive the graupels, the lightning, and the gravity waves long enough to disperse a large enough portion of the cloud, there will still be fatally cold temperatures between them and Regalis. Any windfairy who goes on this mission has almost no chance of returning alive."

Constance turned to face him. She had already swallowed her fear of dying in the same manner that her father had—the way Princess Joanna had. Now she had to help Cambrian through it. Somehow. Quickly.

"We should evacuate," Cambrian protested. "Call out the guards, tell them to abandon whatever it is that they are doing, and begin loading the windships."

"Impossible." All eyes turned to where Marta sat, her face as white as a snowflake. "Four shiploads of guests for the winter festival have arrived this last week alone. The windships that brought them departed as soon as the last piece of luggage was offloaded, eager to beat winter home."

"Dispersing the storm is our only chance," Constance interrupted, her mild tone catching

Cambrian's attention instantly. Reaching out, she gripped him by his forearms. "I only wish…" She found that she could not complete the sentence.

"It will be hard enough to convince the citizens to go into their winter routines without starting a panic," Jasper agreed heavily. He had already weighed the two options and made his choice. It had been simple, really. Evacuation was impossible because there were not enough windships, even counting the military vessels. Sending out cloud chasers, the heavily fortified military vessels designed for this type of work, with every other military vessel currently docked at Regalis to support them, was their only chance. "I will need your finesse with that, son."

Cambrian closed his eyes to shut out their gazes. *Breathe in. Breathe out.*

His eyes popped open. "Launch the windships," he ordered, his hands catching hold of Constance's to prevent her from leaving when she moved, startled, to obey him. "Father, call an assembly. All remaining merchants and citizens in the city are to report to the Mirus Theater, every man, woman, and child-fairy of them! Visiting nobles and those at the castle can meet in the Great Hall. You two," he looked sharply at Constance, then swept Jennings into his command, "come with me."

"What assembly?" Jasper called after his son as Cambrian hurried to the window. "What are you thinking?"

"An assembly of accusation," Cambrian flung over his shoulder as he kicked the windows open. "You will find evidence against some of the traitors buried in the southern end of the herb garden—enough, I hope, to pinpoint their master. At the very least, everyone will be inside where it is safe while you shut down the outer exits and open the tunnels. You handle the Great Hall, Oliver can tell the Mirus Theater." *Where was Oliver?* he wondered for an instant.

"Where will you be?" Marta asked, her hand fluttering to her throat.

"Aboard the *Nadauld*, with Constance and Kuntza." He looked down at Constance, whose grip on his hand tightened in understanding. "Perhaps with his help, we can find a way."

"Go!" commanded Jasper, tripping over a stray dish in his haste to reach the hallway door. "Hurry!" He flew out of the room.

Constance hesitated fractionally on the sill. She locked eyes with Marta. "Please tell my brother I am sorry that I cannot join him for dinner tonight." That said, she allowed Cambrian to pull her out the window and they were gone.

"By your leave, m'lady." Jennings paused, eying the map that Jasper had forgotten on the desk. Scooping it up, he stuffed it inside his jacket, then zipped out the window after Cambrian and Constance.

Suddenly Marta was alone in the room. The

hallway door stood half open, left that way by her husband as he flew to set the assembly in motion. There were still dishes scattered about the floor and a rubbish pile that bore a sad resemblance to the handsome chair she had missed upon entering the room. All was quiet except for the broken windows, which squeaked almost eerily as they swung back and forth, still reeling from Cambrian's blow.

Marta shivered once. It had been on the tip of her tongue to tell them that young Rolf Warner, of the Silver Fairy Tribe's royal house, had arrived unexpectedly on the last windship. Her initial reaction to his visit had been a mixture of pride—that an official Historian had been sent to make a record of their simple celebration—and slight trepidation at how few 'spare' guest rooms she had left at last count. Her eyes closed in pain as she pondered how many fairies were in danger at that exact moment. She hardly dared to think how losing her only son might affect Princess Arabella…

Then Marta's jaw set and she folded her hands in front of her. An assembly of this scale meant gathering well over a thousand fairies. She left to find the triplets and Gemma, pausing only to give the guard instructions to have the windows repaired immediately and the room restored to order.

<u>*The Seeker's Storm*</u> (Bk 5) Excerpt

Chapter 1

As Prince Oliver followed his father from Arnold Mosley's elegant hotel suite, he saw a flicker of movement out of the corner of one eye. The long hallway was lined with statues and ornate paintings, and dotted with recessed doorways that lead to other suites. Curiousity getting the better of him, Oliver signaled for the marine behind him to continue flying forward no matter what. When they reached the next doorway, Oliver slid into it. Careful to stay hidden, Oliver turned back towards Mosley's suite and sank soundlessly into the plush carpet between the beautifully carved planks that framed the doorway. Dropping first to his knees, then down to lie flat, he stifled a chuckle at the idea of trying to explain himself to the hotel guest if the door beside him should abruptly open. Carefully, he edged his face towards the edge of the doorframe. The small party that had escorted him and his father to Mosley's hotel faded away, the sharp click of a window—locking behind them—the last sound he heard. One eye finally clear of the doorframe, Oliver held perfectly still. And waited. The hallway was so still that he thought he could hear the paint on the walls fading in the bright afternoon sunlight.

The motion he saw might have belonged to anyone—a chambermaid, another guest... Oliver was beginning to give in to the feeling of foolishness when a slightly built man-fairy peeked out from behind one of the statues at the far end of the hall. Mosley had dismissed his servants when the king first arrived, which meant the suite should still be empty, Mosley having also gone off to take care of personal business. Oliver's right eyebrow lifted fractionally when the man-fairy slipped over to Mosley's door and glanced furtively around before he produced something from the inner folds of his scribe's robe, and let himself in through the locked door.

More than curious now, Oliver came silently to his feet. Decades of playing hide and seek with his younger siblings contributed to his swift, but soundless flight down the length of the hallway, where he arrived just in time to slip between Mosley's door and its frame. He quickly dropped to his knees in a shadow before it swung shut behind him. From there, he was able to watch as the scribe began searching single-mindedly for something on Mosley's desk.

It was all so absurd that Oliver nearly gave in to the urge to laugh at himself. He had just assisted his father in interrogating Mosley—and unless Mosley was an even more masterful manipulator than the Wood Fairy Minister of the Interior, he had been telling the truth when he denied any involvement in the delay of the winter storms. Now he, Oliver Bijou, Crown Prince of the Sky Fairy Tribe, was hiding in the shadows? Sleuthing was the specialty of his younger brother, Prince Cambrian. Still, Oliver could not shake the feeling that something was amiss here. Mosley might have given a scribe a key to his suites, but…scribe! Another piece of the puzzle fell into place, bringing Oliver to his feet precipitously. Cambrian had recently brought evidence to them that a scribe was involved in the conspiracy.

Startled by Oliver's movement, the scribe jerked to one side. His elbow struck one of the taller stacks, knocking it over in an avalanche of blue, white, and yellow papers that fluttered to the floor. Some fell quite a distance. Others struck the hem of the frozen scribe's robe and landed about his feet.

"Harold Scroggins," Oliver casually scooped up a small volume of poetry from the entryway table beside him, "I arrest you in the name of the crown." As he had expected, Harold flew towards the nearest window. Oliver's arm came up and snapped forward, hurling the hard-bound book towards Harold's back. "Well, that is a first," Oliver murmured to himself as he watched the scribe crumple to the floor, temporarily stunned. "I do not recall ever seeing a book drop a scribe before."

Tugging the window sashes free, Oliver bound his prisoner securely. As he was about to begin searching the desk himself, Harold stirred. Weak blue eyes stared up through his tousled blue bangs, full of unanswered questions for his assailant.

"A thousand pardons for interrupting your search." Oliver, eyeing the stacks of papers that Harold had not yet begun to search, felt that the thousand pardons should be made to him, not Harold. If Oliver had just waited, Harold might have found whatever it was that he was looking for. Anyway, judging by Harold's glare, Oliver's humor was not appreciated. Which gave him an idea. Why not use Harold's expressive face against him? Mosley had already given whatever hard evidence he had to Captain Constance Kimberlite, who had in turn passed the documents on to the crown. That left…what?

"However, since the map has already been removed," Oliver shrugged with one hand towards the door while keeping both eyes on Harold, "your search was already a failure."

Harold blanched. "You have to protect me."

Oliver's false nonchalance melted away. "From whom?" He leaned forward.

"Does it matter?" Harold shot back. "If I do not return with that map…" Words failed him and he began simply shaking his head.

Oliver was accustomed to high pressure situations, but negotiating with criminals was well outside of his usual duties.

"Harold." Oliver waited briefly, then repeated, "Harold." When the scribe finally looked him in the eye, Oliver wasted no time on subtlety. "Your life is balanced on a knife blade.

Tell me what I want to know," he nodded reassuringly, "and you will be protected."

Harold seemed to crumple even further into his capacious robes.

"One problem at a time, Harold," Oliver recommended, folding his arms across his chest and taking a step forward. "If you are convicted of treason against the tribe, that map will be the least of your troubles." An imposing figure at his most casual, Prince Oliver Bijou straightened to his full height, despite the fact that he was holding his breath.

"What do you want to know?"

"Maps are easy to come by." Oliver chose the topic that was nearest Harold's fear, pretending ignorance of the fact that the maps had been subtly altered over the last few hundred years until they were dangerously inaccurate. "So you will tell me what makes this map so important."

Harold's inner wrestle was written in frown lines on his face. At last, he glanced up at the closed curtains and exhaled slowly.

"I could draw that map in my sleep," he said bitterly. "I made enough of them. But this copy," he lifted his bound hands as if to run his fingers through his hair, then dropped them back to his lap in frustration. "It is one of a kind, not meant to be given away." He hesitated, then unconsciously leaned closer. "It is not what you can see that makes it special; it is what is hidden in plain sight."

Oliver inhaled slowly, trying to mask his excitement. Carefully, he questioned Harold, wishing the whole time for a pageboy, or a marine, or anybody that he could send to bring his father and brother to him. The thought that Harold had dared make a secret copy of the treasonous master plan was mind boggling. Even Harold could not explain how it had gotten from his private files into Mosley's hands, but the important thing was that it had.

"Royal Marines!" bellowed a voice from outside the window. "Open in the name of the king!"

"No!" Harold reached for Oliver with both of his bound hands. When Oliver stopped, Harold continued in a whisper, "I know that voice. He is not a marine."

Oliver squatted beside Harold long enough to warn him. "If this is a trick, or you try to cry out to your friends," he jerked his head towards the window, "I will throw more than a book at you this time." Harold's wildly nodding head was all the answer he needed. While a trick was still possible, Oliver dared turn his back on Harold long enough to peer through the place where the closed curtains met. The whole of the outside world was tinged a painful shade of purple by the thousands of tiny fibers protruding from the curtain edges, but unless facemasks had been added to the marine uniform in the last five minutes, something was sorely amiss.

Seizing Harold by his collar, Oliver stuffed

him under the desk, where the knees and feet normally went. Setting the chair back in its place, Oliver draped his jacket over it.

"Remember," he warned Harold in a hushed tone, "the map is well beyond reach." Scooping up the book of poetry he had used to stun Harold, Oliver sprawled on the nearest settee, with just enough time to muss his hair and close his eyes before the outer window splintered open.

"Wha…" Oliver nearly threw the book to one side, as if in an involuntary twitch of fright as three armed civilians stormed through the window. "How dare you!" Coming to his feet, he glared them down.

"Quiet, you!" The nearest of them put one huge hand in the middle of Oliver's chest and shoved him back on the settee. His smirk was evident even through the mask as he watched Oliver flop onto the cushion.

"Leave him," barked one of the others. "Scroggins is all we want."

"And the map," reminded the third, already scanning the room. "Keep an eye on him," she fluttered a hand in Oliver's direction, "but get busy. The sooner we find what we came for, the sooner we can leave Regalis."

Oliver's ears pricked at that. Regalis was in the path of a monster snowstorm, something they had learned just that morning. Nevertheless, the capital city was a much safer place to be than any village or town he could think of…unless they were headed for Aureus? If that was the case, then they might have considerably more time than any of them had guessed, for Aureus was nearly two days away by windship.

"I," Oliver found himself staring down the length of a highly-polished sword blade. Deciding in an instant that deception was his only choice, he swallowed visibly. "I say," he shrank back a little, "Mosley is not here right now. But if you would just tell me what you are looking for…"

"Never you mind," sneered the sword-wielding villain. "You sit," he tapped Oliver on the chest with the point of his sword, "quietly."

Looking wildly towards the one woman-fairy in the group, who was approaching the desk, Oliver pretended to think aloud. "Mosley has an entire book of maps in…" He stopped when the sword point settled firmly against his chest.

"Maybe you can help us." The woman-fairy did not look up from the stack of papers she was rapidly thumbing through. When she had finished scanning them, she dropped them on the floor. "What happened to those papers?" She pointed at the papers Harold had knocked over.

"I bumped into them." Oliver answered without hesitation.

"Tsk, tsk." The woman-fairy picked up another stack of papers and began flipping through them as she flew towards Oliver. "And you did not think to pick them up?" She allowed the papers in her hand to flutter down over Oliver, her eyes narrowing thoughtfully when he continued to meet her gaze. In her experience, fairies who were truly in the wrong place at the wrong time tended to exhibit fear. Spontaneously, and especially when their personal space was invaded. "Who are you?" she asked sharply.

Again Oliver gambled, aware that he had somehow given himself away.

"I am Prince Oliver Bijou, heir to the throne of the Sky Fairy Tribe." He relaxed back into the comfortable settee, sensing that his indifference added to her pique. "Princes," he smiled, "have servants to clean up after them." The thought of expressing that sentiment to even one of the household servants at the Crystal Castle made him smile even more broadly.

"Indeed? A prince, eh?" She sounded more annoyed than impressed. "What a pity that you will not live to inherit that throne."

"No?" Oliver held up one hand, palm towards the windows, as if examining his manicure. "Perhaps if I told you that the map you are looking for is even now being taken to the royal kitchen, to be read near a warm cooking fire," he smirked up at her, "you would not be so arrogant." This time the sword point pressed against his throat, so tightly that Oliver hardly dared breathe. "I assure you, you will never make it to Aureus."

"Overstepped yourself there," the man-fairy holding the sword growled triumphantly. "Why should we wait the winter out buried under snow?"

"Stupid," snapped the woman-fairy, crumpling the last few papers in her hands. "Stupid, stupid, stupid! What else would you like him to know?" By now even the third fairy had stopped searching and was watching the scene play out. "They obviously know about the map. Which means," she continued, her voice temperature dropping by the syllable, "that it is just a matter of time before the timetable, the routes, and the list of the council are in their hands."

"Well, tell him all about it, eh?" sulked the berated man-fairy beside her.

She did not even bother to look over at him, just kept staring at Oliver. "On the other hand, why should we keep secrets from our friend?" Her smile was cold, serpent-like. "Perhaps we can tell you where you will not be spending this winter."

"You mean take him with us?" The poor fool holding the sword opened his mouth to continue protesting, only to choke on air when she turned her icy glare on him.

It was possible that the woman-fairy was about to let loose with another string of derogatory remarks. Oliver did not wait to find out. Leaning back more firmly into the overstuffed settee, he removed his throat from imminent danger.

"Now!" With his left hand, he slapped the sword point away from his body. His right hand shot forward, grabbing the shocked man-fairy by his sword wrist while a squad of marines exploded into the room through the broken windows. Oliver pulled on the man-fairy just until he reflexively tried to jerk his hand free, then released him to stumble backwards into the waiting arms of two husky marines.

Oliver had no sooner completed the move than he realized that the woman-fairy on his left was coming towards him, dagger in hand. Rather than being sensible enough to dodge her attack, he snatched up a heavily upholstered pillow and lunged at her. The dagger, thrust hastily at his attacking form, became embedded in the pillow, allowing him to easily twist it free of her hand. He extended his wings, halting his forward rush in time to escape the force of an adrenaline-fueled marine who struck her from the side, taking her clear to the floor.

"Your Highness," the squad leader, a second lieutenant, confident that things were in hand, saluted him from the far side of the desk. "Reporting as ordered."

"And just in time," Oliver grinned back. He was going to have to remember to thank his father's escort for sending someone to check on things. Gesturing towards the prisoners, he commanded, "Separate them—and keep them separated. Absolutely no communication between them starting now."

It was just as well, he decided, that they were not going to be put in a single cell. The insults they were tossing about as the marines hauled them away would have singed the rust right off the cell bars. It was a waste of energy, too; Harold was the one they should have been blaming, not each other.

"Oh, Lieutenant," Oliver spoke up as the last prisoner approached the window. "Send a carriage back for me, if you would." He helped the prisoner along with a none-too-gentle shove and found himself alone in the room. Well, almost. "Hsst." He bent towards the back of the desk, hovering so that he would not get glass from the windows embedded in the soles of his shoes. "You can come out now."

Arrotz: a town of moderate size located some distance from Regalis.
<u>Origin</u>: Arrotz, Basque for *stranger*
Cachora: the capitol city of the Water Fairy Tribe. (*Pronounced Cash-ora*)
<u>Origin</u>: Cachoeira, Portuguese for *waterfall*
Bijou, King Jasper: leader of the Sky Fairy tribe; husband of Marta; father of Oliver, Cambrian, Lesley, Laura, and Lila.
Bijou, Prince Cambrian: the younger son of Jasper Bijou, King of the Sky Fairy Tribe.
<u>Origin</u>: "The Cambrian Period marks an important point in the history of life on Earth; it is the time when most of the major groups of animals first appear in the fossil record. This event is sometimes called the "Cambrian Explosion," because of the relatively short time over which this diversity of forms appears."
(www.ucmp.berkeley.edu/cambrian/cambrian.php)
Bloomers: a term borrowed from the costumes worn by cheerleaders and other performers to preserve their modesty.
Burdina mines: Iron mines owned by Arnold Mosely, a wealthy, powerful Sky Fairy.
<u>Origin</u>: Burdina, Basque for *iron*
Do'tore: finest restaurant in all of Regalis, save only the king's table. (*pronounced Dough-tore-ay*)
<u>Origin</u>: Dotore, Basque for *elegant*

Graupel: granular snow pellets—called also "soft hail"

(www.merriam-webster.com/dictionary/graupel)

Gyrfalcon Class: most closely resembles the naval sailing ship called "frigate." Carries between thirty and forty cannon; carries a crew compliment of approximately three hundred windfairies; frequently assigned escort and scouting duties.

<u>Origin</u>: "The largest falcon in the world, the Gyrfalcon breeds in arctic and subarctic regions of the northern hemisphere. It preys mostly on large birds, pursuing them in breathtakingly fast and powerful flight."

(www.allaboutbirds.org/guide/Gyrfalcon/id)

Kestrel Class: most closely resembles the naval sailing ship called "corvette." Carries approximately twenty cannon; carries a crew compliment of approximately one hundred windfairies; frequently assigned to patrol the edges of tribal territory.

<u>Origin</u>: "North America's littlest falcon, the American Kestrel packs a predator's fierce intensity into its small body. It's one of the most colorful of all raptors…"

(www.allaboutbirds.org/guide/american_kestrel/id)

Kimberlite, Captain Constance: first seen as the captain of the windship *Falcon* in <u>Silver Verity</u> (Silver Sagas Bk 3).

<u>Origin</u>: "Diamonds are brought to the surface from the mantle in a rare type of magma called

kimberlite and erupted at a rare type of volcanic vent called a diatreme or pipe."
(http://volcano.oregonstate.edu/diamonds)
Kimuxwe: Kestrel-class Sky Fairy Fleet windship, carrying twenty guns. Lost in <u>Troubled Skies</u> (Silver Sagas Bk 4) during an escape from a pirate fortress.
<u>Origin</u>: Lenape for *stealth* (http://www.talk-lenape.org/index.php)
Kuntza: a Water Fairy introduced in <u>Troubled Skies</u> (Silver Sagas Bk 4). Physician and truth-seeker for his tribe.
<u>Origin</u>: (Basque) verbal suffix signifying an abstract act or action.
(Basque-English Dictionary by Gorka Aulestia)
Liviano Wind: a cold, swiftly rising air current that winds through the mountains to the east of the Sky Fairy capitol city, Regalis.
<u>Origin</u>: Liviano, Spanish for *light, fickle, frivolous*
Mirus Theater: the royal theater of Regalis,
<u>Origin</u>: Mirus, Latin for *wonder, amazing, marvelous*
Mosley, Arnold: wealthy, powerful mine owner. Sky Fairy. Named after Benedict Arnold (American Revolutionary War) and Sir Oswald Mosley (WWII).
Regalis: the capitol city of the Sky Fairy Tribe.
<u>Origin</u>: Regalis, Latin for *royal*